Super Chief

A John Tall Wolf Novel

Joseph Flynn

Stray Dog Press, Inc.
Springfield, IL
2019

BY JOSEPH FLYNN

The Jim McGill Series

The President's Henchman, A Jim McGill Novel [#1]
The Hangman's Companion, A JimMcGill Novel [#2]
The K Street Killer A JimMcGill Novel [#3]
Part 1: The Last Ballot Cast, A JimMcGill Novel [#4 Part 1]
Part 2: The Last Ballot Cast, A JimMcGill Novel [#5 Part 2]
The Devil on the Doorstep, A Jim McGill Novel [#6]
The Good Guy with a Gun, A Jim McGill Novel [#7]
The Echo of the Whip, A Jim McGill Novel [#8]
The Daddy's Girl Decoy, A Jim McGill Novel [#9]
The Last Chopper Out, A Jim McGill Novel [#10]
The King of Mirth, A Jim McGill Novel [#11]

McGill's Short Cases 1-3

The Ron Ketchum Mystery Series

Nailed, A Ron Ketchum Mystery [#1]
Defiled, A Ron Ketchum Mystery Featuring John Tall Wolf [#2]
Impaled, A Ron Ketchum Mystery [#3]

The John Tall Wolf Series

Tall Man in Ray-Bans, A John Tall Wolf Novel [#1]
War Party, A John Tall Wolf Novel [#2]
Super Chief, A John Tall Wolf Novel [#3]
Smoke Signals, A John Tall Wolf Novel [#4]
Big Medicine, A John Tall Wolf Novel [#5]
Powwow in Paris, A John Tall Wolf Novel [#6]

The Zeke Edison Series

Kill Me Twice, A Zeke Edison Novel [#1]

Dedication

For Catherine

Acknowledgements

My thanks to Anne, Catherine, Chris, Laura and Susan, who did their level best to catch all the mistakes I made. Any that remain are strictly my responsibility.

Author's Notes

This is a work of fiction. Neither the characters nor the Native American reservations named in the story are real. The Bureau of Indian Affairs, of course, exists within the United States Department of the Interior, and within the BIA its Office of Justice Services is "responsible for the overall management of the Bureau's law enforcement program," but my research turned up no one who has the job description I gave to John Tall Wolf. This mixture of fact and fiction falls under the heading of literary license. If you're a purist who demands complete realism, I recommend you stick to nonfiction, and good luck finding an author in that field who doesn't make mistakes or omissions.

As to a white male writing about Native American characters, that involves a bit of license, too. From my point of view, that license is rooted in our common humanity. If writers were to focus only on characters who shared their own backgrounds, we would establish a regime of literary apartheid.

AL
**Reader
Discretion
Advised**
Contains Adult
Language

Stray Dog Press, Inc.

Super Chief
A John Tall Wolf Novel
Published by Stray Dog Press, Inc., 2019
Springfield, IL 62704, U.S.A.

Author website: *www.josephflynn.com*

Flynn, Joseph
  Super Chief / Joseph Flynn
  256 pg.
  ISBN   978-0-9908412-1-0
  eBook 978-0-9908412-0-3

Printed in the United States of America

PUBLISHER'S NOTE
This is a work of fiction. Names, characters, places, and incidents are either the product of the author's imagination or are used fictitiously; any resemblance to actual persons, living or dead, events, or locales is entirely coincidental.

Book design by Aha! Designs

Super Chief

A John Tall Wolf Novel

— CHAPTER 1 —

San Francisco, California

Merritt Kinney thought he was going to die in his bathroom. Turned out he had the portent of mortality right and was off on the location by only one floor. The case of indigestion that had struck him was the worst he'd ever known. The agony, he felt sure, was courtesy of food poisoning from the new joint down the block.

It took all his self-restraint not to scream. Doing that might cause the downstairs neighbors to think someone was being murdered and call the cops. He decided he was going to sue the restaurant.

In a desperate attempt to divert his attention, he reached back and grabbed the book sitting atop the toilet tank: "Railroaded: The Biography of Theodore Judah."

Judah was the visionary with the first practical plan to build a transcontinental railroad across the United States. He was undone by the corrupt merchants who funded his efforts. The money men tried to buy Judah off, but he wouldn't play along. He boarded a ship bound for New York in 1863 to find new financial backing and expose the corruption behind the railroad's management, but he never made it. He took ill with yellow fever in Panama and died shortly after in New York at age thirty-seven.

The swindlers, who were over-billing the federal government for every mile of track laid, went on to become some of the wealthiest and most revered men in California history.

Kinney knew all that because he'd read the book several times, always hoping for a new ending. He felt his guts spasm and tossed the book in the nearby bathtub to save it from the long-awaited vile eruption. The resulting excreta required three flushes. He felt a great relief in his midsection but was left weak in the knees.

And greatly aggrieved by the stink.

Kinney completed his business and tottered across the room to open the window and let fresh air inside. That was when he saw the car pull up to the curb across the street. Four large men in dark clothes exited the vehicle and came straight for his building.

With an intuitive certainty, Kinney knew they were coming for him. They'd soon be kicking in his door, and if they caught him, he'd die as surely and as young as Theodore Judah had. For the same reason, too. Trying to expose a great crime, but not quite succeeding.

One of the men in the street looked up and saw him in the window. Kinney retreated and grabbed his cell phone. All he could get was static.

Good God, were they jamming cell phone service?

It certainly wouldn't be beyond their means.

A stop-at-nothing billionaire was behind them.

Heart pounding, Kinney fled in the only direction available to him, up one flight of stairs to the building's roof. He tried to use his phone again, hoping to find a signal. He wanted to call the *Chronicle*, tell a reporter everything he knew. All he got, though, was more static.

Frantic, he ran around the perimeter of the roof, looking for an adjacent building to which he might leap. Just as he found the most likely one, the door to the roof opened and the four large men appeared. One of them held a video camera.

Their leader looked at Kinney and knew immediately what his prey had in mind. He smiled and shook his head. "I know what you're thinking ... and it only works in the movies."

Having delivered his warning, the man took out a badge.

"Just in case you've got the wrong idea, we're the police, and you're under arrest for grand larceny. We're going to take you in and book you. All your rights will be observed."

Kinney didn't believe that for a minute. They might well be cops, but he'd never make it to any police station. Even so, he took three defeated steps in their direction.

Then he pivoted and with a running start jumped for the roof of the neighboring building.

He came up short. Fell four stories and died on impact.

The cop had been right. Stunts like that never worked in real life.

— CHAPTER 2 —

Los Angeles, California

Four hundred miles south of the alley where Merritt Kinney's body lay broken, a classic EMD F7 locomotive wearing the classic red and silver war bonnet design of the most popular passenger train in American history gave a blast of its horn and began to pull out of Union Station. A small gathering of local dignitaries, celebrities, business people and train enthusiasts applauded.

Many of them still had glasses of champagne in their hands. They were the hardcore remainder of a party that had started hours earlier in the one custom coach that was pulled by the locomotive. The mayor, city council members, actors from both film and television, a handful of professional athletes, and other affluent people who could afford to pay $5,000 — tax deductible — for an evening of diversion had come and gone.

They all thought the locomotive had a retro cool design. The passenger coach was like a long thin room from an art deco mansion. It had a bar, a bandstand, a dance floor, plush settees and even a bedroom compartment where some serious getting-to-know-you might be done.

Only the door to the bedroom had been removed, so nobody actually got it on. Still, more than a few fantasies had been conceived. Strangers meeting on a train and all that. The band had been a big hit. One of the entrepreneurs present liked the idea of a traveling club. Exclusive as hell. Zipping through the night, letting all the little people gape in awe as it roared past.

The guy chatted with two big-shots, Edward Danner and Brian Kirby, whom he'd heard were dabbling in trains, "You guys know if there are any jet-powered trains yet? Hey, rocket-powered would be even better. All this is really cool, but these days you've gotta have speed, too."

Kirby told the man, "Rocket propulsion hasn't been considered, but a Japanese train has hit 381 mph in a test run."

The entrepreneur smiled and said, "That rocks. I could do something with that."

Danner only rolled his eyes and walked away.

"What's wrong with him?" the entrepreneur asked.

Kirby said, "He was hoping I wouldn't be here tonight. We used to be friends, but that was a while ago."

"I understand perfectly. I've been there. Two guys getting crosswise, it's worse than a divorce. So which one of you screwed the other?"

"I came out on the short end."

The entrepreneur smiled. "Yeah, but you just let him know you'd be getting even, right?"

"Why do you say that?" Kirby asked.

The other man laughed. "Why else would you have anything to say to him?"

As things stood in American railroading, the locomotive of the party train trundled out of Los Angeles at less than a tenth of the top speed of the world's fastest train. Even so, it drew a round of applause. The night's festivities had raised more than $400,000, after expenses, for the new train museum in Chicago where the locomotive was scheduled to spend the remainder of its days. Additional stops along the way east would add over $2 million dollars to the take.

Once the train was out of sight, the small crowd dispersed. Most got in their cars and drove home. The handful that had come from out of town made their way to the private airport in Santa Monica and jetted into the night sky.

— CHAPTER 3 —

Brooklyn, New York

Amtrak Special Agent Maj Olson was awakened in her apartment at six a.m. Not by the alarm on her iPhone, but by the ring tone: a passage from Tchaikovsky's "1812 Overture." The part where the composer inventively wrote a cannon barrage into his composition. Maj sat bolt upright in bed, disoriented for a moment.

Not by the early hour. Six o'clock was her normal workday wakeup time. Only she was sure she had *some* vacation time left. She looked at the date on her phone and saw she was right about that. Christ, it was only the *second* day of her vacation; she had almost two weeks to go.

She hadn't made any plans to travel. She was going to stay home. Catch up on her personal reading and her sleep. But the iPhone continued the cannonade, and she answered the call, saying, "This better be good."

It was. A train had gone missing. *Disappeared.* Not just any freight train. Nor a passenger train. Nor a commuter run. The damn thing was a two-car classic on its way from L.A. to the new train museum in Chicago. Maj had briefly entertained the idea of going to the museum's opening.

She'd decided not to do that. She was going to be lazy. Hang at home. Reevaluate her career choice. Maybe give it one last shot to find a college teaching post she might enjoy. Her Ph.D. from

Columbia in American history ought to be good enough to …

Spend twenty or more years in a classroom?

Well, yeah, but only in the right classroom at the perfect school.

That'd been her plan all along. But she had to admit …

The nature of the call that had awakened her had piqued her interest.

Trains, even the two-car variety, didn't just vanish. The damn things ran on rails and were massively heavy. The best illusionist in the world couldn't make one disappear.

But that was just what her boss, Deputy Chief Steve Chudzik, head of the Amtrak Police Intelligence Division, was telling her.

"The Chicago Museum Special was supposed to show up in Las Vegas at four a.m. Pacific Daylight Time. There was going to be gambling and a party for bigwigs with the proceeds going to the museum. The train was actually due in at 3:30 so it could be prepped for the guests. When it didn't arrive, the Las Vegas cops put up a helicopter to see if there was a problem on the line, an obstruction or something. But there hadn't been any call from the cab crew and the guys in the air saw no sign of the train."

"Damn," Maj said. "What the hell could have happened?"

"That's what you have to find out," Steve told her, "and make it fast."

"You're thinking, what? A theft or terrorism?"

"I'm keeping an open mind. Other people are going with terrorism."

"The FBI?"

"Among others."

"I'll be working with them?"

"Unh-uh. You'll be partnered with the BIA."

It took Maj a second to decode the acronym.

"The Bureau of Indian Affairs?" she asked, confused.

"Yeah, them."

Then the picture became clear. "You don't mean?"

"I do. Someone stole a Super Chief locomotive. What I hear,

the guy you'll be working with is some new poobah over there by the name of —"

— CHAPTER 4 —

Washington, D.C.

John Tall Wolf looked at his name on the door of his new office suite. His title was co-director, Office of Justice Services. He stepped inside. The desk for his secretary was empty. Somebody had known enough to let him make his own hire. Still, he felt uneasy.

He'd never wanted to become an administrator, much less the guy at the top of the pyramid. In his case, though, he wasn't alone at the summit. As co-director, he'd be working hip to hip with his nemesis Marlene Flower Moon. Maybe cheek to jowl would be a better description, he thought. In any case, they'd be well inside each other's comfort zone.

If John had his way, he'd still be a special agent working out of the Santa Fe field office — with the independence of having tendered his resignation on his first day of work at the BIA. Ready at a moment's notice to walk out the door if Marlene ever tried to force him to do something he thought was wrong. Something that might put him in hot water.

Now, however, both a measure of John's independence and his low profile as a rank-and-file government employee had been taken from him. Vice President Jean Morrissey had selected John for the job and President Patricia Grant had approved. Confirmation by the Senate was unnecessary. His new job didn't rank *that* high.

One small comfort of his sudden rise in the world was that he'd had occasion to meet James J. McGill, the president's husband. Sometimes known as her henchman. John liked that description; he also liked the man. McGill knew more than a little about a rush to prominence and had told John to call him if he ever wanted to talk.

The other perks of John's new status were a serious bump in pay and benefits: traveling business class, better hotel accommodations, more vacation time. Rebecca Bramley, a lieutenant in the Royal Canadian Mounted Police and the love of his life, had been all but giddy when she learned of John's promotion. She was in Washington to witness his swearing in by the Secretary of the Interior that afternoon.

John's parents, Dr. Haden Wolf and Serafina Wolf y Padilla, would also be present and couldn't be more proud of their son.

Really, it should have been a shining moment for him, a day of signal achievement.

Still, he felt uneasy and he saw the reason why the moment he opened his office door. Marlene Flower Moon, his co-director, his former boss and the woman he thought might really be Coyote, was waiting for him. It had never occurred to her the polite thing to do would have been to respect his new boundaries. The look she gave him said working with her now would be more of a battle than it had ever been before.

— CHAPTER 5 —

Marlene wasn't sitting in John's chair, but she was standing behind his desk, looking out the window. She turned when she heard him enter and said, "I think your office has a better view than mine, Tall Wolf."

John replied, "I'll trade with you, if you want."

Marlene waited for the kicker.

John added, "After I have your office cleansed and blessed by my mother."

They both knew John thought Marlene was Coyote. The Trickster. The sly shape-shifter that was always creating mischief for its own amusement and to its own advantage. Shortly after his birth, John's adoptive parents had saved him from being devoured by the largest coyote either of them had ever seen. If not in the flesh, John felt sure Marlene had been there in spirit. Had felt cheated out of making a meal of him as an infant.

He also thought she had pursued him in her current human guise when she'd recruited him to join the BIA not long after he graduated from college. Meaning to consume his soul if not his flesh. Maybe, though, she'd take a good bite out of his hide, too. Anyone who saw the incisors in Marlene's mouth would never doubt her ability to rend flesh. Anyone who'd ever worked for or with her would have no trouble thinking of her as a man-eater.

The mood she was in now only reinforced both of those perceptions for John.

"You feel safer with Mommy around?" she asked him.

Serafina Wolf y Padilla was a professor of cultural anthropology at the University of New Mexico. She was also a *curandera* — healer — and a *bruja* — witch. John had managed never to finish worse than even when he went head to head with Marlene, and he usually came out on top. Even so, he took comfort in the knowledge that if he ever suffered as a result of Coyote's scheming, his mother would exact a horrific retribution.

He was also secure enough in his masculinity to admit as much. "Sure, I always feel good with my mom around. Are you going to finally take the opportunity to meet my parents?"

John had invited Marlene to his swearing in, if only to see whether she had the courage to accept. Marlene smiled, revealing her overdeveloped canines.

Coyote was scheming again, John saw. At the very least, she meant to spoil his day.

"The reason I stopped by this morning was because someone at Amtrak hadn't gotten the memo that you now have charge of BIA special investigations and they called me."

"Amtrak?" John asked.

"Intelligence division, the people over there who look at threats to the train lines."

"What happened?" John asked.

"Someone stole a locomotive that left Los Angeles bound for Chicago. It's disappeared."

John looked puzzled. "How do you steal a train? And what would the BIA's interest be?"

Marlene smiled at John's momentary inability to intuit the situation.

"Come on, Tall Wolf. You should be able to answer at least one of your questions."

That was all the prodding he needed. "There's a Native American angle ... somebody thinks the bad guys are Indians?"

"Maybe. What else?"

"The engine itself is relevant?"

"How could that be?" Marlene smiled at him.

She was playing the teacher coaxing the slow kid in class. John didn't let her condescension get to him. He thought about the situation. Terrorist assholes around the world had been using truck-bombs for years. Such improvised weapons had terrible destructive power. If someone ever seized control of a train and filled it with explosives it could destroy the heart of a major city.

But what did that have to do with Native Americans? It hardly seemed likely anyone would use such a weapon against a reservation. Attacking any poor community would only bring global condemnation.

So … he'd asked if the locomotive was relevant and Marlene hadn't said no. That meant it was a reason for him to get involved. What train had he ever seen that was pertinent to a Native American culture?

That question led him to think of where he'd grown up: Santa Fe, New Mexico. His adoptive parents had instructed him in the cultural basics of the local tribe, the Northern Apaches, the people from whom his birth mother had come.

But it wasn't tribal lore that resonated now, it was the name of his hometown.

Santa Fe. Just like the old railroad, the Atchison, Topeka & Santa Fe.

Its most famous train was —

The phone on John's desk rang, surprising him.

He didn't even know his office number yet. He answered the call anyway.

"Special Agent Tall Wolf," he said.

"Soon to be Co-director Tall Wolf," Byron DeWitt replied. DeWitt was a deputy director at the FBI. "You hear someone grabbed a Super Chief locomotive?"

— CHAPTER 6 —

Southwestern U.S.

Alan White River had long ago lost count of how old he was. Keeping track had never mattered to him. He'd known when he was a boy, a man and an old man. Now, he was very old, but he still stood tall. His long, white hair remained full, pulled back from his weathered face. There was still a last rush to what had once been a fierce wind. A will that possessed a core of iron still animated him. He was sure he had everything necessary to perform one last great task. After that, he wouldn't care if his body passed beyond this life.

His spirit would remain, and if he was worthy, it would join the ranks of his ancestors. There he would be more at home and at peace than he'd ever been in this world. To those who survived him, he would have shown that he'd been a man worth remembering.

He told the young warriors who did his bidding, including his great-grandson, Bodaway, Apache for Firemaker, "Let me see these men, and let them see who stole their train."

White River and his band entered a rude mountain shack that wouldn't last another winter.

The four men who'd crewed the Super Chief sat tailor-fashion in a semi-circle and wore blindfolds. White River's men removed the coverings from their eyes. The crew's wrists were left bound behind their backs. White River might have towered over them, looked down on them, asserted his position of power.

He didn't do so. He sat as they did on the dirt floor.

Morning light pushed through the imperfectly joined walls. The rising sun also powered through the one dirty window and made the captives squint. To them, the man who held their lives in his hand was little more than a cloud of glowing white hair and a soft but strong voice. Its tone told them not to mistake old age for weakness.

White River said, "I told my people not to hurt any of you, if they could avoid it. I am told all of you are well. Is that so?"

The senior engineer, Albert Wicker, grimaced.

"You are injured?" White River asked.

Wicker shook his head. "Not hurt, but I need my blood pressure medication."

A yellow plastic bottle with a childproof cap landed in his lap. The senior engineer looked at the label and saw it was his prescription. "Thank you."

White River read the label. Took two pills from the bottle and popped them in the man's mouth. He recapped the bottle and left it in front of Wicker.

Another member of the crew, Dale Brent, a younger man, cracked wise. "So you're not gonna let us die of heart attacks. You're just gonna shoot us, right?"

Bodaway, standing behind Brent, put a foot hard into one of his kidneys. The crewman toppled over sideways and moaned. White River shot his great-grandson a disapproving look and waited until Brent grew quiet.

Without any verbal instruction, Bodaway righted the man.

Then White River said, "You will have food and water. You will have each other's company. You will be watched, but if you do not try to run, we will leave you alone."

White River stood. His shoulders were still broad. They blocked the sun and allowed the railroad crew to see his face. A thousand lines scored it, the sum of which showed he wasn't a cruel man, but neither was he to be underestimated. He could claim their lives with a word or a gesture.

As if reading their minds, he told the crew in an even tone, "If you try to escape, you will die. If you attempt to run and hurt one of my people, you will die badly. But if you cause no trouble you will be released before long. Your train will be returned to you and you will be allowed to complete your journey. Think of these words before you decide how to act."

White River turned to leave but Wicker, the senior engineer, said, "I won't be able to take my pills with my hands tied behind my back."

White River looked at him. "No, you couldn't do that, could you?"

He spoke in a language his captives didn't understand. The bindings were removed from the wrists of each crewman. They all tried to rub the pain away.

White River inclined his head, and one of his men brought several plastic shopping bags into the shack and lined them up against a wall.

"Food and water," White River said. "We will leave you now. You won't see us, but we will be watching you at all times. Remember what I said. You try to run, you die. Maybe in great pain."

For the moment at least, none of the crew doubted him.

— CHAPTER 7 —

Washington, D.C.

Byron DeWitt escorted Maj Olson into the office of the Secretary of the Interior. DeWitt began his introductions with John Tall Wolf. "You'll be working with the new co-director of the BIA's Office of Justice Services, John Tall Wolf."

While shaking John's hand, Maj asked, "You won't be delegating the investigation to someone else, sir?"

She'd already been surprised by having met with DeWitt. The guy was way up the FBI food chain. She thought he'd hand her off to an underling, someone closer to her own pay grade but, no, he explained he'd be working his half of the case and —

John told the Amtrak special agent, "I like to get out of the office. At heart, I'm a working cop."

That message was meant for more than Maj, but she pleased John when she said, "Me, too. I like nothing better than doing field work. I'm a hands-on person."

Maj's claim was backed up by her appearance. Bright, attentive eyes, a long, lean build and strong hands with short nails and calluses that didn't come from pushing paper.

"We should get along just fine," John told her.

DeWitt introduced John's parents and Rebecca Bramley, whom he'd met at dinner the night before, and the soon-to-leave-office Secretary of the Interior, George Kinsley. Saving the headliner for last, DeWitt said, "Madam Vice President, may I present

Amtrak Special Agent Maj Olson, Ph.D. in American History from Columbia University. Special Agent Olson, the honorable Jean Morrissey, the vice president of the United States."

The vice president smiled and extended her hand. Maj took it and did her best not to get into a my-grip-is-stronger-than-yours contest.

Even so, the vice president felt the strength in Maj's grip and asked, "Did you play any sports as an undergrad, Special Agent?"

"I ran track at Columbia, ma'am."

Jean Morrissey beamed at her fellow collegiate athlete. The vice president had played ice hockey at Minnesota. "That's great. Well, we'd better get down to business. Secretary Kinsley has an oath to administer and then we all have a train to find."

Maj watched as John took his oath. She could see he took it seriously, but she thought there was just a glimmer of reservation in his eyes. His parents and Ms. Bramley, though, placed no qualifications on the pride they felt for him.

Ms. Bramley, introduced as a lieutenant in the RCMP, looked like quite an athletic specimen herself. A good match for a big guy like Co-director Tall Wolf.

The Wolfs were interesting looking people, Maj thought. Immaculately dressed and groomed, they were the picture of the American professional class. Still, there was something other-worldly about them. That was the best adjective Maj could find.

And her new partner, if she might think of him that way, was he unusual, too?

Before she could explore that notion, the ceremony was over and everyone was shaking hands, including hers once again. Making her feel she was a full member of the investigation. That was reassuring and still a little hard for her to believe. Government work was normally a matter of hierarchy not meritocracy, but —

At the vice president's suggestion, Secretary Kinsley escorted the senior Wolfs and Ms. Bramley out of his office for the moment and she addressed the three federal employees who would be working under her direction.

"The president," she told them, "has delegated the job of finding this train to me. I don't intend to let her down. I know all of you won't let me down. I'll need daily reports from you, Deputy Director DeWitt and you, Co-director Tall Wolf. Special Agent Olson, I'll expect to see your input, too. We're going to pull out all the stops here. If any of you need resources beyond what you might presently foresee, contact me immediately. I'll make sure you get whatever you need. Without skipping any legalities, I want to wrap up this matter as quickly as possible. Do we all understand each other?"

John and DeWitt said, "Yes, ma'am."

The vice president turned to Maj. "Special Agent?"

"Ma'am, Amtrak has already agreed to provide me with a two-car train similar to the one that disappeared. My thought was to follow the route the Super Chief should have taken and see where I think things might have gone wrong."

Maj glanced at John to see if he was on board with that idea.

He nodded. "That would be a good start to the investigation."

The vice president said, "Very well. Do you have something else in mind, Special Agent?"

"I just had the thought, ma'am, it might be a good idea if I could be provided with a dirt bike. The trail might lead off the rail bed."

For the blink of an eye Jean Morrissey looked as if she wished she could ride along with Maj, but she only nodded. "Whatever you need. Anything else?"

"If I'm not out of line, ma'am," Maj said, "it might also be a good idea to have a helicopter on call."

— CHAPTER 8 —

Flying West

John asked Maj Olson, "Would you like me to call you Doctor Olson?"

She shook her head. "Please don't."

The two of them had just taken off from National Airport in Washington and were headed to Los Angeles International Airport. They were afforded the use of the aircraft the government made available to outgoing Department of the Interior Secretary Kinsley. He graciously had said they were welcome to it; he'd used it only twice during his time in the president's Cabinet.

A Montana oil man, Kinsley normally used his own Gulfstream to save the government money.

Not only had that been more convenient for him, it also allowed him to conduct personal affairs — including those of the amorous sort — when he flew. Kinsley was a bachelor and something of a ladies' man. He correctly assumed that it wouldn't look good for the president if he conducted any high-altitude hanky-panky in a government airplane. What he did in his own flying machine, however, was his business.

His choice of transportation, moreover, conformed to the Department of the Interior's main guideline for travel: Choose the means that provides the best value to the government.

John and Maj were using the plane because they'd interpreted the vice president's directive to proceed with haste not to include the vicissitudes of commercial air travel. It also turned out that the DOI's Office of Aviation Services would be able to provide Maj with a helicopter should she need one.

The FBI, tasked by Deputy Director DeWitt, would provide Maj with a dirt bike in L.A.

She'd asked John, "You want one, too?"

"Sure, why not? If your train can accommodate it."

"That's one of the great things about trains: They can haul just about anything."

Now, she responded to John's question. "Only my mom calls me Dr. Olson, and she does it only when she's trying to fix me up with some guy."

"How has that worked out?" John asked.

"So far, I've been able to elude all prospects," she said with a laugh.

"It's okay then if I call you, Maj?" He pronounced the name to rhyme with Taj.

"That'd be great." She was pleased when people didn't call her Madge. "And do I call you Co-director Tall Wolf?"

"John will be fine."

"May I ask what you'll be doing in Los Angeles while I'm securing the use of the train Amtrak says it will have for me?"

John gave her a look. "Says it will have?"

"My colleagues try their best, but Amtrak is chronically under-funded."

"Give me a minute," John told her.

One of the many perks of not flying commercial was you didn't have to worry about whether you could make a phone call when you felt like it. John might have called Marlene Flower Moon and asked her to lean on whoever it took to make sure Maj's train was waiting for her in L.A. Only after disappearing from his office an hour earlier, there was no telling when or where Marlene might turn up next.

John was sure he could have persuaded Marlene it would be in her self-interest to be helpful on this case. In fact, he had a big idea to suggest to her. But he wanted to test another question. How badly did the vice president really want to see this matter resolved?

He called the White House and identified himself. He was put through to Jean Morrissey immediately. He expressed his concern. The vice president told him not to worry. Dr. Olson's train would be waiting for her by the time she arrived at Union Station in Los Angeles. The vice president would see to it personally.

Hearing that news, Maj was impressed. "That's some pull you've got, John."

"More likely an indication of how serious this situation is," he said.

Modesty aside, John thought being able to reach out to the second most powerful person in the world and get the help he needed was a heady accomplishment. He'd always believed that working collaboratively produced better results. But he'd never been able to reach so high before.

He'd have to be careful. Couple his new promotion with access to the White House and a guy might get too exalted an opinion of himself. Influence always came at a cost. A loss of the common touch if nothing else. He wouldn't want that.

Nothing would please Marlene more than to see his swift rise result in an abrupt crash.

"Thinking deep thoughts?" Maj asked.

John smiled. "Despite our current means of travel, I'm just trying to stay grounded."

"Always a good idea," Maj said. "So what will you be doing in L.A. while I'm getting ready to ride the rails, and should I hold my departure until you're ready to climb aboard?"

John told her. "You keep to your own schedule. As long as I know where you are, I can catch up with you. What I have in mind is to get a list of all the monied folk who paid to see the Super Chief pull out of Los Angeles. They were the last ones we know of to see the train. Maybe one of them noticed something unusual."

Maj gave John an inquiring look. "Or even had something to do with the Super Chief not turning up in Las Vegas?"

John smiled again. "Good to know you're not just book-smart."

"There are a few other working cops in my family. One of them gave me a nudge in the direction of my current line of work. So you think there might be a villain in philanthropist's clothing?"

"Wouldn't be the first time," John told her.

— CHAPTER 9 —

San Francisco, California

Captain Makilah Walsh was known to some in the San Francisco Police Department as an administrative rat. That was, she was the commanding officer of the unit that investigated accusations of procedural violations by the department's cops. Officer-involved shootings and in-custody deaths were her bailiwick.

She'd also put in time as a criminal rat, investigating allegations of criminal conduct by San Francisco coppers. Her reputation in that role inspired awe. She approached the job with the same philosophy the justice system was alleged to apply: innocent until proven guilty. She did her best to find out where the truth lay.

If an officer was being set up by someone with a grudge, she'd give it her all to clear his good name. But if a cop crossed the line, broke the law and disgraced his badge, she'd skin him alive and hang his hide out for all the world to see. Her approach had made her both lifelong friends and enemies.

One of the bad cops, knowing she was closing in on him, decided to get the jump on her and blow Makilah away before she could complete her investigation and hand the DA a gift-wrapped case. In the ensuing shootout, she sustained gunshot wounds to the upper-right chest and both thighs. "Gonna make it hell for me to look good in my bikini," she'd joked to friends from her hospital bed.

Makilah had gotten off only one shot, fired from the ground

where she lay after being wounded. On an upward trajectory, the round had entered her assailant's head at the bridge of his nose, transited his brain and blew out a section of the rear of his skull. He was dead before he knew it, probably while he was still thinking he'd been the better gunfighter.

Of course, Makilah was investigated for an officer-involved shooting. Not only was she found justified in her actions, she was promoted to the command of the administrative rat squad. She took pride in her work and insisted that everyone in her unit do the same. For excellence on the job, she gave out Solid Gold Rat awards: a tie pin, charm bracelet or body piercing ornament, per the officer's preference.

That morning, Makilah started her day with an interview of Sergeant Fabrizio "Fab" Gallo of the Special Investigations Division. SID worked what the department labeled "complex, sensitive and confidential" criminal investigations. The unit often worked with federal agencies. SID was considered a plum assignment staffed by the best and brightest the department had to offer.

Makilah had done her homework before the interview got started. She'd read the initial reports of the attempted arrest of Merritt Kinney at his residence in the city. She'd reviewed the personnel records of the four cops sent to arrest Kinney. She'd also reached out to cops she'd cleared of false accusations to find out tidbits that didn't find their ways into official documents.

Gallo, for instance, had been a ladies' man before he got married, but hadn't played around since. Made sense to Makilah. He'd landed a lady investment banker who not only made an enormous salary but was also very easy on the eyes. A man would have to be a fool to risk that combination just to do some catting around.

Not that there weren't guys that dumb. Some of them just couldn't resist random temptation. Others thought they were so smart they could get away with anything. Makilah hadn't met a cop yet who could outsmart her, but she felt intuitively that she'd do well not to underestimate Sergeant Gallo.

She greeted him with a proffered hand and the offer of something to drink.

"San Pellegrino?" he asked, taking his seat opposite Makilah.

She knew he was joking, maybe seeing how she'd react. Gauging her personality.

Makilah said, "Might take a minute, but I think we can do that."

She relayed the request to her civilian secretary.

Didn't take any time at all. Sally brought in the bottle of Italian sparkling water she kept in the office fridge. The one she drank with lunch every day, as Makilah well knew. Sally brought a glass and a coaster, too. Poured for the sergeant as if he were at a fine restaurant.

Gallo rewarded her with a smile that must have made many a woman flush with pleasure.

Maybe that was how he'd nabbed his banker.

To cap off the moment, Gallo said, *"Grazie."*

Sally, not easily impressed, left on a cloud.

The sergeant raised his glass to Makilah and asked, "You check me out top to bottom, know what kind of water I like to drink?"

"Happy coincidence. What can you tell me about Mr. Kinney's death?"

"Only what's in the report. I'm sure you've read that."

"I have," Makilah said. "Let me hear it from you directly."

Gallo put his glass down on the coaster and told his story.

Makilah reviewed it. "Mr. Kinney fled his apartment in anticipation of his arrest?"

Gallo replied, "I can't say for sure what he was thinking, but it did seem to me like consciousness of guilt."

"It's reasonable to assume, though, that he saw your approach, you and your men. He didn't just happen to be on the roof of his building when you found him."

"The door to his apartment was open when we arrived. Again, that might be interpreted in different ways, but one idea that occurred to me was that, yes, he saw us coming and felt the only way he could run was up. So he went to the roof."

Gallo picked up his glass and took a sip of water.

Makilah felt he was being truthful, forthcoming even, but the way he hedged his answers made her curious.

"I didn't see it in your record, Sergeant, but have you ever been to law school?"

Gallo laughed. "You mean the way I talk? No, I haven't been to law school. But after getting married, well, my wife and I socialize with a lot of people who are lawyers. You think their bad habits are rubbing off on me?"

Makilah smiled. "I'll let you know if that happens. Your report says one of your men videoed your team's movements and your telling Mr. Kinney he was under arrest. Is that right?"

"Yes, ma'am. I have a duplicate of the video file right here. The original was forwarded to your office last night." He handed her a flash drive. "You did receive the original, right?"

"Our tech people have it, yes."

"Nobody diddled it," Gallo said.

"Good to know. Let's see what you've brought me." She invited him to look over her shoulder as she plugged the drive into her laptop. They watched the SID team from the time it entered the building, through the moment Kinney made his futile, fatal leap, and then looking down from the roof to the ground below where there seemed to be no doubt that the man had died on impact.

Nonetheless, the last image and words on the recording were of Gallo calling for ambulance.

"You see anything we missed, anything we didn't do according to procedure?" he asked Makilah.

"Not a thing." Still, she couldn't help but wonder if even an unedited video couldn't be shot in such a way as to distort an in-person view of what had happened. Suspicions were a part of her job. So was testing their strength. Some were easily discarded; others refused to budge.

What she was feeling now lay somewhere in the middle.

"There a problem?" Gallo asked.

"Don't see one," Makilah replied. "Sometimes, I'm just quiet for a minute or two."

"So we're good?" Gallo asked, returning to his seat.

They both knew that question was premature. The investigation was only getting started. Just hearing Gallo ask if he'd be cleared cranked up Makilah's suspicion a notch.

"Who called in the complaint," she asked, "the one that said Mr. Kinney had stolen a trade secret from his company?"

"Arthur Halston, the general counsel of Positron, Inc."

A Silicon Valley high tech company, one of two working on developing high-speed train service between San Francisco and Los Angeles.

"Mr. Halston said he feared Kinney might be working for the Chinese," Gallo added.

That was the first note Makilah had heard that didn't ring true. Yes, the government in Beijing would steal any useful technology it could from the U.S. She knew that from reading both law enforcement bulletins and the business section of the *Chronicle*. But she'd also read the Chinese were *ahead* of the U.S. in high-speed rail. If anything, that was one area where Washington should be stealing *from* the Chinese.

But Makilah had something else in mind.

"Mr. Halston, is he one of the lawyers you and your wife socialize with?"

That caught Gallo by surprise. He looked like he wanted to kick himself for giving too much away. "Yes, he is."

"Do you know anyone else at Positron?"

"I've met Edward Danner."

Now, Makilah had to keep surprise off her face. Danner was the founder, CEO and biggest stockholder of Positron. A billionaire a hundred times over. Rich company indeed for a police sergeant to keep.

"Your relationship with Mr. Halston and your acquaintance with Mr. Danner, were they the reasons you went to arrest Mr. Kinney in the middle of the night at his residence instead of picking him up, say, at his place of work during his lunch hour?"

All the charm and animation that had made Gallo so attractive only moments earlier deserted him. His voice sounded as flat as any perp she'd ever questioned. "That and being told Kinney might be selling vital technology to another country. It was impossible to tell if or when he might run. I used my best judgment."

Perfectly reasonable, Makilah thought, but the mere appearance of the police had panicked Kinney so badly he'd risked his life and lost. Something was definitely wrong with that. The man had to be fearful he'd suffer a worse fate than a simple arrest and a trial in a courtroom.

She closed her computer and said, "Thank you, Sergeant. That will be all for now."

Gallo got to his feet and Makilah could see he wanted to ask his question again.

Were they good? He didn't say another word, though.

He could see they weren't good. Not even close.

— CHAPTER 10 —

Los Angeles

Vice President Jean Morrissey had made good on her promise. The two-car train Maj had been promised was waiting for her at Union Station when she and John arrived. There was a four-man crew in the cab of the locomotive ready to roll. Word had been passed throughout the nationwide rail system. Maj's train had the right of way wherever it went, whenever it wanted it.

Other trains would pull onto sidings for her; she would not do so for them.

Unless that was the way she wanted it.

Fresh cab crews would be made available, if necessary.

The vice president had literally pulled out all the stops.

"Makes me think the woman is expecting big things from us," John told her.

He'd joined Maj at Union Station because the first person he wanted to interview worked there, station master Jack Stanton. Stanton had been among those present to see the Super Chief off. John thought if anyone might have noticed something amiss with the train, it would be him. Stanton hadn't met them when they arrived, but he'd left word he would join them shortly.

"What happens if we fail to deliver?" Maj asked John. "Disappoint the VP?"

"We probably won't get invited to Ms. Morrissey's inaugural ball."

Maj wouldn't mind that. "I don't like to get dressed up anyway. But I was thinking more of professional consequences."

John had wondered about the possible repercussions, too. Not with any trepidation. His promotion had fallen out of the sky on him far more than it had been earned. He told Maj, "There's always private sector employment."

She made a face.

"What?" John asked. "You like working for Amtrak?"

"I couldn't find a teaching job I liked; that's why I became a cop. But I'll tell you that story another time. I'm going to talk to the guys driving the train. They might be nervous, what with the other crew disappearing. Nothing reassures big strong railroad men like a female Ph.D. with a gun."

"And a badge," John said with a smile. "Don't forget the badge."

"Right. Why don't you check out the passenger car? Tall as you are, you can call dibs on the bigger bed, if there is one."

With the division of labor established, John climbed into the passenger car. It was furnished at a level comparable with a hotel earning a rating between two and three stars: clean, comfortable, suitable for middle management. Someone must have missed the memo that he was something of a big shot these days, he thought. That or the BIA didn't cut much ice with Amtrak.

Still, there was more than enough space for two federal employees to coexist and do their jobs without any discomfort. There were two work stations with desktops the size of card tables, electrical connections to recharge computers and smartphones and a decal on a window proclaiming the coach had wireless connectivity. A group of four large facing seats made small conferences possible. A kitchen area featured a compact fridge — stocked with soft drinks and spring water — a coffee maker and a microwave oven. A cabinet was stocked with sweet and salty snacks and, John was glad to see, herbal tea, boxes of dried fruit and granola bars.

There were two lavatories, one shower stall and two sleeping compartments. The beds were the same size so there was no point in claiming dibs. At the back of the car was a storage area, primarily used, John assumed, for luggage and office materials but now partially filled with two dirt bikes. Yamaha YZ450Fs, John saw. The motorcycles looked fast and expensive.

The vice president really was giving them no reason to fail.

She probably had an army attack helicopter on standby for them, too. If John remembered right, the top model of that weapons platform was the AH-64D Apache Long Bow. An aircraft named after his own people. Some of them anyway.

He'd no sooner sat down at one of the work stations and started reading the list of people who'd attended the send-off of the Super Chief when his phone rang. Nice clear signal, too. Marlene was calling.

"I wanted you to be the first to know, Tall Wolf, I'm going to resign my position with the BIA."

"You get another movie gig?" he asked.

Marlene had acted as co-producer on Clay Steadman's latest, and probably final, film "Texas Mean."

"No. I haven't decided what I'm going to do next."

"May I offer a suggestion?"

Marlene laughed. It wasn't a happy sound, more one of calculation. Something that might accompany a plan for revenge. One that might include him.

"Sure, Tall Wolf, tell me what I should do."

"The Secretary of the Interior is resigning. I'm sure you know that."

"I do."

"I think you should try for the job. Then you could be my boss again. Nominally, at least."

"You are a sonofabitch."

Despite the criticism, John could tell the seed of ambition was already planted.

"You really think I could get a cabinet post?" Marlene asked.

"Do you think Native Americans stole the Super Chief?" he replied.

On his last case, a series of bank robberies, a multi-ethnic crew, none of them Native American, had masqueraded as Indians.

Marlene said, "Yes, this time I do."

"So do I. My sense is there's some large grievance involved."

"That list goes back centuries."

"My point exactly. You could be helpful sorting things out. Make the difference between failure and success."

John's flattery was transparent, but Coyote did enjoy her vanity. She also wasn't one to pass up opportunity.

"You always have been good about sharing credit, Tall Wolf."

"Do my best to give it away."

"But it keeps finding you anyway, Mr. Co-director."

His promotion still stung Marlene.

"If we succeed this time," he said, "the moment would be right for me to suggest to higher powers that you'd be the right person to succeed George Kinsley at DOI. Darling of Washington that I am, someone might even listen to me."

After a pause, Marlene said, "Why would you do that for me?"

"Half the fun is figuring it out, right?" John asked.

Marlene laughed. "You're right. That is part of our game."

She agreed to table her resignation and help him.

Not everyone was fully on board, though. Maj joined him in the passenger car with some news. The station master, Jack Stanton, had to deal with a family emergency that was worse than first thought. He wouldn't be available for an interview that day. Maybe not even tomorrow. Stanton would get back to John as soon as he could.

Not a good way for the investigation to start, John thought. Especially with the No. 2 at the White House cracking the whip. Never one to fret, though, John decided to be philosophical.

"Okay," he said, "I'll spend my time talking to the local fat-wallet railroad aficionados."

"The ones who came in from out of town, too," Maj reminded him.

"Them, too," he agreed.

John said goodbye to his new colleague.

He stood on the platform and watched her train pull out of the station.

Hoping he wouldn't have to go looking for her, too.

— CHAPTER 11 —

Washington, D.C.

FBI Deputy Director Byron DeWitt met with the vice president in her office at the White House, just down the hall from the Oval Office. He wondered if he'd have been dealing directly with the president if her time wasn't being taken up by a possible impeachment being brought ever closer to reality by the Republicans in the House of Representatives. A long-time student of China, its culture and languages, DeWitt remembered a favored curse from that land: May you live in interesting times.

Things were fascinating all right. A two-car train was missing. None of the dispatchers in the nation's rail system had been able to locate it in the fifteen hours since it had failed to arrive at its scheduled stop in Las Vegas. That meant its transponder, radio and even the cab crew's cell phones had been shut down.

Still, DeWitt thought, the damn thing ran on rails. The locomotive weighed a hundred tons. To lift it off the tracks, you'd need a crane with a boom over a hundred and fifty feet long. Such an exercise wouldn't exactly be inconspicuous. Even if somebody managed to lift the Super Chief off the tracks, where the hell would he *put* it?

And what would the point of that be?

So far neither DeWitt nor anyone else at the FBI had managed to answer those questions.

What seemed far more likely in their surmises was the stolen locomotive was going to be the delivery vehicle for a terrorist payload. At the moment of the train's departure from L.A., they knew that the engine was pulling only one passenger car. But that didn't mean whoever was behind the theft couldn't also have helped himself to any number of empty freight or tanker cars.

The old Super Chief trains used tandem locomotives to pull a dozen passenger cars. DeWitt's research people were working on seeing what one engine could pull. Even if it were only three or four cars, their capacity to carry fertilizer or fuel bombs would be —

"Bad news?" The vice president looked up at DeWitt from behind her West Wing desk.

She'd just put down her phone after speaking with the president. DeWitt hadn't been listening overtly or had even given the conversation much of his attention. Still, he'd heard what sounded like the decision to begin the impeachment proceedings was now on the House calendar.

DeWitt responded, "In this case, I'm afraid no news is bad news, and the lack of information only makes imagining what might be going on worse."

"Nothing on your end or from Tall Wolf or Special Agent Olson?"

"We've done background checks on the cab crew in the Super Chief. None of them has a criminal record or known association with any radical group. Two of them aren't even registered to vote. All of them according to co-workers and neighbors are good guys. All of them are married with at least one kid and said to be good husbands and fathers."

"What about the station master or other people working at Union Station in L.A.?"

DeWitt sighed.

"What?" the vice president asked.

"Jack Stanton, the station master, checks out clean, too, but his older son, Patrick, a high school athlete, collapsed today after running a track practice. They thought he'd be okay because he revived quickly. Then in the school nurse's office he lost consciousness again. The last I heard he was in an ambulance on the way to the hospital. His prognosis is uncertain."

"Damn," Jean Morrissey said. She had no children, but she definitely empathized with athletes. The possible loss of the station master's son prompted a thought. "Even if the crew and Mr. Stanton are all good guys, might anyone be threatening their families?"

"We're looking into that right now, Madam Vice President."

"Good. You have had contact with Tall Wolf and Olson, right?"

DeWitt nodded. Said John had called him fifteen minutes ago. Told the vice president of the efforts Tall Wolf and Maj were making.

"You're the clearing house on all this, Byron. As soon as the FBI or your colleagues learn something of substance, you let me know immediately. Any time, day or night."

"I will," DeWitt said.

"You brought the list of scenarios, the ways terrorists might use a train?"

"I did." DeWitt took his laptop and a flash drive from his attaché case.

He rose from his chair, placed the computer on the vice president's desk and was about to start his presentation when she put a hand on his and said, "One thing before we begin."

"Yes?"

"In speaking with the president just now I was given another assignment."

DeWitt felt a flash of empathy. Jean Morrissey's burdens must be second only to the president's. He supposed that was appropriate to her position. "Is there any way I might be of help, Madam Vice President?"

"In fact, there is. There's a state dinner at the White House tonight. Ordinarily, the president would not let politics, even the threat of impeachment, interfere with that. The visiting head of state, however, is not one of her favorites. The event is more of an obligation than a pleasure. She asked me to stand in for her."

DeWitt found that amusing but kept a straight face.

"And the way I might be of help?" he asked.

Jean Morrissey told the deputy director, "I need a date."

— CHAPTER 12 —

Los Angeles

John Tall Wolf called Marlene Flower Moon and said, "This is not a *quid pro quo* for my helping you with the cabinet job, but I need a favor: the name of an L.A. restaurant with star power. The kind of place ordinary people would have to book a table months in advance and big shots get in just by showing up."

"What makes you think I'd know of any place like that?"

John stroked his former boss's ego. "Come on, Marlene. Is there a restaurant anywhere that wouldn't let you waltz in just on your looks alone?"

She laughed. "How long have you been avoiding my advances, Tall Wolf?"

"I'm different. Has anyone else ever turned you down?"

"No." A note of anger singed the margins of the reply.

"Of course not," John said. "So where did Clay Steadman take you out to eat when you were here working on the post-production of 'Texas Mean'?"

"Gio."

"As in Giovanni? Italian?"

"Tuscan cuisine." Marlene told John the name of the A-list movie star who was the money behind the place. "That's an open secret, but you're not supposed to mention his name there or you'll never be allowed to come back."

"No problem," John told her.

"You're supposed to come for the food."

"Is the food good?"

"Excellent."

"Does the place have a private room, and if it does can you get it for me on short notice?"

"You mean immediately?"

"Yes."

"Why should I?"

"Because, despite what I just said, my heart will be more in it when I push for you to become the next Secretary of the Interior."

Marlene laughed. "So you're not a hundred percent altruistic, Tall Wolf."

"We all have our flaws."

Marlene understood he was implicitly criticizing her as well as himself.

The favor Tall Wolf was asking for was trivial. No more than picking up a phone.

Even so, she hesitated before agreeing.

She was supposed to be the one who twisted people around her finger, but with Tall Wolf it more often worked the other way.

He added, "If we wrap up this grand-theft locomotive quickly, you'll like the way I'll campaign for you, give you a *big* share of the credit."

She didn't doubt it. He'd done it often enough in the past. Tall Wolf never worried about covering himself with glory — he even went out of his way to hide his achievements — and the bastard still managed to get ahead in the world. He'd already stolen half her job-title.

Still, Marlene knew she'd have no chance of landing the cabinet post without Tall Wolf's help. Bowing to pragmatism and repressing a growl, she said, "All right, Tall Wolf, I'll make a call."

"I'll need the address, too."

She gave it to him and John relayed it to the driver of the cab he hailed.

John felt a Q&A session with the local people who'd seen the

Super Chief depart Union Station would go much better if he could give them a little good food and drink. That and provide them with a story of being treated to hors d'oeuvres where the glitterati dined. From everything he'd ever learned of Los Angeles, status was the true drug of choice.

He also thought if he overreached with his new government credit cards maybe he'd get knocked back down a peg. His plan was not only to help Marlene climb the bureaucratic ladder. He wanted to scoot back down a couple of rungs.

Put enough space between the two of them, maybe she'd obsess less about him.

— CHAPTER 13 —

Southwest U.S.

Alan White River stood with three other Native American tribal elders — chiefs when they were talking amongst themselves — and half-a-dozen younger men. Included in the latter group was White River's great-grandson, Bodaway, also known as Thomas Bilbray in the white man's world. The men gathered under a canopy of broadleaf trees. The foliage shading them was far thicker than what nature had provided.

Bodaway was a structural engineer, an honors graduate of Georgia Tech. He'd learned many interesting things about drone technology from his classmates who'd gone into aeronautical work. An example being the amazing resolution of their cameras. The army had one that could resolve fine detail in an object as small as six inches from an altitude of twenty thousand feet.

Spotting a Super Chief would be duck soup.

At Bodaway's direction, layers of pruned branches in leaf had been entwined with the living limbs of the trees overhanging the area. The supplements would soon wither and their dead leaves would fall, but the camouflage and concealment would last long enough for White River's purposes. The prize they had stolen would not be seen from above by either drones or satellites.

The classic Super Chief locomotive and its elaborate passenger car stood motionless before the onlookers, resting on a length of track no longer than the two cars. No rails connected them to any other line. To Bodaway, the rail cars looked like a train enthusiast's ultimate Christmas gift. Something Neiman Marcus might dream up for a billionaire.

Horace Black Bear, one of the chiefs, saw things differently.

"If it was up to me, I would destroy this iron beast. Beat it to death with my own hands and a good war club."

The old chief turned to Bodaway, his eyes asking if such a thing would be possible.

"You could destroy the electronics in the cab" Bodaway said. "Keep it from moving. But it's not going anywhere right now."

Black Bear frowned, as if it was impertinent of Bodaway to dash his hopes.

White River came to his great-grandson's aid. He said, "I have promised that the train would be returned, once we are done with it."

Bodaway said, "Grandfather, we *could* take the locomotive apart. Return it one piece at a time. Take a century or so to do it."

Black Bear and the others looked at Bodaway, some of them clearly intrigued.

Then Bodaway grinned and said, "But where would the fun be in that? All of us would have gone to our ancestors by then."

White River, who had other plans for the locomotive, clapped his great-grandson on the shoulder and laughed. The others joined in.

Their amusement grew when Bodaway added, "Besides, if we drag things out that long, even the government people might be able to find us."

— CHAPTER 14 —

Los Angeles

John Tall Wolf watched the waiters in the private dining room at Gio make sure everyone had the appetizers and wines of their choice and then leave. John got by with a bottle of San Pellegrino. Marlene had not only come through with access to the restaurant and its largest private dining area, a favored venue for show biz after-parties, she also got Clay Steadman's production company to foot the bill.

Suspecting that Marlene was trying to set a trap for him, John almost called the whole thing off. Accept the fact he'd have to do a great many individual interviews. In a very short time to accommodate the vice president's sense of urgency.

Then Marlene told him, "Look, Tall Wolf, you had a good idea, appealing to Angelenos' love of celebrity, but you didn't take it far enough. Some of the people you want to talk to might think of Gio as a restaurant they've already left behind. You attach the name of one of the biggest stars in town, though, you'll get everyone on your list."

John had read about attaching the right elements, e.g directors and actors, to get a movie greenlighted in Hollywood. So he could understand Marlene's logic. But he disliked losing the chance to overspend his government budget. Not that he knew what that was.

Marlene turned out to be absolutely right. Eating at Gio on Clay Steadman's tab? Everybody John wanted to see showed up.

Now, they'd all have a good story to tell their friends.

John gave his guests their fifteen minutes of fame by association. Then he stood up and said, "My name is John Tall Wolf. I'm your host for the evening and also the co-director of the Office of Justice Services of the Bureau of Indian Affairs."

The illumination in the room was artfully moderate. The food looked great and the diners looked as good as they ever would. John didn't need the Ray-Ban sunglasses he wore outdoors on all but the most overcast days. He kept them on anyway. With his height and wearing the shades his presence was imposing. He had everyone's attention.

"I asked all of you here this evening because you are the people who saw the Super Chief off at Union Station last night. "

Now he had them curious and leaning forward. Looking left and right, nodding in recognition. Same crowd all right — and they all had the same unspoken question: What was going on? News of the Super Chief's disappearance had yet to be revealed.

Byron DeWitt had intervened with cops in Las Vegas and Amtrak had told the train people to keep mum. The intended guests had been told there had been a breakdown on the rails. Americans had no trouble accepting the idea of trains being delayed or even canceled.

John said, "All I can tell you at the moment is that a crime has been committed."

He'd called Byron DeWitt with the suggestion that they limit information to any third parties — such as the gathering at Gio — but tell no outright lies. At some point, the news would come out and the investigation might depend on public cooperation.

The deputy director was an easy sell on that point. Adding to John's growing appreciation of the woman, Vice President Morrissey agreed. They'd tell the story, most of it anyway, when they could.

A man to John's left raised his hand.

"Yes?"

"Can you tell us if this is some sort of hate crime?"

"What would make you think that?" John asked.

"Well, the train was the Super Chief; you're from the Bureau of Indian Affairs."

"You think there's some slight against Native Americans here?"

"I don't know. That's what I'm asking."

"Without going any further into the details of what happened, I don't think that's the case."

"Maybe it has to do with another kind of hate," a woman on the other side of the room said.

"What other kind?" John asked.

"People who hate rail travel. They might vandalize the Super Chief, if that's what happened."

John didn't affirm or deny the woman's speculation.

He asked, "Who hates rail travel?"

A second man said, "The airlines."

"Auto makers," said a second woman.

"Highway contractors," came another voice.

"Oil companies," offered a third woman.

John held up his hand like a traffic cop. Clearly, a gathering of rail fanciers felt they had enemies.

"As I've said," he told the gathering, "I can't comment further on speculation right now. What I can assure you of, though, is that as soon as the matter is resolved, the substance of it will become public knowledge."

"Unless Washington decides to cover it up," a new speaker asserted.

John lowered his glasses to the tip of his nose. He looked at the man and then at every corner of the room. "You help me, I'll help you. You'll get at least the basics of the story from me, if not from anyone else."

He raised his Ray-Bans and said, "What I'd like to know now is if anyone here saw anything suspicious or even just out of place either at the farewell party or as the train pulled out of the station."

People looked around at each other, shook their heads or shrugged.

The man who asked the initial question about a hate crime

told John, "If something bad happened to that beautiful old train, you could do worse than to look at competing economic interests."

John thanked everyone for coming, told them to enjoy their food and wine. He added that he was sorry but he didn't think Clay Steadman would be dropping by. Then he left the restaurant.

He was waiting at the entrance for a taxi when the only other person who'd been drinking sparkling water came through the door, gave him a look and offered her hand. There was a card in it. John took it.

Ellen Feazell, Los Angeles Times.

"You probably don't want to tell me any more than you told the others, do you?"

"I can't, not now. Were you at the station?"

"Yes."

"Any chance you saw something you'd care to share? I'll even keep it off the record, if you want."

Ellen grinned. "How long have you been waiting to use that line with a reporter?"

"Just occurred to me."

"But you're not willing to trade: what I saw for what you know."

John looked her in the eye. He decided she really had something, wasn't just trying to play him.

"What goes around comes around," he said, "but not necessarily immediately."

It was the reporter's turn to assess character. In L.A., bullshitters were more common than smog. But she'd seen this big guy's eyes when he'd let his glasses down. Of course, he could just be one more actor, and she'd hate herself for being naive enough to trust him.

Sighing, she decided to take the risk.

"Here's the strange thing I saw at Union Station: Edward Danner was talking, albeit briefly, with Brian Kirby."

John searched his memory for the names, managed only superficial recall. He'd seen Danner and Kirby in print or online but couldn't recall the context. Ellen saw she'd have to help him.

"Two of the deepest-pockets in Silicon Valley, and that's saying a lot. Danner heads a company called Positron; Kirby's company is Deft Play. That help any?"

"Only a little," John said.

"All right. Short story time. Danner and Kirby, roommates at Stanford. Danner, computer science; Kirby, finance. Partners in a start-up right out of school. Start-up blows up. Each blames other. Best friends become worst enemies. Won't speak or even look at one another."

"And they were talking at Union Station?" John asked.

"Yeah. I knew I couldn't get close enough to listen in without being obvious so I didn't try."

"You think they were patching things up?"

The reporter shook her head.

"Why not?" John asked.

"Body language was wrong. They've been competing fang and claw the past twenty years. It was easier to imagine one of them throwing a punch than extending a hand."

John asked, "You think they were taunting each other? Trying to psych the other guy out. Could they have some kind of business face-off coming up?"

"It's under way. Those two moneybags are competing to see which of them — are you ready for this — will get to build the first high-speed rail line between L.A. and San Francisco."

John thought about that and came up with a question. "Who looked like the top dog? Could you tell?"

Ellen nodded.

"Kirby looked like he was having the better time."

John's cab arrived. He gave the driver a twenty, but told him to find another fare. He accepted a ride to the airport with Ellen. The two of them had more to talk about.

— CHAPTER 15 —

San Francisco

The main business campus of Positron, Inc, was in Cupertino, California. Silicon Valley. Edward Danner, however, kept his personal office in San Francisco's Financial District on First Street. He had a one hundred and eighty degree view of waterfront when the fog was in abatement. It was an easy drive from his Pacific Heights home.

Taking in the sparkling forest of the city's high rise buildings that night, Danner's mind momentarily drifted from his own problems to the current topic of proletarian outrage in the city: the skyrocketing cost of housing. The mob complained, accurately, that soon only the wealthy would be able to afford to live in San Francisco. Danner agreed completely.

He didn't object to the situation, though.

He considered it to be urban renewal at its finest.

The city had become too gorgeous for just anyone to live there. His own parents, an orthodontist father and housekeeper mother, would be hard pressed to buy a nice house in town. That was just the way things went. Not everyone got into the best prep schools or universities. Not just anyone got to live in San Francisco. Even some among the entrepreneurial class. Despite popular myth, not everyone who launched a high tech start-up became a billionaire and …

That was where Danner's thoughts veered back to his personal problems.

Brian Kirby, as he had for the past two decades, was trying to destroy him. Show Danner that he'd been responsible for their failed company back when they were just kids. Only this time the prick had found the means to do it. Thanks to that idealistic little shit heel Merritt Kinney.

Danner wished he could have *thrown* the bastard off his lousy apartment building.

As it was, his only pleasure lay in viewing the police photos of the runt's broken body.

Arthur Halston had shown him the pictures. Halston was both Danner's personal lawyer and Positron's chief counsel. There was not a subatomic particle's gap in their lawyer-client privilege. Given that shield, Danner told his attorney almost everything he planned to do and listened to the lawyer's counsel before he acted. Not that he always *followed* Halston's advice. The man was educated and grounded in the law.

Danner had long ago formed his own *modus vivendi:* The more money you had the fewer rules you needed to follow. He was now so rich it was the rare occasion when he didn't do exactly as he pleased.

Not that the government couldn't come after him if it chose to do so. But when you were truly rich the authorities tended to target your corporate identity not your precious pink backside. There was the rare exception, of course. Ken Lay was convicted of fraud after Enron came crashing down. He avoided serving a long stretch in prison only by dying of a heart attack while awaiting sentencing.

Still, it wasn't often when justice got personal with a billionaire. But as that prick Kirby had told Danner yesterday in Los Angeles, he might well join the VIP jailbird club. Kirby had promised to send him a cake to mark the anniversary of every year of jail time he served.

Kirby had learned that Danner kept a detailed private journal of both his personal life and his business dealings. There wasn't a chance the greatest hacker in the world — Chinese, Russian or American — would ever be able to crack his journal. He'd done the inconceivable for a tech mogul and committed his innermost secrets solely to ink and paper.

It was nearly as quaint as if he'd used a quill and parchment.

"You're sure you didn't misplace the damn thing?" Halston asked.

For just a second, Danner felt like pitching his lawyer out his forty-eighth floor window.

He'd answered that question twice already. The third time wasn't going to be the charm. He just glared at Halston by way of response.

"All right, all right," the lawyer said. "You're likely correct in thinking Merritt Kinney took it."

"*Stole* it," Danner said.

"Yes, stole it. The problem, however, is the police search of Kinney's apartment didn't turn up your journal. Neither did the examination of his safe deposit box."

"He gave it to Kirby. The bastard knows what I've —"

Halston held up a hand. He didn't know *everything* his client had committed to paper. Nor did he want to know. If he had to participate in Danner's defense in a court of law, he wanted to do it with as unburdened a conscience as possible. He chose to examine his client's assertion.

"Is Brian Kirby foolish enough to receive stolen property?" Halston asked.

Danner frowned. "No, he's much too smart for that, but he knew … things he shouldn't."

Halston appreciated Danner's avoidance of criminal specificity.

The lawyer said, "There's no crime in listening to one person speak of another."

"There is if you learn about a crime and keep it to yourself." Danner was pretty sure he had that point of law right.

"Accessory after the fact, yes," Halston agreed. "But how might we prove that? My investigator looked all day but couldn't find a connection between Kinney and Kirby, much less any hint that Kirby put Kinney up to stealing your journal."

Danner took the seat behind his desk. He sought inspiration in staring at the floor in front of him. "No, Brian didn't reach out to Kinney. There was no way he could have known I kept a journal."

"You didn't keep one in college?" Halston asked.

Danner shook his head, still looking down.

From that posture, he said, "Merritt Kinney was the security officer tasked with watching the cleaning crew when they worked in my office. He was the last person in this room on the last day I made a journal entry. The next day in Los Angeles, Kirby knew too damn much. Kinney must have told him. There's no other explanation."

"Is it possible Mr. Kirby will be content merely to make you squirm?" Halston asked.

Danner laughed and looked up at his lawyer. "Not a chance."

"Then we might consider the idea that Mr. Kirby told Kinney to turn himself in to the police ... after perhaps showing your journal to a news outlet."

That idea gave Danner a jolt. Then he shook his head again. "The story would have broken immediately, and you'd be posting my bail."

"Is there anyone else Mr. Kirby might have suggested Kinney give the journal to, some person or group who would be shocked by the contents and would feel compelled to go to the police regardless of the consequences for you?"

That was when the light dawned for Danner. That conniving sonofabitch, Kirby, he thought. Yes, of course, there was a group just like that. The recent beneficiaries of a million-dollar grant from him.

"The new train museum in Chicago. That's where Kirby had Kinney send the journal."

Halston brightened. "If that's the case, I can call the museum director right now. Tell him stolen property — proprietary business information — has been sent to him. I'll say I'm obtaining a court order instructing him to leave the package unopened." The lawyer's face fell. "Oh, shit. That will work only if the museum hasn't received and opened it already. If the journal was sent express delivery —"

Danner shook his head. Enemy or not, he knew Brian Kirby as well as anyone alive. "It hasn't arrived. The journal wasn't sent express delivery. I know how Kirby sent it."

"How?"

"He got someone to put it on the Super Chief for him. Kirby not only knows my secrets, he wanted to see me watch them pull out of Union Station."

Danner's phone buzzed, an internal call from the security desk in the lobby.

Halston answered. "Yes?"

He listened for a moment, looked puzzled and then turned to Danner.

"There's a pair of SFPD patrol officers in the lobby. They have a federal official from the Bureau of Indian Affairs with them, a man named John Tall Wolf. He'd like to speak with you."

Danner told his lawyer, "Hang up."

— CHAPTER 16 —

San Francisco

John arrived at San Francisco International Airport after the short flight from Los Angeles. He'd had to fly commercial because the Secretary of the Interior's plane had mysteriously been summoned back to Washington. John immediately suspected mischief on Coyote's part.

He sent a text to Marlene: *Maybe you can help me find the plane that was detailed to me. If VP should discover someone is causing delays in investigation ...*

There'd be no chance that person would ever become a member of the cabinet.

He didn't need to spell that out for Marlene. He just bought a ticket to San Francisco.

He'd identified himself as a federal agent to the Transportation Security Administration people at LAX. He'd even gone so far as to use his new co-director's title. It took fifteen minutes for his bona fides to be verified; the Bureau of Indian Affairs was a low-profile agency. Few of his federal colleagues came into regular contact with it.

Once John had been recognized as one of the good guys, and a fairly significant one, he was privately introduced to the undercover air marshal who would be aboard the flight. The man knew better than to question John's right to be armed. He only said, "If something bad happens, I'll take the lead, right?"

"Sure," John said.

"You don't use your weapon unless I go down."

"Not even if I have the opportunity to *prevent* you from going down?"

That made the marshal think. "Only if you're good enough to hit the bad guy and not some grandma from Pacoima."

"Right. Unless *she's* the hijacker."

The marshal grinned. "Yeah, unless that."

The flight went smoothly: no one charged the cockpit; there wasn't even any turbulence. John did use one perk of his federal status. He went back to the galley and discreetly made a phone call to the San Francisco Police Department. He explained he was working an investigation and would need to speak with a prominent local citizen, Edward Danner. Would it be possible to have a couple of San Francisco's finest act as his escorts.

Always best to get the local cops to buy in early, John felt.

Culturally sensitive department that it was, the SFPD knew all about the Bureau of Indian Affairs. As John was a senior BIA official and had politely requested help, the cops would be only too happy to assist him. Officers Chang and Gilhooley, both female, met John at the airport and drove him into town.

"Big fish you're going after," Gilhooley said.

"You want to try the man's home or office first?" asked Chang. She was driving.

"Let's try his place of business first," John said. "If we're lucky, we won't have to disturb him at home."

Turned out, Danner didn't want to be disturbed at all.

The security guard at Danner's workplace, wearing a look of surprise, told John and the two cops, "The guy just hung up on me."

"Danner?" John asked.

"Don't think so. Sounded more like his lawyer, Mr. Halston."

John exchanged a look with the cops and quick-stepped outside. Chang and Gilhooley followed. Chang asked, "You think Danner is trying to duck you?"

"Pretty much, yeah," John said. He was looking at the entrance to the building's garage. The overhead door was down, but John expected it to go up any moment. "We might have to follow the man home."

Chang jogged back to her patrol unit and turned the motor on.

A moment later, John and Gilhooley heard a far larger engine roar into life. They looked up and saw a helicopter lift off from the office building's roof. It turned south and was soon out of sight.

Wasn't a cop in the world who liked it when somebody skipped out on them.

So Gilhooley asked, "You want me to call for a CHP aviation unit? Intercept the guy?"

John shook his head. "No need for drama. That might not even be Mr. Danner up there."

Gilhooley looked highly skeptical.

"Probably is," John conceded.

And he thought Maj Olson might be right.

Maybe, in the end, they would need their own aircraft.

— CHAPTER 17 —

Southern California

Maj Olson's train had barely cleared Union Station in L.A. when a thought occurred to her. Maybe whoever had commandeered the Super Chief had taken it into dark territory. That was the railroad term for a section of track that wasn't controlled by signals: mechanical or electrical signs that told the engineer what lay ahead. Dark territory track didn't tell the engineer a safe speed at which he might proceed or whether he should get onto a siding to avoid a collision with an oncoming train. It was closer to nineteenth century railroading than twenty-first century.

In dark territory an engineer might have to rely on a track warrant to guide him. A warrant was a verbal report of conditions that lay ahead received from a dispatcher by radio or phone contact. Warrants were also used to grant main track access from smaller lines. They might contain time restraints. Make your move only within a specified period of time, perhaps a matter of minutes.

This method was effective up to a point, but compared to the direct traffic control system used on main lines it was a decided step down in safety. In dark territory, there was no way for a dispatcher to control the switches that led onto main tracks or to detect misaligned switches, broken rails or runaway trains.

Worse still, runaways weren't detectable on a line with no signals. The result could be a wreck of tragic proportions, such as the one that occurred in Lac Megantic, Quebec in 2013. A runaway train carrying a cargo of crude oil derailed in the Canadian town causing explosions and an inferno that killed forty-two people.

Despite such hazards or maybe because of them, Maj felt dark territory might be just the place for whoever stole the Super Chief. The thieves could maintain communications silence with dispatchers, disable their GPS transponder and become functionally invisible.

Maj asked Don Prosser, the senior engineer on board, "What do we have in the way of dark territory around here? Anything?"

"Miles, miles and more miles," he said, made uneasy by the question. "All of it belongs to Union Pacific."

"Really?" Maj hadn't expected that. Usually, you found dark territory in the middle of nowhere. Places where towns and even people were few and far between. Not adjacent to the second biggest city in the country.

Prosser said, "Really."

His lack of enthusiasm for what he felt might be coming was obvious.

The other guys in the cab, Prosser's fireman Dean Spaneas, and the relief crew of Ed Fenwick and Leo Taylor, didn't look too cheerful either.

Fireman was an archaic description on a diesel train. There was no firebox to feed with fuel. On a diesel, the fireman monitored controls and assisted the engineer. The brakeman, Fenwick or Taylor, whichever one wasn't resting, operated the brakes and assisted in switching tracks.

Trainmen were a traditional lot. They liked their structure and revered their union rules. They knew the conductor was the ultimate authority, had overall control of the train and its crew. That was another point of discomfort for the guys in the cab. This train had no conductor, except for Maj. Now, she was a federal agent and that carried some weight. So did the fact that she was the only one of them who was armed. They'd seen her sidearm and the case she'd bluntly told them held an M-4 carbine.

"Yeah, just like the one combat troops use," she'd said in response to Taylor's question.

Still, she was a female and younger than any of them.

The crew's notion of a woman's place was stuck in the fifties, the 1850s.

But they'd been told by the CEO of their company: "Do whatever she tells you." Before they could complain to their union, the president of their brotherhood said the same thing. So Don, Dean, Ed and Leo were stuck.

Maj knew that, and she wanted to make things as agreeable for the guys as possible, but she had to follow her instincts. She said, "We'll be careful. We've got cell phones and radios, right? We'll get track warrants for everywhere we go."

Don Prosser told her, "There are plenty of places around here you can't find a cell signal. Even radio contact gets sketchy."

"Huh," Maj said. "Then while we're still in a 21st century locale, I'll make a call. Have some satellite phones delivered first thing tomorrow."

That was the best she could do for the moment.

So off they went into dark territory, spending the day traveling from Long Beach to Colton in the Inland Empire and Calexico in Imperial County on the border with Mexico.

The first stop in Long Beach was far too built up to hide a Super Chief. The city was part of the L.A. to San Diego megalopolis. Of course, Long Beach was also a major seaport. Giant cranes on the docks were as common as crabgrass in a back yard, and they could lift even a locomotive. Put a Super Chief in the hold of a ship and no one would notice until it came out again, maybe on the far side of the world.

Maj gave that idea some thought, but rejected it. She didn't see a foreign interest involved in the theft. Anyone who had the money necessary to steal a train and ship it off to another country could as easily have made a legitimate purchase. She felt intuitively the crime was committed by … she was about to say to herself, "Americans."

But with John Tall Wolf involved it was obvious someone thought *Native* Americans could be involved. Were involved? She'd have to talk with the BIA man about that. He might have insights that would help her efforts.

No stranger to collaborative academic efforts, Maj didn't need to be the lead author on the write-up of how this case got solved, but she would appreciate some recognition. From what she'd seen of Tall Wolf, she thought he'd be good for that.

The rail terminal in Colton was relatively small and easily surveyed. The local officials were forthcoming and candid. No, they hadn't seen a Super Chief roll through. Everyone with a pair of eyes would have noticed that full headdress custom paint job on the locomotive. They did admit that only a skeleton crew worked the overnight shift and … well, they could get distracted.

No one came right out and said their colleagues might fall asleep in wee, dark hours but the implication was clear. They probably would have 'fessed up if Maj had pushed them, but she didn't see the point of embarrassing people unnecessarily. She could always come back and have a heart-to-heart talk later, if things came to that.

As Maj's two-car train rolled southeast, the desert landscape became more primal. For all of California's huge population, there were vast areas of the state that were largely uninhabited. In places, the train line paralleled stretches of highway so isolated and lonely it was possible to imagine the next vehicle you saw might as easily be a covered wagon as a car.

Maj had Prosser pull onto a siding in Calexico's tiny rail yard at sunset. The train should be safe there for the night. She had Leo Taylor help her offload her Yamaha dirt bike.

The crew had noticed there was another motorcycle on board.

"Who's that one for?" Prosser asked

"We might be joined by another federal agent, a guy from the Bureau of Indian Affairs."

"Yeah?" It took the senior engineer only a moment to make the intuitive leap. "Did Indians steal the Super Chief?"

"Maybe. I think it's possible."

Dean Spaneas hesitated before asking, "Are these Indians, you know, hostile?"

Maj grinned. "Well the thing about any thief is he can get very possessive about the things he steals. Never likes to give them back."

The trainmen laughed without humor. Prosser said, "Yeah, ain't that a pisser?"

"Without a doubt."

"You think you'll have to use your gun?" Ed Fenwick asked.

Maj said, "Hope not."

Prosser asked, "Should we be armed, me and the guys?"

"Fair question. Any of you have training in shooting at people who are shooting at you?"

They all shook their heads, except for Taylor.

He was non-responsive. Maj wasn't sure how to take that.

"We just don't want to wind up like that crew on the Super Chief," Prosser said.

"Tell you what," Maj said. "We'll stop somewhere quiet and lonely tomorrow. I'll let each of you pop off a few rounds with the M-4. See what you can hit. That make you feel any better?"

They all liked that idea. Prosser, Spaneas and Fenwick went off to find a place for dinner, chattering like teenagers about the prospect of firing the assault weapon. Taylor, the junior man, stayed behind to guard the train with a large wrench. The others would fetch his dinner.

The crew wanted to make sure nobody stole their train.

Maj fired up her bike. Rode out of town into the gathering darkness.

A thought tiptoed to the edge of her consciousness, something from the year she was doing research for her dissertation. She couldn't pin it down right away. But she thought it had something to do with track construction. She didn't push it.

The road ahead veered to the left. She leaned into it. A glance showed she was already doing eighty. Man, the Yamaha could fly. She gave it more gas as she hit the straightaway.

There were a billion stars overhead but not another vehicle in sight.

All sorts of dark territory surrounded Calexico.

She wondered if Tall Wolf had made any progress that day.

— CHAPTER 18 —

San Francisco

With one of the billionaires who interested him having flown the coop, John Tall Wolf went to call on the other one, Brian Kirby. Officer Chang had an interesting tidbit to share with John as they reached the street with some of the grandest houses in Pacific Heights.

"That one's Danner's place," Chang said.

The house was dark behind its wrought iron fence and half-acre of lawn. Didn't look like Danner had parachuted in. John asked, "Either of you officers know if this fine home has its own helipad?"

Neither cop did, but Gilhooley said, "I'll check Google Earth. If the guy hasn't pulled a Dick Cheney, we should be able to see if there's a place for a chopper to land."

The former vice president had browbeaten Google into not showing an aerial view of his official residence while he was in office. Probably hadn't wanted the voting public to see what he'd been doing, John thought.

A moment later, looking up from her tablet, Gilhooley said, "No helicopter access."

That was when Chang made her interesting comment. "This is Switzerland."

"Pardon?" John asked, looking at another huge house.

"Nickname for the innocent rich lady who lives between Danner and Kirby. I hear she takes a strictly neutral stance regarding her neighbors. Her real name is Erika Bergdahl."

"Sounds Swedish," John said, "but they have a history of avoiding other people's fights, too."

The last mansion on the block belonged to Brian Kirby.

The lights were on.

Someone used a remote control to open the gate to the Kirby property before Chang could press the intercom button and announce their arrival. Another thing cops hated was someone getting the drop on them. The two uniformed officers exchanged a look. Gilhooley's hand went to her weapon. John stepped out of the car before the tension could escalate.

"I'll take it from here," he said.

"You don't want us to go with you?" Chang asked.

John gave them his cell phone number; Gilhooley put it in her tablet.

"Give me a call in ten minutes." He gave them passwords: one for all clear, another for bring help. "When I get back, I'll share whatever I can about what happens in there. And lunch for both of you is on me. Well, it's on the federal government. So think up something good."

The two cops could live with that plan.

Chang parked her patrol unit athwart Kirby's driveway nonetheless.

Nobody was going to drive off the property without their okay.

"San Francisco police?" Brian Kirby asked, standing in his open doorway. "Or are you FBI?"

"Bureau of Indian Affairs," John replied.

Kirby blinked and then grinned. "Well, that's interesting. Would you like to come in?"

"I would, thank you. Is that a Modigliani?" John asked, regarding the painting in the entryway. Kirby turned his head toward the painting and said it was. While he was looking the other way, John flashed an okay signal to the SFPD patrol unit. He'd bet at least one of the cops saw it, and wouldn't bother making their previously arranged call.

John stepped inside and Kirby looked back at him. "You like art?" he asked, closing the door behind them.

"Sure, mostly representational, but some abstract stuff, too."

Kirby led John into a nearby room. It was surprisingly cozy for such a large house. An unlit fireplace and four wing back chairs placed around a circular table all but filled it. A square cut-glass decanter and two snifters were centered on the table. Kirby gestured John to a chair and sat opposite him.

He said, "I expected someone to come calling. I thought I'd offer my visitor some very good brandy, but …"

Seeing his discomfort, John said, "You're not sure that's wise with a Native American."

"Yes." Confession may have been good for the soul, but it hadn't put Kirby at ease.

"Of course, the idea that I can't handle alcohol might be considered insulting," John said.

Treading carefully, Kirby asked, "Is it?"

"Well, this is a tricky situation. I don't know if there's a graceful way to handle it, but welcoming me into your home is a good start. In my case, drinks are no big deal. I've never had alcohol, don't care to know how I'd react to it. I'm happy with sparkling water, if that's available."

Kirby smiled and nodded. He made a circular gesture with his right hand, as if doing a magic trick. The drink John requested didn't appear out of thin air, but a young woman with high cheekbones, blue eyes and gleaming sable hair brought a glass of sparkling water within a minute. John and Kirby both thanked her and she left the room.

Kirby poured himself a measure of brandy and raised his glass.

"Your health and mine," he said.

"Mutual success as well," John replied.

They sipped their drinks and John said, "You said you were expecting a visitor, and now we're being observed?"

The charming young woman must have seen Kirby's gesture, overheard John's drink request.

Who else was watching? Security, surely. Legal counsel, most likely.

Kirby admitted as much. "We are. Should I offer your colleagues outside some refreshment?"

"I'm taking care of them. We'll leave it at that."

"Of course. You're here about Edward Danner?"

"I am." John told Kirby about Danner's hasty departure from his office.

The man laughed. "That Eddie, he's something."

"He has a history of making quick exits?"

Kirby took another sip of brandy. He looked at John.

"I know you must have done some spadework before arriving here. Why don't you tell me what you know, so I won't have to cover what you've already learned?"

John didn't mind a repetition of the facts, so he gave Kirby only the bare outline he'd first heard from Ellen Feazell, the *L.A. Times* reporter.

The venture capitalist nodded and put his glass on the table. He crossed his right leg over his left and folded his hands on his lap. He looked at the ceiling for a moment as if to arrange his thoughts in the proper order.

"All right. You have the broad strokes right. Now, let me fill in the details. Edward Danner has one of the brightest minds in the field of nanotechnology. The next big thing in science is how to make things ever smaller. You've heard of this?"

John nodded but didn't say a word.

Kirby continued "As you know, we were roommates at Stanford, each of us bent on becoming the next icons of high technology, Eddie by doing the basic science and me by providing him with all the funding he needed to get our business off the ground.

"Venture capital is in my blood. My father founded one of the first modern firms providing start-up money to smart people with world-altering ideas. That was forty years ago. He brought me into the business in a very small way when I was ten. I did routine office chores for a couple of years and then I noticed how many bright ideas got hatched in people's garages. So you know what I suggested to my dad?"

John said, "You suggested he buy a garage building company?"

Kirby clapped his hands and laughed. "Bravo. That's just what I did. I thought if garages were where people did their inventing, let's build more garages. My dad bought a local company. Sold first-rate garages at mid-range prices and cleaned up. He cut me in for a share of the profit. I told him I wanted my money reinvested in whatever ideas he thought were good bets."

"And that was your first step to getting rich," John said.

"A millionaire before I got to high school. By the time I met Edward Danner, it was tens of millions. I was so sure Eddie was on the track of an enormous breakthrough …" Kirby sighed. A look of regret filled his eyes. "I wanted to launch my own venture capital firm with a walk-off home run. I talked my dad into dissolving the trust fund he'd set up for me and letting me use that money, too. I sank every penny I had into the company Eddie and I were going to start. You know what happened next."

"Not the details," John said.

"It was a mistake in the science, Eddie told me. An equation or some damn thing didn't work the way he thought it would. You remember those two guys who thought they had cold fusion whipped? It turned out they weren't even close. It was like that, but only up to a point. Anyway, I lost all my money."

"And then?" John asked.

"I begged my dad for a job and wouldn't take anything more than room and board for pay. Within a year, Eddie got his science right, found new funding and made a killing. Nano-science is now involved in everything from killing cancer to creating lighter, stronger building materials than anything we've ever known, and Eddie's company, Positron, is in the thick of just about any application you can imagine."

John said, "Looks like you've made quite a comeback, too."

"I learn from my mistakes," Kirby said. "I thought Eddie would cut me in for a share of Positron after all the time and money … all the friendship I invested in him. He didn't even return my phone calls. I took that to heart, and now I do due diligence better than anyone I know. Yeah, I came back all right, but I paid the price, too."

"Tell me what you and Danner had to talk about at Union Station," John said.

A smile lit Kirby's face. He uncrossed his legs, emptied his snifter and poured more brandy.

"For the past twenty-three years, Eddie and I haven't spoken a word to each other even though we live so near to each other."

"Who got here first?" John asked.

Kirby laughed. "I did. Understandably, we've never had any further business dealings. But two years ago we became direct competitors for the first time."

"In what way?"

"Each of us is vying to build the first high-speed rail line between San Francisco and Los Angeles."

"A railroad?" John said, leaning forward.

"Yeah, like nothing this country has ever seen. True high-speed rail travel like they have in Europe and Asia." A gleam came into Kirby's eyes. "Maybe even faster."

"Who's ahead?" John asked.

"Technologically, my team."

"What other measure is there?" John asked.

Kirby had his own question. "Do you have the power to make arrests, Mr. Tall Wolf?"

"That and a license to take scalps," John said.

Kirby laughed, delighted. "Perfect. Eddie doesn't know for sure, but he's an intuitive thinker as well as a first-class scientist. I'm sure he knows his team is running behind."

"How can you know that?" John asked.

"It took me some time to figure out what happened with the company Eddie and I tried to start, but I finally did. The SOB didn't make any mistake in the science; he sabotaged his own work. Why would he do that? Because he and I were going to be equal partners. He drove a much harder bargain with his new backers. He controls Positron and has three-quarters of the equity."

"So he sold you out for money, after waiting long enough to make it look like he found a legitimate fix for the so-called problem?"

"Right, but money was only part of his motive. I thought there had to be more. It wasn't like we were interested in the same girl, though. Or longed for any other one of a kind consideration. We'd never done anything to slight each other. Not that I was aware of, at first."

John said, "But you finally came up with something."

Kirby nodded. "The light dawned after I thought it might be something to do with ego. Eddie and I were both top of our class in our respective disciplines, but a long time ago, before we'd even met, I found out I beat him at something that was very important to both of us."

"What's that?" John asked.

"As kids, we were both into building model train sets. There was a national competition to build the most creative and efficient track layout within specific parameters. You know, so spending money wouldn't be the determining factor. I won, and like any good young egotist, I never even bothered to look at who came in second. Turns out it was this kid from suburban L.A."

"Edward Danner."

"Yeah. Now, we're doing it all over again, only this time with real trains."

"And Danner's afraid you're going to beat him again."

Kirby nodded and sipped his brandy.

"So he's cheating?" John asked.

"Doing things that could get him locked up, I was told. I'll be happy if you're the one who arrests him."

"But what does all this have to do with the Super Chief? Anything at all?"

Brian Kirby told John just what the connection was.

— CHAPTER 19 —

Southwest U.S

The Indians had brought blankets to the crew of the Super Chief, but that didn't keep them from shivering in the cold of the night. There were far too many cracks and gaps in the tumble-down shack where they were being held to keep out the cold air. The temperature wasn't quite down to the point where they could see their breath frost in the air, but it was close to that.

Truth was, they couldn't see much. The night was clear and the sky was filled with stars, but illumination was minimal for men who were used to electric light. The engineer, Albert Wicker, sat leaning against a wall where the protection from the cold, steady wind was a bit more solid than elsewhere.

Dale Brent, the relief engineer whom Bodaway had kicked in the lower back for cracking wise had been complaining ever since that he'd suffered internal damage and had to pee every ten minutes as a result, told the others, "I've got to go again."

He'd been the first one who'd needed to relieve himself. The Indians had left them an empty plastic milk jug. The kind that could hold a gallon.

Brent had looked at it the first time he had to piss and said, "What, are we all supposed to use that? The stink would kill us in nothing flat. And what if we have to shit?"

So far, all of them seemed to be constipated, but they took his point.

"You might get shot," Bob Clarey, the crew's fireman had said the first time Brent had been about to step outside.

"Better than having my appendix burst," Brent replied.

"Your bladder," said Rick Engram.

He was the crew's brakeman and the youngest crew member by twenty years.

"What?" Brent asked.

"Your bladder's where you hold your piss not your appendix."

"Jesus, like I give a damn. All I know is I've got to piss and I'm going outside to do it. I don't care if they shoot me."

Brent did just that, but he didn't go too far. The men inside could hear his stream hit a rock. Hear him moan, too. Somewhat from pain, it sounded, but with relief, too. No one shot Brent, but when he returned he said there had been blood in his urine. Nobody went outside to verify that.

They all did make individual trips later to address their own needs and in an unpremeditated fashion wound up using the same small area to relieve themselves.

Now, deep into the night, Brent was headed for the door again. This time he said, "You know what? I hope those bastards do shoot me. It'd be better than putting up with much more of this shit."

He stepped outside.

The others waited, on edge, wondering if Brent had just tempted fate. Maybe their captors would cut them less slack at night when a man might be more tempted to make a run for it. They heard no crack of gunfire, though, and Brent came back unharmed.

The others also scurried out, individually, and returned to the meager shelter of the cabin.

A minute or two later, Brent told his companions about his latest pee.

"I'm out there thinking I might be squirting nothing but blood by now. With all the stars in the sky, I thought I might be able to see if that was the case, but I was afraid to look. Just pointed my eyes to heaven, and damn if I didn't think it was beautiful. I should've paid more attention to nights like this when I was a free man."

Brent gave a hard look to each of the other members of the cab crew.

"Then I asked myself how I got to be where I am. The last thing I remember, we were all pulling out of Union Station in L.A. The next thing I know, we're all here, bunch of goddamn Indians holding us prisoner. Threatening our lives. How the hell did that happen?"

Shrugs and silence were the only replies.

Brent continued, "That old Indian bastard, their chief or whatever, he said they'd give us our train back if we behave, let us take it to Chicago. That means they must have it, and in working condition, too. So how'd the Indians bring the train to wherever the hell we are now?"

Brent had the others thinking hard now.

It was amazing the things a man could figure out while taking a long, hard piss.

Brent said, "One of us, and it sure the hell ain't me, had to help those bastards."

Wicker, Clarey and Engram all looked at one another. Each of them had wrapped himself in a blanket. Clarey was seated on the floor next to Wicker. Engram was on his feet, wedged into a corner.

Brent continued his line of reasoning. "When we left L.A., three of us each had a cup of coffee poured from the same thermos. Only man who didn't was you, Rick."

Wicker and Clarey got to their feet. Brent took a step toward Engram.

"I can't handle caffeine is all," Engram said. "I woke up here tied up just like the rest of you."

Brent laughed. "That was supposed to make you look good, wasn't it? Of course, if one of us was to make a run for it, you could warn your friends outside, couldn't you?"

Brent lunged toward Engram with his hands extended, as if to choke him. Both younger and quicker than his would-be assailant, Engram sidestepped the attack and threw his blanket over Brent's head. He shot the gap between Clarey and Wicker and ran out the cabin door.

The three men he left behind heard Engram shout something in a language they didn't know. Brent threw off the blanket and ran after Engram. He'd only just cleared the doorway when a bullet hit the exterior wall next to him. He ducked back inside. Three more rounds slammed into the decrepit building, but they were fired to intimidate not to kill.

That didn't keep hypertensive Albert Wicker from having a heart attack.

He dropped just like a man who'd been drilled right between the eyes.

— CHAPTER 20 —

San Francisco

The next morning, with Officers Chang and Gilhooley off duty, John Tall Wolf took a taxi to Erika Bergdahl's Pacific Heights mansion. He pressed the intercom button at the gate to her property. He was just about to try again when a woman's voice came through the speaker. Her English was slightly accented by Scandinavian tones.

"Yes, who's there please?"

John thought his new title would play better in the upscale neighborhood. "Co-director John Tall Wolf, Bureau of Indian Affairs." He added for clarity, "I'm with the federal government, ma'am. If you're Ms. Bergdahl, I'd like to speak with you briefly."

"You are Native American?"

"By birth if not upbringing."

"Which tribe?"

"Northern Apache and, I think, Navajo."

"And you were raised by?"

"My father is Caucasian, my mother is Latina and also has native blood."

His pedigree apparently passed muster. The woman told him, "I'm working in my garden behind the house. Follow the driveway." She buzzed him in.

John did so. He found a woman wearing a chambray shirt, jeans and scuffed sneakers. She held a trowel with a good point on it in her right hand. If he'd been an intruder scamming her, he could see her using the garden tool as a weapon.

"You're Erika Bergdahl?" John asked.

"I am. Sometimes also known as Switzerland, I am told."

She smiled. Erika was nearing fifty, John thought, and aging as gracefully as anyone could hope. Her face glowed with health and the faint lines at the corners of her eyes and mouth only made her features more interesting.

John offered her his card to buttress his claimed identity.

Erika read it and told him, "This says you are a special agent."

"Recently promoted. The new cards haven't been printed yet. Might not even ask for any until I use up the old ones."

She liked that, and stuck her trowel into a pot filled with soil.

"May I offer you a glass of lemonade? I have to warn you, though, I like it quite tart."

"So do I," John said.

Erika led the way up to the veranda adjoining the house. John half-expected her to summon domestic help to provide the refreshment, but a carafe of lemonade already rested on a glass-top table. Four glasses sat next to it. She offered John a seat and poured for him.

He waited until she sat before raising his glass. *"Skol."*

She smiled and waited for him to sip his drink.

John did and said, "Just the way I like it."

Erika nodded, pleased by his approval, and took her own drink.

Putting her glass down, she asked, "Am I a person of interest to the government?"

"Only in the hope you might help with an investigation."

"So, if it's not me, is it my neighbors?" She tilted her head to one side and then the other.

Maybe it was insignificant, but John noted she'd indicated Danner's home first.

"Yes, ma'am. I can't go into detail, but can you tell me what you think about Mr. Danner and Mr. Kirby?"

"They are very rich, of course, but I'm sure you know that."

"I do. What I'd like is your impression of their character, if you have any awareness of that."

"Well, each of them has offered to buy my home."

"But you're still here. So money isn't an issue to you."

"Not as far as remaining here is concerned. I am an immigrant, albeit a wealthy one. I have found my place in America and I intend to remain here. Right where I am."

John thought about that. "Have Mr. Danner and Mr. Kirby accepted your position with good grace?"

"Mr. Kirby has. All he asks is that if I ever change my mind I give him the first opportunity to bid on this property."

"And Mr. Danner?"

The look that flashed in Erika Bergdahl's eyes confirmed for John the idea that she'd happily gut anyone who threatened her well-being. Beneath her twenty-first century gloss, pulsed Viking blood.

"Mr. Danner ... he is proof that even the well-off can have a pesky neighbor."

"Persistently pesky?"

"Until my lawyers obtained a restraining order."

"Would your feelings about your neighbors, then, incline you to trust Mr. Kirby more than Mr. Danner?"

"I am the heir to a shipping fortune, Mr. Tall Wolf. My father was at least as ruthless as either of my neighbors and likely more so. I would expect both Mr. Danner and Mr. Kirby to be relentless in pursuit of their interests. Mr. Kirby would accomplish his goals with more élan; Mr. Danner would be more rude. Simply put, I would trust neither of them unless I knew my goals aligned exactly with theirs."

John liked that analysis. Thought it might be helpful.

"Would you mind if I ask a few more questions about your background?" Erika said. "My interest is academic, you see. I am a cultural anthropologist at San Francisco State."

John grinned. "Really? My mother is in the same field."

He gave Erika his mother's name and university affiliation. Spoke to her for five minutes.

— CHAPTER 21 —

Washington, D.C.

"You can not trust Tall Wolf, not for a minute," Nelda Freeland said to Marlene Flower Moon. "He's a devil."

Nelda was Marlene's niece, and could not have borne a closer physical resemblance to her aunt had she been her daughter. Nelda had been the acting director of the BIA's Office of Justice Services while Marlene was on a leave of absence to make a movie with Clay Steadman. Tall Wolf had been absolutely dismissive of Nelda's new position of authority.

Once Marlene had returned to Washington, Nelda had been obligated to take a step back on the organizational chart.

Worse, Tall Wolf as the new co-director of the OJS, was now Nelda's superior.

Giving the younger woman two reasons to hate him.

And suspect him of having a diabolical nature.

Marlene, who'd been looking out her office window, had heard her niece's accusation and gave it little heed. A more prosaic but not insignificant concern occupied her thoughts.

"The view out Tall Wolf's new office window is really *much* better than mine."

Anyone who had ever clawed her way up the ranks of any hierarchy knew such symbols mattered. The scenery outside a pane of glass could easily be a forecast of career prospects. Soaring towers and monuments might be hints of future greatness. A view of an alley with a Dumpster spoke for itself.

Marlene's vista wasn't half bad; it just wasn't as grand as —

Tall Wolf sent a text to her phone. Almost as if he'd known she'd been thinking of him.

His message read: *Are you planning to take Nelda with you when you get your cabinet post? If not, I just spoke to someone who said there's a plum job coming open at the National Museum of the American Indian. Thought you'd like to know.*

Marlene showed the text to her niece, who recoiled in fear. Her suspicion of John's link to the infernal was confirmed. Then Nelda crept back because the museum was a part of the Smithsonian Institution, and a top job there with Native American cachet was nothing to be shrugged off. Even at the cost of one's soul. Wheels began to turn in Nelda's head.

"Would you rather work at the museum than for me?" Marlene asked.

Nelda's immediate impulse was to say of course not … but there was no fooling Auntie.

"If you were to stay here, second to Tall Wolf in everything but name, yes, I would."

The younger woman emphasized her point of view with a pugnacious set of her jaw.

Marlene admired her for that. Looking out for yourself was a matter of basic survival. Not lying about it, showed courage. It also warned the person higher up the ladder that a new threat might be coming from below.

"Perhaps you're right."

"You don't think I'm disloyal?" Nelda asked.

"You're loyal to yourself. As you should be. It's my job to give you a reason to be loyal to me."

"You'll bring me with you if you become Secretary of the Interior? Give me a slot above Tall Wolf?" Nelda was always one to hedge her bets.

Marlene laughed. "How much good did that do you with Tall Wolf the last time, when you were acting director?"

"Not one bit," Nelda said with a pout. "But if you become a cabinet member —"

"Tall Wolf won't care at all. Besides, he has the ear of the vice president."

Nelda mulled that over. "He's not —"

"No, he isn't, but she is looking for a man. She knows she can't run for president as a single woman."

"What about you, Auntie? Do you still want to be president? Would you marry to win the Oval Office and turn the White House Indian Red?"

Marlene gave her niece a look, reminding the younger woman there was *nothing* she wouldn't do to reach her goals, no matter what they were. She dismissed Nelda and started working her phone, putting in calls to Indian chiefs — Native American tribal leaders — around the country. Tall Wolf, damn him, had put the bug in her ear to become the next Secretary of the Interior.

That would be an important executive position to add to her résumé.

She knew she would never beat Jean Morrissey in a head-to-head race for the Democratic nomination to be president. The thing to do would be to appear to be a good soldier working for Morrissey, all the while sabotaging her behind the scenes. Then, in the next presidential election, she could make her move.

First, though, she had to snag that cabinet post. Get the Native American power structure behind her. Only she ran into trouble immediately. None of the important men and women she called across the country were available to speak with her. They were all out of town on business.

What business, Marlene wanted to know.

The flunkies taking her calls couldn't or wouldn't tell her.

Something big was going on, something Marlene didn't know about.

She couldn't abide either her ignorance or her exclusion.

She got busy on changing all of that fast.

— CHAPTER 22 —

San Francisco

Makilah Walsh looked up from her office desk at police head-quarters and saw the biggest Indian she'd ever seen in her life. Oops, she thought. Political correctness was mandatory in San Francisco city government. Biggest Native American. The guy must've been as tall as that old-time movie actor, Will Sampson. Only with those Ray-Ban sunglasses and the sharp suit he had on he looked like might have just stepped out of a fashion shoot.

"Captain Walsh?" he asked.

"Yes," Makilah said.

"The officer at the security desk said he'd call up to let you know I was coming."

Makilah rolled her eyes. "I didn't get any call. The department is switching over from AT&T to a system Google Voice is putting in for us. At least, that's what I think I was told." Standing, she added, "The bugs are still gumming up the works. They say they're working to fix emergency calls first."

"Makes sense."

"Of course, if I didn't live so deeply in my own little world, I might've *heard* your approach." She extended her hand. "You know who I am. So who're you?"

Shaking her hand, he said, "John Tall Wolf, Bureau of Indian Affairs."

"Really? A special agent?"

"Co-director."

"My, my. Well, please have a seat, sir. Would you like something to drink?"

"I'm good, thanks." John sat in Makilah's guest chair.

She returned to her seat. "You sure you're in the right place, Mr. Co-director? I handle investigations of possible procedural violations by SFPD officers."

"Please call me John, and I have some information that might be of help to you in the matter of the death of a man named Merritt Kinney."

Makilah sat back in her chair and stared at her visitor. "Okay, John, I'm happy to have any help you care to offer, only I'm stumped how a bigwig from the BIA knows about Merritt Kinney or how you found your way to me."

John said, "A confidential informant pointed me your way. He told me Kinney worked for one of your town's tech moguls, Edward Danner."

Makilah remembered Sergeant Fab Gallo telling her he'd met the high and mighty Danner.

She wanted to hear more of what this mysterious Native American fed knew.

But not right there in her office where anybody passing by might see them.

If she faced the possibility of going up against a billionaire who'd gone rogue, she wanted to be very careful. She was still a year out from her pension being vested. No way was she going to lose that.

"How about I buy you breakfast somewhere nice, John?" she asked.

John countered with: "How about you take me to the late Mr. Kinney's apartment for a look-see, Captain?"

— CHAPTER 23 —

Southwest, U.S.

Alan White River met with a half-dozen of his fellow tribal leaders in the plush celebrity car the Super Chief locomotive had been towing. They sat around a polished teak table in ergonomic leather chairs. The old men's flannel shirts, blue jeans and boots were at odds with the furniture and other designer flourishes surrounding them. It was clear none of them was completely at ease.

But Bodaway, the firemaker, was.

He looked completely at home. He was doing his best, in fact, not to seem like he was enjoying his surroundings too much. With each glance around the car, though, he was making mental notes of furnishings he'd someday own.

"I've never even been in a casino this nice," Donald Leaning Elk told his peers.

Henry Bald Eagle smiled and nodded. "This is the first time in years I'm wondering if I've got cow flop on my boots."

Three of the other chiefs laughed and made similar jokes.

White River let the others go on for a moment. He knew they were all nervous. Sitting there among the white man's luxuries made plain the wealth of the powers they'd dared to confront, the seriousness of what they'd done. If they were called to account for their theft in a federal court, they wouldn't be the only ones to suffer. The people who had trusted them with positions of leadership would also be tainted.

Then again, each chief had joined in the conspiracy with the assent of the elders of their tribes. Native American politics could be as divisive as any others, but on this issue there was complete agreement. The plan Alan White River had set in motion would be the redress of a longstanding and agonizing grievance: the harm the railroads had done to their people.

At an opportune pause in the nervous good humor, White River said to his great-grandson, "Bodaway, what news do you have?"

The others fell silent and turned to look at the young man.

"Wicker and Brent, the trainmen, were alive when the ambulances arrived to take them to the hospital."

"Not the same hospital," Andrew Hardwood said.

He'd been one of the leaders not to join in the uneasy joking. Hardwood took matters every bit as seriously as White River. He was Apache and in his native tongue his name was Cochise.

"No," Bodaway told him. "Not the same hospital nor even the same state. Still, by releasing these men rather than treating them ourselves, we've narrowed the area where the FBI will search for us."

The lines of concern deepened in the faces of all the older men.

Bodaway had suggested they keep both Wicker and Brent, have them treated by the tribe's doctors, but the only physicians they'd been able to contact were general practitioners and both of them had said Wicker needed a heart surgeon and Brent probably needed a nephrologist. Bodaway had thought if the two men died, so be it. They'd become only the latest casualties of a conflict that had begun centuries ago.

The elders, however, had overruled him. They'd intended to spill no blood. They didn't want any angry spirits haunting their dreams. That made Bodaway laugh, but only to himself. The chiefs had their own purposes in stealing the Super Chief, but they weren't his.

He'd only wanted to show that it could be done. He had already taken a trophy from the passenger car. That would be payment enough for what he'd done.

Still, he loved his great-grandfather, and had done his best to buy him and the other old men all the time they would need to achieve their goals. Wicker and Brent had been stripped of all identification. Both men had been unconscious when they were loaded into their respective ambulances. Assuming they had both gone into surgery, it would be some time before either of them was in full possession of his faculties.

As for the third non-complicit member of the train crew, Bob Clarey, it was decided he should be released, too. But Bodaway had offered an idea to which the elders had agreed. Clarey was dosed with Rohypnol, put on a private airplane and flown to Louisiana. He'd been deposited in a dive bar in Baton Rouge, left at a table with a bottle of cheap bourbon and a glass.

When he regained his senses, he'd have no idea of where he was or how he got there. He also had no ID on him, and if he claimed he'd been kidnapped on a train in Los Angeles … well, it'd be sometime before the cops would believe him. More time would be required to confirm the claim, but even if everything happened with unexpected speed it would still create a geographical diversion the FBI would be obliged to investigate.

Bodaway felt comfortable everything would work out for the best.

The Native Americans were the good guys in this Western.

They'd come out on top this time.

Only White River brought up a concern Bodaway hadn't foreseen.

"I was told Marlene Flower Moon tried to call me this morning. She was informed I was away on business, but not where I was. She left a message saying she might be nominated to be Secretary of the Interior. She wants my support."

He left it to the others to take the next step.

Hardwood got there first. "She must have called all of us. That woman leaves nothing to chance."

"Not being able to find any of us at home will make her very suspicious," White River said. "She must be searching for us right now. Trying to find out what we are doing."

Bodaway saw that prospect frightened the elders far more than any worry about the FBI.

He said, "This woman is just a bureaucrat, a would-be politician, isn't she? Why worry about her?"

White River knew his great-grandson would laugh at the idea Marlene Flower Moon was really Coyote. The young man's heart put him inseparably with his people, but his mind was indivisible from his education in the white world. Bodaway wanted to beat them at their own game.

The old man chose his words carefully.

"She is a force to be reckoned with, a woman none of us has ever known to fail."

Bodaway saw all the old men nod. Even Hardwood agreed.

"All right," Bodaway said, "she's smart and she's powerful. So what? Why would she have any reason to oppose what we're doing?"

"She may not," Hardwood conceded.

The others nodded hopefully, except for White River.

"There is no way to know what is in that woman's mind," he said. "All we can be certain of is she will find us before the white men do. And there is one other thing."

"What?" Bald Eagle asked.

White River began to tell the others what he knew of John Tall Wolf.

Bodaway leaned forward and listened intently.

— CHAPTER 24 —

San Francisco

Here we are," Makilah Walsh told John as they arrived at Merritt Kinney's apartment.

Before leaving police headquarters, Makilah had shown John the video recording Sergeant Fab Gallo's team had made of their attempt to arrest Kinney. She plainly expected him to make some comment on what he'd seen. John told her he'd reserve judgment for the moment.

Kinney's place was so small a nickel tour would have been price gouging. The living room, dining area and kitchen were contiguous. A man John's size might have sat at the card table with his dinner, used one hand to change the TV channel without a remote and grabbed a drink from the fridge with the other. The bedroom was over-furnished by nothing more than a twin bed and a tiny dresser. The bathroom was a claustrophobic's nightmare.

"Barely room to turn around" John said of the lavatory. "Trying to towel off in here must bruise your elbows just about every time."

"It's got a window and a bathtub," Makilah told him. "With the rents in this town, this apartment isn't half-bad."

John said, "The window's open."

"You look at what's on the floor around the toilet, that's a good thing."

Dried splotches of feces circled the bowl like a vile necklace.

"Yeah," John said. "But who opened the window, Kinney or SFPD?"

Makilah said, "I don't know. I'll find out."

"If it was Kinney, that would explain how he heard or saw your cops coming. If his underwear shows signs of a hasty retreat, that should clear up the window being open."

With a thin smile, Makilah nodded. "I imagine it would."

John lowered himself to a squat and looked at the book he saw in the bathtub. His movement nudged Makilahh to the threshold of the room. Looking over John's shoulder, she said, "The man must've been reading while he was taking care of his business."

"Mmm-hmm." John took a notebook and pen out of a coat pocket. Both he and Makilah were wearing nitrile gloves to preserve the crime scene, but he didn't touch the book. Only wrote down the title and the author's name. A big shot like him, he should be able to charge a copy of the book to his official credit card.

Makilah asked, "You think that book has something to do with all this?"

John stood up and gently urged the police captain backward so he might exit the room.

"You've been very patient," he said. "Let's step outside and I'll tell you what I know. Well, some of what I know, anyway."

Makilah took John to Union Square, bought him an iced green tea with mint, instead of the breakfast she'd offered earlier, and had a Snapple Kiwi Strawberry for herself. They sat on the plaza at a table for two under a green umbrella. Looking like the couple of cops they were, passersby gave them a wide berth. They kept their voices down, but didn't have to whisper.

John told her about Edward Danner flying the coop on him.

"Maybe he just had to be somewhere in a hurry," Makilah said.

"Is that what you'd think if you went to see someone and he jumped in his helicopter?"

"You put it that way, no."

"So I went to see Brian Kirby at his house."

The SFPD captain gave John a look. "You just drop in on a billionaire and he opens his door for you?"

"I had reason to believe he was expecting a visit from someone with a badge."

Makilah smiled. "Someone's been whispering in your ear."

"I'm easy to talk to, get along with people well. Anyway, what Mr. Kirby told me is that Mr. Kinney called him asking if he'd like to have Mr. Danner's personal journal. Kinney also told Mr. Kirby that Mr. Danner used the journal to explain his part in a number of crimes. In his own handwriting, as it were."

"Sonofabitch. No, wait just a minute. Why would Danner do that? Screw himself."

"Take a guess," John told her.

Makilah took a hit of Snapple to aid her imagination. "He must *want* people to know what he did, just not right away."

"Posthumous publication is what I'm thinking," John said. "That also makes me wonder if he has any children to consider."

Like any good cop, Makilah had at least a passing knowledge of the high and mighty in her jurisdiction, who they were when they let their hair down, what kind of mischief they might get up to when they thought no one was looking.

"Word is Mr. Danner is gay, when he finds the time for anything but his work. He has no children I've ever heard about."

"That's one fewer constraint on how he'd like to be remembered."

Makilah nodded. She drew another conclusion from what John had told her.

She said, "Brian Kirby must not have bought Danner's journal or he wouldn't have said anything to you. He had to know he'd be guilty of receiving stolen goods."

"Kinney didn't offer the journal for sale; he wanted to *give* it away, but Kirby understood taking possession would still place him in jeopardy."

"So if he doesn't have it, who does?"

"Kirby said he suggested that Kinney 'do the right thing' with it."

Makilah's smile was sardonic. "Well, wasn't that civic minded of him? But I still get the feeling you might have a better idea of what *the right thing* is than I do, John."

"I probably do," he admitted, "but I can't say for the moment."

"Not even a hint? I mean, I did buy you a green tea with mint."

"Well, the thing that strikes me about what happened when your officers went to arrest Kinney was that he overreacted fatally. He was panicked when the most he should have been worried about was finding a good lawyer. He found a small team of SFPD cops who acted professionally to be menacing. Why was that?"

"And your answer is?"

John said, "I'm not sure, but I'm going to read a copy of the book that wound up in Kinney's bathtub. Who knows if something in it didn't contribute to his being overwrought?"

"Maybe I should read it, too," Makilah said.

"One thing I can tell you," John said, "if you have any uncertainties about any of the cops who went to arrest Kinney, you should pass the word that Danner might be involved in a very big federal investigation. Nobody will be getting off easy. If they have any knowledge about Danner that could substantiate Kinney's claim that the man is a criminal they ought to come forward fast. Before judges start handing down sentences, and they can still get some consideration for, you know, doing the right thing."

Makilah laughed. "I'll do just that. And I'll stay in touch if you will."

"Deal," John said.

— CHAPTER 25 —

San Francisco

Cullum Walker, CEO of The Museum of American Railroading in Chicago, told Arthur Halston, chief counsel of Edward Danner's Positron, Inc., "I promise you, sir, any stolen property found aboard the Super Chief or its passenger coach will be returned to its owner immediately. If, as you say, that includes any personal documents, the confidential nature of their contents will be respected completely."

Yeah, sure, Halston thought. That sounded good, but it was human nature for people to take a peek at things they weren't supposed to see. Be they stock tips or a comely neighbor. And if Walker or someone in the museum's mail room didn't leave a greasy thumb print on a page of Edward Danner's personal journal, how would Halston know if the pledge of privacy had been honored?

Well, there was one way. If the cops or feds descended upon Danner in large numbers, that would be a pretty good clue someone had read whatever the hell Danner had been loopy enough to commit to writing. Genius, Halston thought, was not a seamless gift. In many cases, it was shot through with moments of jaw-dropping idiocy.

Just look at what Danner had done last night. Absconded from an interview with an official of the Bureau of Indian Affairs. Jumped into his helicopter, dragged his lawyer with him and fled into the night sky. All he had to do was greet the man with a bit of courtesy and say on the advice of his attorney he would not be answering any questions.

That would have been that. No fuss, no muss. If the fed had gotten pushy, Halston would have come out swinging. Figuratively, of course. But he would have quickly erected a wall of legal protections that the man from BIA … that still bothered Halston. If the federal government had a bone to pick with Danner, why not send the FBI?

Wouldn't that have been a more intimidating move? Would Edward have dared to duck them? You dodged the BIA, you could plead, reasonably, that you were simply avoiding an annoyance. Even if a judge didn't agree with that notion, it was likely a juror or two would, and that was all any good defense lawyer needed.

So why … an unwelcome thought occurred to Halston.

The BIA showing up at the same time Edward Danner's personal journal was smuggled onto a train called the Super Chief? Now, there was an element of symmetry. But only if …

"Mr. Walker," Halston said, "is there any reason why the federal government should be looking into the train headed to your museum?"

The man's eagerness to please vanished. "I can't talk about that."

"But you do know about it." A declarative statement not an interrogatory one.

"I can't talk about that either. If we find anything belonging to your client, it will be returned expeditiously."

"Even if the government wants to take a look?"

"Good-bye, Mr. Halston." The museum chief ended the call.

Halston woke up his desktop computer and Googled "Super Chief Troubles."

A link to that morning's online edition of the *Las Vegas Review-Journal* displayed the headline "Super Chief Unable to Make Scheduled Stop Here." Halston clicked on the link but the story was short and offered only one additional bit of information. *No reason was given for the classic train's failure to make its scheduled stop in Las Vegas on its way to Chicago. Promoters of the event here said they were told it was unclear whether the train would make any of its other interim stops.*

Looked to Halston like the damn thing had, what? Gone missing?

With Edward Danner's personal journal hidden somewhere aboard?

A chill ran through the attorney, almost as deeply as the fright he'd felt last night in the helicopter. Danner knew he disliked flying in airplanes and *hated* the very idea of flying in helicopters. Nonetheless, Danner had coerced Halston into accompanying him to his vineyard in Sonoma, taking the long way by first heading south and then looping back over the ocean.

At night. Into a fog bank that rolled in.

Halston had been a wreck by the time the pilot made a feather-soft landing.

Danner had laughed at what he'd called Halston's misplaced anxiety.

The attorney's older, beloved brother had been an Army helicopter pilot in Vietnam. His aircraft had been shot out of the sky when Halston had been in middle school. He'd had nightmares for years, lurid imaginings of how horrible Richard's death must have been. They'd faded eventually, but last night, after reaching home, the horrors had returned with a vengeance. He'd been in the co-pilot's seat next to his brother. Their chopper was hit by an enemy rocket. Richard reached over and took his hand.

Told him, "The crash is where the pain ends."

The all-consuming fire, Halston saw, was where it began.

He had awakened screaming.

Now, the unexpected jangle of his telephone produced a yelp.

It took a long enough time for him to find his voice that the party on the other end asked, "Are you there, Arthur? This is Brian Kirby calling."

That left Halston nearly as breathless as the helicopter flight had. Kirby was the main enemy. The Soviet Union to the U.S. during the

Cold War. It would have been possible for either Kirby or Danner to destroy each other if they'd wanted to go all out, but they, too, would have been subject to the trap of mutually assured destruction.

So far any impulse to kill the other guy had been restrained by a reluctance to commit suicide.

Brian Kirby had never called Halston before, and the lawyer was sure he wouldn't be the bearer of good news.

"How did you get my number?" he asked.

"My chief counsel gave it to me, after Edward Danner tried to subvert him. Danner promised him your job if he sold me out. Gave him your number so he could fire you personally."

That news shook Halston to his core — but was it the truth?

Just then, after being made to endure the helicopter flight, he was inclined to think it was.

"Are you offering me the job of being your chief counsel?" Halston asked.

"Don't be foolish. My guy's loyal and ten times the lawyer you are, but I've always thought you were much too decent a man to be working for Eddie Danner."

As far as Halston knew, Kirby was the only man who dared to use the familiar form of Danner's first name. "What do you want then?"

"Just giving you a heads-up. Merritt Kinney told me what's in Eddie's journal, and you're not going to like it. Your damn fool boss has teed himself up for prosecutors from … well, from San Francisco to L.A. I'm sure the feds will be looking for a handle on him, too, and I bet they'll find one. Now, you could spend the next five years trying to keep Eddie out of prison and lose, maybe even raise a suspicion or two that you're party to his crooked plans. Or you could bail out now while the bailing's good."

Halston had no idea of whether Kirby had learned how his brother Richard had died, but the metaphor of escaping a doomed aircraft resonated for Halston.

He almost asked what alleged crimes Kirby was talking about, but his legal training asserted itself and told him he didn't want to know. It was enough for him to understand that Kirby wasn't simply doing him a favor, he was trying to hurt "Eddie" by denying him the assistance of his senior lawyer.

Nonetheless, Halston said, "Thank you."

He hung up and tried to remember the name of the BIA man who'd come by last night.

John Tall Wolf, that was it.

Halston drafted a letter of resignation.

Then he called the BIA to see how he might contact Tall Wolf.

— CHAPTER 26 —

San Francisco

John called FBI Deputy Director Byron DeWitt from the Bureau's office at San Francisco International Airport. The special agent on duty was initially reluctant to let John use the dedicated land line. He'd have more than egg on his face if he let someone without the right federal weight dial out from that phone.

Admitting to John that he'd never worked with the BIA before, he said, "It's nothing personal, you know. Just being careful."

John believed him. "No offense taken. Why don't you place the call? I'm sure the deputy director will take it."

DeWitt did. He also told the special agent where John rated in the federal hierarchy. Instructed him to give John any privacy he might request.

The FBI special agent acquiesced, but now he gave John a look.

As if to say, "You might have told me what kind of clout you have."

"I don't like to throw my weight around," John replied to the unspoken rebuke.

He'd found it much more effective to let others establish his power and perks.

He asked DeWitt, "You find any terrorist angle to the Super Chief's disappearance?"

"Nothing so far, neither foreign nor domestic. How're you doing?"

"I've got the uneasy feeling this one does involve Native Americans."

"Based on intuition or something more?" DeWitt asked.

"Intuition is a bit bloodless as a description. You're a California guy, so you'll understand when I tell you I'm feeling a bad vibe."

DeWitt laughed, but he said, "Yeah, I know all about vibes. Place great faith in them, too. If native people are involved, what's their point?"

"Well, it's a bit late to derail the iron horse from intruding on their land. There's probably not a lot of hope at this late date that the federal courts will compensate them for treaty violations either. Still, the feeling I get is some grievance is about to be aired."

"Won't look good if the train rustlers go public before we can grab them," DeWitt said.

"Yeah, I might even get busted back to special agent."

"Come on now. Even a salt-of-the-earth guy like you must take some joy in privilege."

John said, "Well, I do like high-end hotels so my feet don't hang off the bed."

DeWitt laughed again. "What's your next step?"

"Telling you about a complication," John said.

He informed DeWitt what Brian Kirby had told him about Edward Danner.

That and the story of Merritt Kinney's woefully short rooftop broad jump.

DeWitt summed up neatly the story he'd just heard. "So we have dueling billionaires here. One of them has committed a string of bribes to politicians the length of my home state to get advantageous rights-of-way to build his high speed rail line. The other guy, also striving to build his own high speed line has this motherlode of dirt on his competitor dumped in his lap by a guy now dead."

"Uh-huh, that's pretty much part one," John said.

"The subsequent parts being?"

"Well, Edward Danner, my guess is, will do everything he can, legally or otherwise, to stop his journal from falling into anyone else's hands. And it won't be much longer before he finds out the Super Chief isn't making its regularly scheduled stops."

DeWitt said, "That ought to send a chill down his spine."

"Maybe motivate him to send his own team out to look for the train, too, don't you think?"

"Now that you mention it, yeah. Thing is, we government types are supposed to frown on competition."

"Yeah, but you and I didn't exactly come off an assembly line, did we?" John asked.

DeWitt had a serigraph of Chairman Mao hanging in his office at the J. Edgar Hoover Building.

"I suppose we both have our quirks," DeWitt admitted.

"So what I was thinking is why don't you assign some people to keep an eye and an ear on Danner. If he hires some investigators, have your people follow them. They might find the train first. You know how some people in Congress think the private sector is so much more efficient than we are."

"I like the idea," DeWitt said. "It's always a pleasure working with you, John. What's the other thing you'd like the FBI to do for you?"

"As cooperative as Brian Kirby was, I think the man might actually be trying to play me."

"A move I'm sure he'll come to regret."

"The one thing I didn't buy was the reason for his breakup with Danner."

John told DeWitt about Kirby besting Danner in the model train competition.

"Does seem a bit thin as a reason to start a feud," DeWitt said.

"Yeah, but what if …" John offered a new slant on the situation.

DeWitt told him, "You are a devious thinker, John. I've never heard of anything like that, but I'll have someone look into it."

— CHAPTER 27 —

Gila Bend, Arizona

Maj Olson had her crew pull their two-car train onto a siding on the outskirts of town. The line carried light traffic at that time of day. Pulling off the main rail, she'd figured, ought to give them an hour or two to just sit and chill — though the day in the Southwestern desert was hot as blazes. Well, they weren't lacking for fuel and both the cab of the locomotive and Maj's coach were air conditioned.

She looked out a window and saw a whole lot of nothing. Not that someone who understood the flora and fauna of the environment would see it that way, she was sure. Still, to her eye, it was humps of unwelcoming mountains, vast stretches of sand and sparse gray-green desiccated vegetation, including some of the most forlorn palm trees she'd ever seen. Even the pale, cloudless blue sky looked like it had been drained of all moisture.

Jeez, she could almost *feel* her skin drying out.

At thirty-one, she wanted to keep her dewy pink complexion a little while longer.

She'd like to keep her job, too, at least until she could find one that was more engaging. Her future with Amtrak looked as bleak as the outside world. She didn't think she was going to find the Super Chief. The bad guys had too much of a head start, the country was so damn big and —

The flash of insight she'd had last night, the thought about track construction, suddenly gained a second element: Irish laborers. She knew from her academic research, of course, that Irish immigrants played a key role in the building of the first transcontinental railroad. They were among the most prodigiously productive workers on the eastern two-thirds of the project. Chinese labor did the heavy lifting on the western section.

But for some reason the Irish were the ones her subconscious was telling her were important. She didn't know why. But she felt sure the two parts fit together and would lead her to the answer she wanted, or so she hoped. The fact that part of her mind, maybe the best part, hadn't given up the chase encouraged her.

She was smiling when Don Prosser, the senior engineer of her crew, knocked and entered her coach. He had two bottles of root beer in hand and offered her one. Maj took it and said thanks.

Prosser said, "The guys and I would like to know how much more layover time we've got."

"Let's say another thirty minutes."

"That long enough for you to show us a little shooting?"

Maj glanced out a window. Decided that, yeah, it would be safe to let off a few rounds.

Wasn't anything to damage out there that she could see.

"Sure, why not?" she said.

The grizzled train driver grinned like a kid who just got the car keys.

Maj picked up the case holding her M-4. She brought her Beretta along, too, and formed up the crew, facing south, away from any sign of civilization. She looked out at the desert landscape for a target. She saw cacti in various sizes and shapes. There were even a few yellow and red blossoms on low-lying plants. But she didn't want to kill any vegetation that might be meaningful to local people or protected by federal law for all she knew.

There weren't any animals moving in the heat of the day that she could see. That was okay. She didn't want to kill any critters either.

She spotted a rock about the size of a family pizza pan about ninety feet out from where she and the guys stood. The interesting thing about it was the rock was mostly a pale orange but right in the center the color condensed to a deep red. Giving the effect of a bull's-eye.

Maj didn't think anyone could object to their shooting a rock, and she thought it was distant enough not to have to worry about a ricochet of rock chip or bullet fragment coming back to bite one of them.

She said to Don, "You guys are more interested in the M-4 than the sidearm, right?"

Prosser, Dean Spaneas and Ed Fenwick nodded.

Leo Taylor told Maj, "I'd rather shoot the handgun."

Maj found that interesting, but agreed to give each man the weapon of his choice. She pointed out the rock in the distance. All the men agreed they could see it clearly.

She said, "I want each of you to aim for the red spot, okay?"

Prosser seemed a bit daunted, being asked to hit the smaller area.

"Aren't we kind of far away to go for that?" he asked.

Maj told him, "The effective range for the M-4 is six hundred meters. What I'm asking you to hit is a gimme. Here look."

She pulled the bolt to clear the weapon, seated a loaded magazine in its well, pulled back the operating rod, fed a round into the chamber, brought the stock to her shoulder, set the weapon to individual shots and released the safety.

Maj told the others what she was doing at each stop. Then she emphasized, "You do not put your finger on the trigger until the moment you are ready to shoot. The rule is —"

"Off target, off trigger," Leo Taylor said.

Looking at him, Maj said, "Yeah, exactly." She turned her gaze to the rock and continued, "Tilt your head until your eye closer to the gun is looking straight down the barrel. You want to look straight past the rear sight, not to either side of it and — "

She squeezed off a round. A chip of rock flew out of the middle of the red spot on the rock. The sounds of the weapon firing and the round hitting the rock echoed in the heated air. In an even voice, Maj said, "And that's how it's done."

There was no hint of boastfulness in her voice. The shot was an easy make for anyone who'd had even a bit of training. But she didn't relinquish the weapon to anyone else yet.

"Now, before you guys try your hands, let me hear any ideas you might have had about what happened to the Super Chief."

Prosser said, "Dean and me, we think it could be in Mexico."

"Why Mexico?" Maj asked. The thought had occurred to her, too, but she couldn't work up any enthusiasm for it.

"Well, it's close," Dean Spaneas said, "and being a foreign country, getting it back could be damn hard."

"Lotsa cars stolen in border states wind up there," Prosser added.

"But you can resell cars," Maj said. "Who's going to buy a classic locomotive?"

Ed Fenwick cleared his throat.

"Yes?" Maj asked.

"I hadn't really thought about Mexico or any other place yet, but what Don and Dean said makes sense to me, only I don't see the Super Chief being resold. What if it was grabbed for one of those drug cartel bosses they've got down there? He wants the train to move his drugs or whatever. From what I know, that engine could pull ten or twelve cars. That's a lot more freight than any semi could haul. It'd be an economy of scale, you know."

Maj thought about that. She supposed a big-time drug boss in Mexico could bribe his way down any rails he needed to run. Put a lot of guys with their own assault rifles on board to deal with any would-be train robbers. Maybe even arm them with Stinger missiles to defend against an air assault.

"Okay, I can admit that *might* be a possibility," Maj said. "But why not buy any old locomotive? Why take the risk to snatch the Super Chief?"

Fenwick said, "Well, they're pretty superstitious down there, aren't they? And they've got their own Indians, I believe. An engine with that 'full headdress' paint job and the name Super Chief could be big magic. Nothing scares people more than their own imaginations."

Shrewd psychology from a train driver, Maj thought. And the guy hadn't even needed to go to grad school. She turned to Leo Taylor.

"What do you think?" she asked.

"I think the guys have part of it right, but they're taking things a little too far."

"What do you mean?"

"I think the Chief is in a foreign country, all right, but one we've got right here in our country."

"What the hell does that mean?" Prosser asked.

Maj answered for Taylor, "By federal law, Native American reservations are sovereign territories."

"That's right," Taylor said, "and whatever magic the Chief might have south of the border could be even bigger on our side."

Her head bobbing in agreement, Maj liked the idea.

It seemed to work as an element with the puzzle she was working out in her subconscious. Track construction, Irish laborers and an Indian reservation. Somehow, they all fit together for her.

She honored her commitment and gave all the men their shots at the red rock.

Prosser, Spaneas and Fenwick all hit the rock; Prosser and Fenwick nicked the red spot with their final rounds. Taylor put three rounds into the red, a much more difficult shot with a handgun than a carbine. He might as well have come right out and told her: He'd had either law enforcement or military training before going to work on the railroad.

She was going to ask him about that but …

Then she got a text from John Tall Wolf: *If you have the time, please call me.*

— CHAPTER 28 —

Rolling East of Gila Bend

When Maj responded to John's request for an update, he asked her, "What are you doing?"

"Right now? Chugging toward New Mexico, cleaning my M-4 carbine and my Beretta."

That surprised John. "You've had occasion to discharge both firearms?"

Maj explained it was only target practice with the crew and why they'd felt the need.

"Perfectly reasonable," John said. "After one train crew disappears, yours won't want to be the next to go. How'd they do?"

"Three weren't bad for guys who'd claimed never to have fired a carbine before."

"Did you explain things are different when someone's shooting back?"

"I will," Maj said. "That and when your target is also moving, and when it's dark outside, maybe even foggy or a high wind is blowing. I'm going to get around to that, but I'm going to let them feel good about things for a while."

"Aren't there four guys in your crew? What about the last one?"

"He's the interesting one. Leo Taylor. I'd like you to take a special look at his background, if you don't mind."

"He shot better than the others?"

"Way better, and he chose to use my sidearm, too. I've got the feeling he has military or police experience. Besides his marksmanship, he looked more at home with a weapon."

John paused for a moment, and Maj asked, "What?"

"I haven't said anything yet, passed my surmise along, but I'm thinking there had to be an inside man on the Super Chief crew. That'd be the most efficient way to take over the train. A whole lot easier than galloping alongside the locomotive on a horse and making a stuntman jump into the cab."

Maj laughed. "Yeah, you're right. I should've thought of that. Don't you think the FBI is checking that out?"

"Undoubtedly. But they might not find out what I have in mind, namely that one of the crew has Native American blood. Not that he'd have to look it. Some tribal leaders look white and have Anglicized names. I want to see if I can turn up a little more information on that possibility before I talk to Deputy Director DeWitt."

"How're you going to do that?" Maj asked.

"My co-director, Marlene Flower Moon, knows every indigenous person from Nunavut to Tierra del Fuego. I'll ask her."

"You two have a good relationship?"

"It's one of mutual self-interest; things usually work out."

"Good. Let's you and me have one of those. I'll tell what some of my guys' conjecture about where the Super Chief is."

She told John about the train being taken to Mexico to run drugs.

"Huh," he said. "I suppose it's possible. Just didn't occur to me, but it's worth checking out."

"Maybe you'll like this one better. It fits with your notion of a crew member being Native American. It's the possibility of the thieves hiding the Super Chief on a reservation. Sovereign territory, right, and there's a sense of irony to it as well. What do you think?"

John was silent long enough for Maj to ask, "You still there?"

"I am. I've thought of that possibility, too, but it's not one I like."

"Why not? Being BIA, it seems like you'd be right at home

with it."

"Too close to home for comfort. I've made a point of never working on a rez."

"Oh, sorry. Didn't mean to push the wrong button."

"Who thought of that idea?" John asked.

"Leo Taylor, the guy who's good with a handgun."

John said, "I'll get Marlene to take a real close look at him. One more thing."

"Yeah?"

"You're the only one on your train who's armed, right?"

"As far as I know, yeah," Maj said.

"Well, keep your carbine locked up safe and your sidearm on your person."

"You think Taylor could be trouble?"

"Only if the thieves are brilliantly well organized, but better safe than sorry."

"Words to live by," Maj said.

— CHAPTER 29 —

Northern New Mexico

So all this is our land, but we used to have so much more," Bodaway said. "Really, the whole continent belonged to Native Americans."

Alan White River and his great-grandson sat cross-legged on a ledge near the crest of a mountain. They looked out on an aspen forest below and other mountains in the range that stretched to the horizon. The sky was a sapphire blue. The air was thin and cool. The drop-off, mere inches in front of them, was thousands of feet.

"We don't own the land," White River reminded the younger man. "We are only its caretakers."

"Yeah, custodians. A position of both responsibility and power."

"In equal measure, but even before the white men came, power meant more to many."

Bodaway nodded, self aware. "Guilty."

White River said nothing, only let his eyes close.

"I'm sorry great-grandfather. I'm intelligent, but I don't have your wisdom. That's why I always try to follow your advice."

The old man opened his eyes. "But I won't always be with you."

"Not even in spirit?" Bodaway repressed a smile.

White River had no trouble sensing the younger man's amusement. Bodaway's father had sent his son out into the white man's world to be educated, to be successful in a modern sense. As Thomas Bilbray, Bodaway had succeeded only too well. His grasp of mathematics and science was intuitive and deep. A gift from a far greater spirit than the boy could ever imagine.

That was the problem. Bodaway recognized no authority higher than his own ego.

He respected his elders, did as he was asked, but he was sure when his time came he would make far more effective plans to … what? Retake North America from the outsiders? White River knew better. The world had changed, as it always did, and the past could never be recaptured.

"Yes, I will always be with you in spirit," White River said, "often to your dismay, I am sure."

Bodaway didn't like the sound of that, being crowded by a ghostly conscience.

One of the lessons he'd learned in the white world was the best defense is a good offense. He said, "Maybe I should be the one who pays for stealing the train, not you."

"A sound idea," White River said, "provided I am not alive when they come for us."

Alan White River had stayed in school only long enough to learn how to read, a habit he had cultivated throughout his life. He'd also learned how to read people early, too. See the thoughts that lay behind their words and the shadows that darkened their souls.

"I will share your decision with the other chiefs," the old man added.

Now, White River was sure his great-grandson would do all he could to make sure his revered elder didn't die before he could assign all blame to himself for the theft of the Super Chief. Otherwise, Bodaway would have no choice but to keep his word. The boy was intelligent, beyond question, but in matters of cunning he still had much to learn.

Bodaway did his best to keep his anger at being outmaneuvered off his face, but his eyes gave him away … until he took a deep breath and let his displeasure go as he exhaled. White River was pleased to see that the boy was learning, but he kept his face impassive.

"How can you be so sure any law enforcement people will find us?" Bodaway asked.

"We've let the train crew go. *You* pointed out the disadvantage of doing that."

White River watched as Bodaway cursed himself silently. The boy had just overlooked a point he himself had raised. Of course, their problems would have been far worse had they killed the crew as Bodaway had considered doing.

White River gave his great-grandson something else to think about.

"The greatest danger is always the one that comes from within," he said.

Bodaway's mind riffled through a mental file of images, starting with himself, moving on to the other chiefs and the ordinary people who knew what they'd done. The number was large and getting bigger fast. Native Americans who'd achieved political standing and moderate wealth were already making their way to the reservation where the two men sat on their mountaintop.

In this day and age, Bodaway was mildly surprised that what they had done didn't already have its own Facebook page. But he dismissed all of the potential candidates for betrayal ... until he got to the one he'd learned of only recently: Marlene Flower Moon.

"Is that who you mean?" he asked White River. "A woman who would use your capture to achieve political advancement?"

White River laid a gentle hand on Bodaway's leg. "I know you will not believe me, but that woman is truly Coyote. The Trickster who plays us all for fools for her own pleasure."

Bodaway didn't even try to hide his feelings now. He all but rolled his eyes.

So White River gave him something else to think about. "You've heard me mention the name John Tall Wolf. I've learned about him just these past few years."

"What's so special about him?" Bodaway asked, expecting more mystical hokum.

"It's said his mother left him to die as an infant. Coyote came along to make a meal of him, but a man and a woman saved the child, drove Coyote off. Now, Tall Wolf and Coyote regularly scheme against each other and to everyone's surprise Tall Wolf seems to be winning."

Bodaway needed a point of clarification. "But Tall Wolf is real, a flesh-and-blood man?"

"Yes, and I can feel him hunting us, getting closer by the minute."

Bodaway nodded.

He thought to himself: Wouldn't it knock everyone on their asses if I did what Coyote couldn't do? Eat John Tall Wolf for breakfast.

— CHAPTER 30 —

Chicago

John flew east after speaking with Maj Olson. The Secretary of the Interior's plane had been returned to him with no explanation. Not that he'd expected one. Coyote never admitted to making a mistake nor offered any apologies.

With an increasing sense of certainty, John was coming to agree with the notion that the Super Chief had been taken to a Native American reservation. Which one didn't really matter, not to him. He didn't want to set foot on any of them. Nonetheless, he sent Maj a text message.

Please see if any rez has a rail link that might accommodate the Super Chief.

She'd responded: *Already working on it.*

Then John called his mother. Told her of the situation.

"Are you worried?" she asked.

"About what I might do, yes."

"Because you're still angry."

"Yes, I'm still mad."

John had found out his birth mother had died some years ago, but the idea that she'd left him as an infant to die of exposure, had stood by and watched as Coyote tried to knock him from the sepulture where he lay and eat him, that rage never went away. It was the one point in his life where his emotions ruled him, and he didn't like it.

Even if the woman who'd given him life was no longer alive, her family was and they were the people whose disapproval had forced his mother to abandon him. Marlene Flower Moon had told him his grandmother and a cousin, both of whom considered John a potential rival for political power in their tribe, still lived on the rez.

He wanted nothing to do with them nor the place where they lived.

He had been made an outcast and he liked it that way.

It was his greatest stroke of luck to be found and saved by his true parents, and he would always live in their world.

So he was surprised when he spoke with his true mother, Serafina Wolf y Padilla, and she told him, "John, the only hold the past has on you is the one you allow it to have. You may come and go freely wherever you wish. You are your own man, a strong and accomplished one at that. You make your father and me proud of you every day we open our eyes. If you have any enemies, they should fear you. And if they're foolish enough not to realize that, I will make them fear me."

And that was that. He was a sworn federal officer, trained in self-defense and marksmanship, rising swiftly in the government hierarchy. If all that wasn't enough, his mom would step in and kick some ass.

He had to laugh at himself, which made him feel much better.

He still wouldn't *choose* to work on a rez, but he could make an exception if necessary.

Now, he stood in a large empty room in a new Chicago museum which hoped to open its doors for the first time in the coming week. With him was Cullum Walker the CEO of The Museum of American Railroading.

"I don't suppose you've come to bring good news," Walker said.

"The federal government has committed many resources to find the Super Chief you've been promised, if you consider that good news."

"I'm happy to hear that, but I'll feel better when we recover the train. An empty space like the one we're in doesn't draw much of a crowd."

"The museum is a non-profit, right?" John asked.

"It is, but we do have overhead: a payroll to meet, keeping the lights on and so forth. We need a steady and predictable cash flow."

"How did the Super Chief figure into that picture?"

"As a featured attraction. It was an iconic passenger train. In its heyday, it had enormous cachet as the primary means of carrying big movie stars and other notables from here to Los Angeles. It had, in a word, glamor. That's how we mean to portray it. Celebrity is always a big draw. I hope we'll still be able to do that."

The empty room was certainly big enough for a crowd. Either people who simply paid their way into the museum or hired the space for private parties. In either case, John could imagine the patrons ranging from the comfortably middle class to the wealthy and renowned.

Might even be a spot where contemporary movie stars got together for a special occasion.

On the other hand …

"Has your museum had any contact with Native American organizations?" John asked.

Walker sighed. His face sagged into a gloomy expression.

"Yes, we have."

"Not a happy conversation?" John asked.

"A definite difference of opinion, I'm sorry to say. The purpose of this museum is to celebrate the development of American rail travel. The railroad in the nineteenth century was the equivalent of the Internet in the twenty-first century. It spread communication and commerce, bound the nation together in a way that had never been seen before."

John said, "The objection to that point of view was?"

"That we didn't sufficiently display the devastation the railroads wrought on native peoples, how lives were lost, land was stolen and treaties were broken."

"But all of that is true," John said.

In a quiet voice, Walker agreed, "Yes, it is. But it's not what we chose to emphasize."

"Did you give the Native American point of view *any* consideration?"

"We did, yes."

"But not as much display space as, say, this area for your Super Chief?"

"No, the room we set aside for the Native American experience with the railroad is considerably smaller. It's very well done and historically accurate, but smaller."

"An afterthought?"

"No, it was in our plans from the beginning and it refers anyone with a greater interest in the subject to The Museum of the American Indian in Washington."

That was interesting, John thought, the very place he'd suggested to Marlene that she consider as a job opportunity for Nelda Freeland.

"Did the way you handled this matter result in any protests from the Native American community, either locally or nationally?" John asked.

"It has, on both levels. We've been taken to task repeatedly."

"But peacefully?"

"Yes, of course." Then Walker got John's drift. "You think that's why the Super Chief was stolen?"

"It's certainly something to check out," John said.

"But you are hopeful the train will be recovered?"

"Hopeful? Sure. Was there any name, among the people who objected to your … understatement of the Native American experience, that stands out in your mind?"

Walker nodded. "One, a man named Alan White River. He was the most persistent, but he was always polite and well spoken. A formidable thinker, given the way he writes. Under other circumstances, I'd have been happy to meet him."

"But for all of his powers of persuasion he got exactly nowhere," John said.

"I'm afraid the direction for our museum was set before we heard from him. After that …" Walker could only shrug.

It was John's turn to sigh, but he kept it to himself.

Looking at the large empty room anew, he asked, "How do you plan to get the Super Chief and the passenger car in here? Are there trucks big enough to do the job?"

"I don't know about that, but right out that window, what do you see?"

"A river," John said. "The Chicago River?"

"Yes, the North Branch of it. There's a rail bridge over the river about a mile away. The plan is to stop the train there and use a crane to put the locomotive and the passenger car on barges, float them down here and use another crane to bring them in here."

"Where there's a will, there's a way," John said.

Walker smiled. "Right, but eventually we plan to build our own rail spur right up to the building. We're fundraising for that right now."

— CHAPTER 31 —

Flying west

John watched his plane leave the lights of Chicago behind. He was all but certain now that Native Americans had stolen the Super Chief. He likely even knew the name of at least one of the ringleaders: Alan White River. The museum CEO, Cullum Walker, had provided him with a complete file of all the people who had objected to the museum's underplaying all the sorrows that the building of America's railroads had inflicted on its first inhabitants.

Some other names might be revealed as important, people who played leadership roles in the plot to steal the Super Chief, but as of that moment, Alan White River was the man who stood out.

John picked up his phone and called Marlene Flower Moon. He was less than surprised when she didn't answer and his call went to voice mail. "Marlene, this is John. We have a lead in the Super Chief theft. We need to look at a man named Alan White River, tribal membership unknown, but my guess is he's someone you must have encountered in some context. He was described to me as highly intelligent and articulate. Please call back as soon as you can."

He broke the connection, uncertain how soon or even if he'd receive a reply.

It depended, he thought, on how much Marlene believed he'd push her for the position of Secretary of the Interior. That and whether his support would actually mean anything. He thought it might, and he was certain if he hadn't raised the possibility of advancing Marlene's career he'd never again receive any help from her.

He'd only just put his phone down when it rang.

Answering, he said, "Tall Wolf."

But it wasn't Marlene, it was Byron DeWitt.

He told John, "We've found Albert Wicker."

John placed the name. "Lead engineer on the Super Chief, right?"

"Yeah."

"Where is he?"

"Recovering from heart surgery in Cheyenne, Wyoming. He was dropped at the hospital by an ambulance that turned out to be stolen."

Ignoring Wicker's condition or prognosis for the moment, John asked, "Any video of the ambulance crew?"

"Yeah, a couple of cowboy-looking types who'd be more at home working a ranch than providing medical care."

John said, "Stand-ins, guys hired to drive the ambulance and alert the ER staff at the hospital."

"That's our thinking," DeWitt said. "But the hospital people our agents in Wyoming talked to said Wicker had received some professional care before he got to them. There were meds in his system and he had an IV line in place."

"So whoever hired the cowboys also had at least one doctor on the payroll, too. Does it look like Wicker is going to make it?"

"Outcome uncertain is what we hear. What's obvious, though, is whoever grabbed the crew could have just let the man die, buried him somewhere he never would have been found. Kept their chances of being found much lower. What's that say to you?"

John replied, "That they know they can't hide forever, and they don't want a capital murder charge filed against them when they're caught."

"Yeah, but beyond that," DeWitt said, "it gives them higher

ground, if they have a political statement to make. Lets them say: 'See, we did our best to save this guy's life. We really aren't so bad.' It's probably a public relations move as much as a humanitarian gesture."

John said, "I can see that. I've got a name for you to check out."

He told DeWitt about Alan White River. "I tried to reach Marlene to ask whether she knows the man, and I'm sure she does, but she didn't answer my call."

"Still peeved about your promotion?" DeWitt asked.

"Most likely. She knows I didn't seek it, but it's still got to rankle."

DeWitt said, "I'll see if I can reach her. Maybe she'll take my call."

John said he'd transmit all the information he'd received from Cullum Walker to DeWitt.

The deputy director added, "I had one other interesting call to-day; it came from Arthur Halston, former chief counsel of Positron and Edward Danner's former personal lawyer."

"The man has cleared out?" John wanted to make sure he had things straight.

"Yes, he has. He said he couldn't reveal any information that would violate lawyer-client privilege, but he plainly wanted the FBI to know he was distancing himself from Danner. He said he tried to call you first but couldn't reach you through the BIA bureaucracy."

Marlene's doing. John didn't even bother to voice his conclusion.

He focused on another point. "Halston's call leaves us to wonder if he knows Danner is breaking the law or just has his suspicions."

"I'm checking on Halston's background right now to see which would be the better guess, but it's clear he wants to be outside the splatter zone when the doo-doo hits the fan, and my people are checking out the accusations Brian Kirby made to you."

"I think I might be able to help you get a clearer picture on Halston," John told DeWitt.

"Good. Turning back to Wicker, you think there's any significance to his turning up in a town with a Native American name?

I have to tell you I'm leaning toward the Super Chief thieves being Native American."

"Yeah, me too," John said. "It also looks like the thieves haven't made it out of the Western U.S. They've helped us a lot on that score."

DeWitt said, "Yeah, that and Alan White River are our two big clues right now."

After a momentary pause, John said, "I just had a thought. Cullum Walker told me the train museum in Chicago is going to have a rail spur built right up to its door. You think our train-nappers might've constructed their own section of track? Leading to a place where they might hide the Super Chief?"

DeWitt whistled. "If they're that sharp, we might have a hard time catching them."

"Yeah, but we have some things to work with. I'm thinking there had to be an inside man on the train crew to grab the thing in the first place. You've thought about that, right?"

"I have," DeWitt said. "It's the only way I can realistically see it happening."

"So you're looking into the other crewmen's family backgrounds and criminal histories, if any."

"We're doing that, too."

"Well," John said, "let's take things a step farther. Can you peer into the database for FAFSA?"

It took the deputy director a moment to grasp the acronym, and even then he wasn't sure he had it right. "The free application for federal student aid? Is that what you're talking about?"

John said, "I am. If the thieves had themselves a train driver, maybe they have some other expert Native American help. Say someone who knows how to build railroad tracks. A guy who went to a tech school and has some kind of applicable engineering background. Say a graduate from the past ten years who needed a Pell Grant or some other federal aid to get his degree."

"Damn," DeWitt said, "that's good, John. If I didn't know you were so happy working with Marlene, I'd ask you to come join our shop."

John laughed. "Yeah, Marlene and me, joined at the hip."

So where are you headed next?" DeWitt asked.

"Back to L.A.," John said, "I want to talk to that station master I missed the other day."

— CHAPTER 32 —

San Francisco

Captain Makilah Walsh sat at a corner table in Emiliano's, an Americanized version of a Mexican cantina, on Jones Street. A large tintype photograph of Emiliano Zapata hung behind the bar. Honoring the spirit of the leader of the Mexican peasants' revolution, the prices of food and drink at the place were kept reasonable, for San Francisco anyway.

The result was a patronage composed of the remnants of longtime city dwellers doing their best not to be pushed out by new-money techies and the lower ranks of those same arrivistes just getting their toeholds in town. The tension between the two groups was palpable, but the peace was maintained by the bar staff and a doorman, all of whom were well muscled and had waxed mustaches Zapata himself would have admired.

Besides that, popular lore had it that there was a *pistola* or two stashed behind the bar.

There was no question that Makilah had her duty weapon on her hip under the cover of her T Tahari Connor blazer. Stylish but priced within reach of an honest cop. Sergeant Fab Gallo walked through the front doorway, and Makilah felt certain he was armed, too. Only his weapon was concealed by a leather jacket that looked like Hugo Boss to her. Had to crowd a thousand dollars for that bad boy.

A gift from his rich wife would be the charitable guess, Makilah thought. Cops like her, though, being a suspicious lot, gravitated to other inferences. Like the sergeant had income beyond his police salary, possibly from disreputable sources for providing questionable services. Gallo spotted Makilah and came her way.

He was no sooner seated than a waitress arrived with two bottles of Negra Modela and a pair of pilsner glasses. The waitress removed Makilah's empty glass, already laced with drying foam. The captain hadn't had an earlier drink; the glass was a prop, but if Gallo chose to misinterpret, fall for her act, so much the better.

Gallo glanced at his bottle of beer and said, "I usually drink wine these days."

Makilah thought: Goddamn San Francisco. Wine-sipping cops. She repressed a laugh.

All she said was, "You can order wine. I'll drink your beer."

Wasn't hard to read between those lines, what she was calling him: Pussy.

Gallo said, "No, that's all right. I can go with beer tonight."

He poured his beer into the glass. Even let it build a nice head. The way a man would.

The guy was nervous and she was going to see if she couldn't give him some angina. She hadn't really expected to hear from John Tall Wolf again. After he'd gone his own way in Union Square, she had done her best to carefully check him out. She had a cousin who worked for Homeland Security. Not that he'd ever told her exactly what he did there.

She didn't really care. The fact that he'd come up with the goods on Tall Wolf told Makilah that her cousin had some juice. "Man was just promoted to co-director of the Office of Justice Services. They're the cops for the BIA. In itself, that doesn't say much. The whole Department of the Interior is kind of a backwater where cops and spooks are concerned."

Makilah felt her cousin was holding back on her and told him so.

"Okay, what's special about this Tall Wolf guy is he's scored points with the White House, coming through on some big jobs that were important to a lot of people. Vice President Morrissey was at his swearing in. She's supposed to be the juice behind this guy, and the way things are going now, with all the talk of the president about to be impeached, that means a lot. Tall Wolf's also supposed to work hand-in-glove with a deputy director at the FBI, guy named Byron DeWitt. That says a lot, too. The feebs don't like to share with anybody most times, barely talk to the CIA the way they're supposed to. But here's this guy from the BIA, and they're all buddy-buddy."

Just hearing Tall Wolf's story gave Makilah chills. A guy that high up the ladder and he'd come across to her all polite and full of professional courtesy. If she wasn't sure someone like that must have a woman in his life, she would have made a move on him.

Only he called her back, just like he said he would.

He let her know that Edward Danner's personal and corporate lawyer, Arthur Halston, had quit on him and called the FBI to let them know he was putting daylight between himself and the tech billionaire as fast as he could. Maybe, Tall Wolf suggested, she could use that fact with any of the cops who looked into Merritt Kinney's death — if she thought someone was holding back something he shouldn't.

Gallo took a tiny sip of his beer and asked, "So what can I do for you, Captain?"

"Listen real close," Makilah said.

She told him about Halston deserting Danner and how the FBI, the White House and God only knew who else was looking at the billionaire for something crooked on a scale that produced consecutive life sentences. That or maybe a rendition to a CIA dark site outside the country.

The captain knew she was laying it on thick, but she was certain Gallo had something to hide when she saw fear darken his eyes. Maybe he wouldn't be water-boarded but he could wind up behind bars. Never a pleasant prospect for anyone, especially a cop.

"Now, Sergeant Gallo, I'm going to advise you of your Miranda rights."

She did so as the man tried to measure just how deep the shit in which he stood was.

Whether he'd disappear into it or have more heaped upon him.

"Do you understand your rights, Sergeant? In addition to your constitutional protection, you know, of course, that your union will provide you with a lawyer. Before you answer, let me tell you that you're not even under arrest. You can walk out of here right now — or you can do what Arthur Halston did and try to position yourself to your best advantage."

Gallo suddenly found his beer to be more inviting. He took off the top half of his glass.

"What do you want to know?" the sergeant asked.

"Whatever you have, you can tell me," Makilah replied.

"Danner offered me fifty thousand dollars, splitting it with my team as I saw fit, if I found something in Merritt Kinney's apartment, and returned it to Danner."

"What was it Mr. Danner wanted?"

Tall Wolf hadn't told her that. Must've wanted to see if she could find out for herself.

"He said it was a leather-bound book."

"Containing what?"

"He didn't say. But he swore he'd know if I read it, and if I did, I'd never …" Gallo finished his beer and then his thought. "I'd never work for him again. Worse than that, he'd destroy my career and my wife's, too. See to it that we'd both wind up homeless."

As a threat, Makilah thought, that wasn't half-bad.

Might be worse than just shooting somebody.

"Did you find the book?"

"No." The mix of emotions in Gallo's voice was easy to read. Disappointment that he hadn't earned what he'd probably thought was an easy bundle of money. Relief that his involvement in Danner's scheme hadn't gone any farther than it had.

"You told Mr. Danner of your failure to find what he wanted?"

"Yes, Captain."

"Did he ask you to keep trying?"

"He did, but I told him I couldn't do it. If I found stolen property in the course of the legitimate exercise of my duty and returned it to him without doing the usual paperwork … well, that could be smoothed over."

"Especially for someone with Mr. Danner's money," Makilah said.

"Yeah, but I told him no way could I freelance a private investigation while I'm on the job."

"How'd he take that?"

"He got mad for maybe ten seconds. Then he thought it through and said it'd be better if he used a private investigator."

"Did he say who that was?"

Gallo gave her a name.

"Anything else you feel it would be wise to share with me, Sergeant?"

Gallo laughed. "Only that I liked that beer more than I thought I would. Can I go now?"

"Leave your duty weapon and your star with me. You'll be on desk duty until I speak with my superiors."

He handed them over, no fuss. Trying to show how cooperative he could be.

"This is going to stay within the SFPD, isn't it?"

"I don't know, Sergeant, I honestly don't."

Gallo left, looking like a man who needed another drink.

Something stronger than a beer.

One thing Makilah was sure of: She owed John Tall Wolf a return call.

— CHAPTER 33 —

Northern New Mexico

The moon passed its zenith and the hour was late for an old man, but Alan White River was out walking through the forest land on the reservation. Enough light pierced the tree cover for him to find a clear path and not stumble. Wouldn't do for him to trip and break his neck now. If he did sustain some mishap, it would be a sure sign that his ancestors and even greater spirits did not approve of the plan he'd conceived and dared to set in motion.

So far, though, no supernatural forces extended a foot to trip him. He took satisfaction that his aged legs still carried him wherever he wished to go, uphill or down. His senses of smell and hearing still functioned well, too. He gathered all the scents about him, from the fertile odor of the earth to the ever changing redolence carried by the breeze.

All this would be lost to him soon. He would be confined in a concrete and iron cage after being convicted of stealing the train the white men mockingly called the Super Chief. Honoring the engine of so much destruction and despair among native peoples. White River thought it would be better if such compliments remained forever silent.

Just as he would remain quiet when the police and the courts asked who had helped him with his plan.

He would not say a word. All punishment would be his. Well, his and anyone who visited the new train museum in Chicago.

The people who visited the train there would also know pain and sorrow such as they had never imagined. But all that was in the future.

Now, and for some time, White River had sensed the beast that was stalking him. Many a fearsome predator roamed the wilderness of New Mexico. Their number included bobcats, mountain lions, black bears and ... coyotes. The creature following him might have been any of their kind.

Not that his aged frame would provide much meat for anything more than a young fox.

But he knew the animal watching him was interested in more than a meal.

He stepped into a glade where the lunar glow shone like a spotlight and there she was, Marlene Flower Moon. For a moment, he thought she was nude. As stunningly beautiful as she was, he was long past the time when a woman might arouse him. He blinked, as if to confirm what he was seeing. Now, he saw she wore a dress of finely worked doeskin.

"You should have come to me, White River," she said.

The old man smiled.

"Isn't that what I've just done?"

Her voice hardened. "Come to me from the start."

The old man shrugged. "We are a patriarchal people."

Marlene stepped close and looked down at White River. He couldn't remember a time since childhood when a woman was tall enough to do that. Then, in a matter of seconds, she seemed to grow before his eyes. A giantess. Not at all pleased by the lesser being in front of her.

The old chief refused to cower. "Kill me, if you wish, but then you will share in the destiny of what I have started."

The truth of his remarks cut the woman, if that was what she was, down to size. She still loomed over him but in the proportions of a normal person not the fearful exaggeration of a mescal hallucination.

"I am here now," Marlene said, "and it is your good fortune

that I approve of what you've done, in outline if not in every detail. I will be watching you. If I see anything that displeases me, you will be the first and perhaps the last to know. If I think you're going too far, I will stop everything you've done. Then I'll let you live with all your regrets. You and all the other *patriarchs*."

White River knew he was about to be dismissed. The woman might vanish as he watched just to show him what her powers were. But there was a point he wanted to raise, a warning to offer. He raised a hand, asking her to wait.

"What?" she asked.

"I consulted many spirits before I started this journey. All the signs were favorable except one."

Marlene's eyes grew huge and her pupils narrowed to vertical slits.

"Do you mean me?"

"No. I am concerned about my great-grandson, Bodaway. He made the taking of the train possible. But he might prove our undoing by going too far. His heart doesn't understand what we will do, and his mind rejects it."

Marlene laughed, making a sound far too wicked for any human throat to produce.

"A college boy, yes? A believer in only the sliver of nature science can touch."

White River nodded. "This is true. I fear he might go too far, but I need him to return the train."

"Would you have me speak to him?"

"I would be grateful."

"So you need me after all."

"Of course, I always knew you'd come."

Marlene laughed again, this time with bitter irony and in a human register.

"You remind me of someone else, old man."

"John Tall Wolf?"

An edge crept back in Marlene's voice. "You know of him?"

"I saw him in a vision."

"So you *are* close to the spirits."

"Not as close as I'd like."

"But you fear neither death nor capture."

"My only fear is for Bodaway. I sense he will challenge Tall Wolf and lose more than a fight."

That was when all human form disappeared from the woman. Coyote stood fully revealed and enormous, leaning in close to White River, fangs bared and eyes afire. The creature's breath was vile as it spoke to him.

"Tall Wolf is mine, and no one else's," Coyote warned.

Moving so fast his eyes could not follow, the Trickster turned and was gone.

When White River awakened, the rising sun in his eyes, he saw he had slept in the glade.

A white man might think he'd had a nightmare and nothing more.

White River knew better. He had to seek Bodaway. Warn him of the danger he faced.

From both Tall Wolf and Coyote.

Find some way to convince the young man both threats were real.

Perhaps the stench of the beast, still strong upon him, would be persuasive.

— CHAPTER 34 —

Los Angeles

Jack Stanton, the station master of Union Station, opened the door of his home in the city's Los Feliz neighborhood. The residence was a Spanish Revival beauty with stucco walls and a red barrel-tiled roof set in a landscaped garden against a hillside. With Stanton was a handsome middle-aged woman in a blue business jacket and skirt. She didn't wear a wedding ring but she held a leather folio in her left hand.

She extended her right hand to the tall man standing in front of her.

"Patricia Derby. I'm Mr. Stanton's lawyer, and you are Mr. Tall Wolf?"

John nodded. "Co-director of the BIA's Office of Justice Services, but I still think of myself as a special agent, especially when I'm doing field work. May I come in, please?"

Not budging for the moment, Ms. Derby said, "Just to be clear, you are a federal officer and lying to you would be a crime?"

"Right both times," John said.

He waited to see if he'd be admitted to the house.

If not, he'd inform the lawyer he'd have LAPD watch Mr. Stanton's house until he could return with a material witness warrant and take her client into custody. Ms. Derby, unable to see John's eyes, protected against the bright Los Angeles sun by his Ray-Ban sunglasses, still managed to correctly assess where her client's best interests lay. She stepped aside, gesturing to Stanton to do the same, and they allowed John to enter.

They led him into the home's living room, gestured him to take a seat in a wing back chair, while they sat side by side on a leather sofa.

Derby said, "Unless I direct Mr. Stanton to speak directly to you, I will be answering all your questions. Will that be satisfactory? If not, I'm afraid we'll be unable to cooperate."

John smiled. "Why don't we just give things a chance? Maybe it won't be too painful."

Stanton seemed to relax a bit; Derby only looked more guarded. Nonetheless, she agreed to proceed.

Looking at her, John asked, "What was the nature of the family emergency that called Mr. Stanton away from his job?"

"His son, Patrick, had an adverse reaction to a prescription medication during track practice. He lost consciousness twice. He seems to be improving but remains in the hospital for observation."

"My best wishes for a full recovery," John told Stanton. Turning to Derby, he said, "May I have the name of the hospital and the boy's doctor, please?"

Derby provided them.

"Were you on your way to be with your son when I arrived, Mr. Stanton?" John asked.

Derby gave her client a hard look — telling him, in effect, to keep quiet.

She told John, "Patrick is resting comfortably, the last we heard, and his mother is with him."

"I see," John said. "I understand that Mr. Stanton has a younger son, Michael. Where is he right now?"

"How is that relevant?" Derby asked.

"Well, is he with his mother and brother at the hospital?"

"He's traveling to a baseball tournament," Stanton said, breaking discipline.

Derby gave him a scolding look.

"Again," she asked John, "what does that have to do with

anything?"

John held his hands wide, a man just being reasonable.

"If Patrick is resting comfortably, and has his mother for company, and Michael feels free to play baseball, what's the reason Mr. Stanton is at home in the company of his lawyer instead of doing his job at Union Station?"

Neither Derby nor Stanton said a word

John turned to Derby and asked, "Did Mr. Stanton contact you for professional help before or after his son was admitted to the hospital?"

"We talked at the hospital. I'm Patrick's aunt."

For John, that was a mark in Stanton's favor. If he had sought out legal representation during a family crisis, that would have increased the impression of acting from a guilty conscience. Even so, something was bothering the man, and John felt sure he knew what it was.

Still addressing Derby, John said, "The Super Chief run from L.A. to Chicago wasn't paid for by any particular railroad company, was it?"

The lawyer shook her head. "No, it wasn't."

"So how was the crew for the train assembled?"

Stanton's face tensed, telling John he was on the right trail.

Derby started to whisper in Stanton's ear, but John cut her short.

"Ms. Derby, Mr. Stanton, it's the considered opinion of a number of federal investigators that the only way the Super Chief could have been stolen was if one or more members of the crew was in on the plan. The FBI is running background checks on the crew as we speak. One member of the crew has suffered a heart attack, and the last I heard it was uncertain whether he'd survive. The situation has gone from bad to worse."

Both the station master and his sister-in-law looked far more worried now.

John continued, "It occurred to me that Mr. Stanton, as the station master at Union Station, might have been afforded the honor of picking the crew for the Super Chief run from a list of volunteers."

Unable to restrain himself, Stanton nodded. Derby didn't chastise him.

"What I need to know, to speed the investigation along, and maybe save a life or two, is whether any member of the Super Chief crew pushed to get his place on board."

Derby looked at Stanton and nodded.

He said, "Rick Engram. He said it would be an honor he'd always remember. He wanted it bad."

"How bad?" John asked. "Did he offer you any personal incentive?"

John thought Derby might object, but she remained silent.

"He did. Five thousand dollars."

"Did you take it?"

Stanton shook his head. "What I told him was, I didn't need or want any money. Wouldn't take any. If he wanted to do anything to show his appreciation, he could make a donation to my son's baseball team."

"Didn't five thousand dollars strike you as a lot of money to get that assignment?" John asked.

Stanton shrugged. "People who love trains will spend all sorts of money indulging themselves."

John couldn't argue with that. He'd made a request of Byron DeWitt hoping to prove just that point.

"As far as you know, did Engram follow through on his end of the bargain?"

Stanton nodded. "He did." Then the station master gestured to a gift box standing on the end table next to the sofa. "And that came shortly before you arrived. Looks like it might be a bottle of Scotch to me, but I didn't ask for it."

John thought it might also be something with more kick than a hundred proof.

Learning there was no one else in the house, he hurried Stanton and Derby outside. He didn't feel certain that a bomb had been sent to silence the station master, but he wasn't going to take any chances. They waited outside while the LAPD bomb squad was called and went inside to make a definitive determination.

John took the opportunity to ask Stanton directly, "If you didn't take a bribe, and I believe you didn't, why didn't you come forward immediately with the information about Rick Engram?"

The man's face went red with embarrassment. "I still screwed up, didn't I? I just hoped the train would be found without my dumb-ass move coming out."

John sighed. The high cost of personal vanity always confounded him.

To make the punishment fit the crime, he told Stanton and Derby they'd have to do the interview all over again with the FBI making a record of it. He'd see if he could have the LAPD bill the fool for the bomb squad's work, too. That'd have to cost a whole lot more than five grand.

He called Byron DeWitt to let him know what he'd found out. Save the FBI the trouble of looking at the wrong members of the Super Chief crew. That was when DeWitt told him, "We found another member of the Super Chief crew in another hospital. Dale Brent was suffering from a ruptured kidney. The organ had to be removed. Brent told the docs he'd been kicked in the back by an Indian."

"Damn," John said.

"Yeah, overt violence rears its ugly head."

"Where's the hospital treating Brent?"

"Flagstaff, Arizona."

"Looks more than ever like the train's still in the Southwest."

DeWitt pointed out, "That still covers a lot of ground."

"Less than before, though."

— CHAPTER 35 —

Northern New Mexico

WHat's your white name?" the old Native American woman asked.

She stood barely five feet tall but her back was ramrod straight. Her face was seamed with nearly as many lines as that of Alan White River. Her eyes were as dark as a raven's wing, showing no light of mercy and precious little humanity. This was a person to be feared, if not for the strength of her own limbs then for those who would do her bidding with no hesitation.

One such specimen stood to her right, perhaps a foot-and-a-half taller, decades younger with broad shoulders and big hands, but going soft at the jawline and around the middle. Signs of power yielding to privilege as the years passed.

Visiting the two in the old woman's home was the subject of the old woman's question, another man, younger than the big guy, showing no signs whatsoever of middle-age spread.

"My white name is Thomas Bilbray," he said.

"Your voice and English are smooth," the old woman told him. "You've been to white schools for many years."

"That's true."

"Are you one of them more than one of us?"

"I was for some time. Then my father and grandfather died. The only elder left to guide me was my great-grandfather, Alan White River."

The old woman's expression eased just a bit.

"I know of him. Wise as a spirit, some say."

"Far wiser than me, but perhaps closer to the next world than this one."

"What is your real name?"

"Bodaway."

The old woman laughed, the emotion being all the more powerful for being so unexpected.

"Firemaker. A fine Apache name."

"Yes, mother."

The big man at the old woman's side flinched, fought unsuccessfully to keep a scowl from his face. He'd expected to see the stranger humbled or at least dismissed out of hand. Instead, he'd been complimented on his name, and had dared to presume the greatest of familiarities with the old woman.

She smiled at the stranger, Bodaway, as she'd never smiled at him.

"Do you now know who you truly are?" she asked Bodaway.

"No, but I believe I am finding my way."

"You found your way to us," the big man said, "but for what purpose? Maybe you're an enemy posing as a friend."

Bodaway opened his hands in a gesture of supplication. "I'll tell you why I'm here, and you may decide what to do with me. I've come to claim the life of John Tall Wolf. To kill him. So he won't interfere with my great-grandfather's plans. I was told you might be interested in helping me."

The old woman stared at Bodaway now, looking for any sign of deceit or treachery.

Finding none, she nodded in satisfaction. "We are interested. My grandson, Arnoldo, and I are most interested in that. Tell us what your plan is."

Bodaway explained his idea to Maria Black Knife, John Tall Wolf's grandmother, and to Arnoldo Black Knife, John's cousin. They both listened closely to what he had to say.

— CHAPTER 36 —

Ruidoso, New Mexico

Maj Olson climbed onto her dirt bike at first light. Her train had stopped for the night on a siding not far from the southern New Mexico town. Don Prosser, the senior engineer, had reported their position to the nearest dispatcher. He'd confirmed their right to park wherever they wanted, and the dispatcher took into consideration any adjustments to through traffic he might have to make.

Now, Prosser, standing alongside the train, looked at Maj and asked, "How long'll you be gone?"

"Can't say. I won't stop to pick any wildflowers, though."

"You gonna leave us unarmed while we wait?" Dean Spaneas said.

Train crews in the U.S. typically worked unarmed. Then, again, thefts of trains, especially ones that simply disappeared, had been unheard of — until the Super Chief had vanished. Now her crew was involved in the hunt for that train. Maj could see how the guys might continue to be on edge. No longer content to depend on the contents of a toolbox for protection.

Well, Prosser, Spaneas and Ed Fenwick were nervous.

Leo Taylor looked cool and relaxed even in the gathering early morning heat.

She asked Leo, "Cops or military?"

"Both," he said. "Marines and San Bernadino PD, but only a year with the cops."

"Why'd you leave?" Maj asked.

"Thought it was a better idea than killing my sergeant. Caught on with the railroad through my brother-in-law."

"You have any problems with these other guys?" Maj meant the rest of the train crew.

"Unh-uh," Leo said. "They're salt of the earth."

She'd been planning to ride with only her sidearm for protection. She got off her bike, went into the passenger car and came back with the M-4 slung over her back and her badge on a lanyard around her neck. She handed her Beretta to Leo.

"You'll have to make do with one magazine," she said.

"That's plenty," he replied.

She told Don Prosser, "You're in charge of the train; Leo has the final word on security. Everybody good with that?"

They were but Prosser returned to his original question, "Is there any limit to how long we wait for you to come back?"

She said, "If I'm not back by nightfall, call John Tall Wolf at the BIA or Byron DeWitt at the FBI and have them come look for me."

Maj got back on her bike and rode off on a small state road to the east, disappearing into the rising sun.

There wasn't a member of the crew, just then, who didn't have both admiration for Maj and impure thoughts about her.

A mile down the road, she veered north into rolling grassland. Mountains stood watch in the distance. Maj thought she remembered a fellow Columbia student, who'd hailed from Albuquerque, talking about going skiing near Ruidoso. It was the wrong season for that, but the place was still as scenic as you could ever want.

She tried not to let the natural beauty distract her. She was looking for something far more prosaic, industrial and unlikely ever to appear on a tourism poster: abandoned railroad tracks. A line to nowhere, forgotten when the last person to use it had long since taken his final ride. Probably overgrown by native vegetation by now, as nature always overcame man's constructs anyplace where it wasn't kept at bay.

The dirt bike held up well after hitting countless rocks and ruts, but it didn't jolt across any rail lines either camouflaged by tall grass or simply overlooked. If human endeavor had intruded on that patch of countryside, she saw no sign of it. She pushed on until the muscles in her legs and backside begged for relief. Not wanting to admit to any hint of personal weakness, she rationalized a return to a paved highway by observing her gas tank was down to a quarter full.

Once she was back on a state road, she stopped the bike and took a long pull of water from her canteen. She looked up at the bright blue sky as if she might see a sign from heaven. When that didn't happen, she muttered, "Damn."

The Mescalero Apache Reservation wasn't far away. She had been hoping to find abandoned railroad tracks with signs of recent use that would suggest the stolen Super Chief had been taken to the nearby sovereign Native American territory. She'd find the train, get the credit and maybe make a move to a more glamorous job somewhere else in the federal government. With a big raise, of course.

But that didn't look like it was in her immediate future.

She pulled out her iPhone, was pleased to see it pulled a signal and opened an app to find the nearest gas station. A map appeared with directions, distance and time of travel. Maj laughed. Settling the West would have been a lot easier with information like that available.

She headed off in the proper direction.

Maybe, she thought, somebody had written an app to locate stolen trains.

Then the recurring thought, the one about track construction and Irish laborers, came roaring to the front of her mind. Hell, maybe looking for old track was entirely beside the point. Maybe the thieves had laid down their own new rail.

She felt pretty sure, though, Native Americans wouldn't hire the Irish to do the job.

Maj opened up the throttle. She wanted to bounce this idea off Tall Wolf. But not from the side of the road. She'd just busted past eighty miles per hour when a New Mexico State Police patrol unit burst from a speed-trap and took up chase.

That was when Maj remembered she had an assault weapon strapped to her back.

She slowed, stopped and raised both hands.

Without looking back, she called out, "Federal officer."

— CHAPTER 37 —

High above southern New Mexico

John Tall Wolf didn't mind flying in jet planes. He enjoyed the amenities found in the executive aircraft used by government and private sector poobahs. For speed and comfort, they couldn't be beat. Helicopters were another matter. He'd once been told, and had believed from the moment he'd heard it, that helicopters had all the glide characteristics of an anvil.

If *anything* went wrong in a chopper, there wasn't going to be a soft landing.

Despite his misgivings, he was on his way from Albuquerque to Ruidoso, where he'd learned Maj Olson's train was waiting, in an AW 109 Power helicopter on loan from the Special Operations Bureau of the state cops. Looking down from a height of several thousand feet, he thought he should've rented a car. Not that the pilot seemed the least bit perturbed. The sky was blue, the air was calm and the guy at the controls seemed to be humming.

Now, if he just didn't have a stroke.

Then the pilot's voice came through John's headset. "Got a phone call from a police captain in San Francisco. She wants to be patched through to you, sir. You want to take it?"

Makilah Walsh, John thought. "Yes, please."

"Just speak normally. Your mike will transmit your voice."

John was wearing a headset that let him communicate with the man to whom he'd entrusted his life. "Right."

A beep sounded and John heard Makilah. "Co-director Tall Wolf?"

"Yes."

"I have some news bearing on your investigation, sir."

"Just a minute, Captain." John looked over at the pilot, got his attention. "Are you listening to this call?"

The pilot turned red with embarrassment. Flipped a switch. "Not anymore."

"Knowing what I say here would only be a burden to you. You'd want to tell people what you heard, but if you did, it would get out and damage your career."

The pilot bobbed his head. "Just you and the other party now, sir."

He flipped another switch.

"Go ahead, Captain," John said, "we've got privacy on my end."

"Mine, too. I spoke with Sergeant Gallo, the supervisor of the raid on Merritt Kinney's apartment. He told me last night that Mr. Kinney stole a personal journal from Edward Danner's office. I advised the sergeant that it was in his best interest to continue to cooperate with the department and the federal authorities in this matter. He took my advice to heart. This morning, the sergeant told me he's learned that the private investigation firm, SearchCo, has been hired by Mr. Danner to find and retrieve his journal. I trust you can pass this information on to anyone else who needs to know."

"I can and will," John said. He thought Byron DeWitt could compel the firm to cooperate. That or just have his people follow the SearchCo investigators. Seize the journal as soon as the thing was found.

"One more bit of good news, sir," Makilah said.

"What's that?"

"It shouldn't take all that long to find Mr. Danner's property. There's a tracking chip embedded in the binding."

"Well, isn't that … convenient?" Or was it, John thought.

Makilah heard the hesitation in John's voice.

"Something wrong?"

"Well, it's just that if there's a hidden tracking device maybe there's something else."

"Like what?"

"A bomb maybe, just a little one. Something that can shred a document beyond reconstruction. Maybe blow off someone's hand in the process."

"Damn, I never heard of anything like that."

"Me neither, but if I can imagine it, maybe someone else did, too. A rich man would want to protect what's his, keep the competition from seizing it. We don't want anyone to get hurt."

"No, sir. No one beyond those private eye types anyway."

John laughed. "Maybe not even them. Just something to think about. Perhaps Sergeant Gallo can inquire discreetly about that possibility."

"Yes, sir. I'll get him right on it."

"Good work, Captain."

"Thank you, sir."

John heard Makilah end the call and he gave the pilot a thumb's-up.

"You're done with your call, sir?"

"I am."

"I had another call regarding you from one of our highway patrol units."

John asked, "One of your people wants to talk with me?"

"Not personally, sir. The trooper stopped a woman who was carrying an assault rifle and speeding on a dirt bike. She claims to be a federal officer working for Amtrak. Our guy never heard of such a thing; neither have I, but she knew your name and asked for you."

John said, "She's for real. Her name is Maj Olson. Let's go see her."

— CHAPTER 38 —

New Mexico State Highway 48

The road where Maj had been stopped held no other traffic for a mile in either direction. The helicopter pilot made sure of that. He set his compact aircraft down on the blacktop. John hopped out, keeping his head down. After completing a safe flight, he wanted to avoid the irony of being decapitated. He hurried over to the state police car as the chopper lifted off.

Once the downdraft and the roar of the flying machine had dissipated, he shook the state trooper's hand and introduced himself. "John Tall Wolf, BIA."

"Ernie Rios, state police. This woman says she knows you."

John noticed an M-4 carbine lying across the back seat of the patrol unit.

Maj, wearing a frown, sat facing backward on the saddle of her dirt bike.

"She does," John told Rios.

"And Amtrak really has its own cops?"

"They do. She's from their intelligence division."

Rios started to look uncomfortable. "That make her a big shot?"

"Pretty much, yeah. We both got our marching orders out of Washington. Very high up."

"Well, hell," the trooper said. "Blasting down the road on her dirt bike, packing that assault weapon, she looked more like some bad-ass chick out of a low-budget movie."

John went with that. "So you're saying Special Agent Olson could be a movie star?"

Rios was quick on the uptake. He understood John had just handed him a way out. "Oh, yeah. I mean, she's got the looks."

Maj snorted.

"She *definitely* has the attitude," the state cop said. "And she rides that bike like a pro."

"I see what you mean about the attitude," John said. "She did identify herself, though, right?"

"Absolutely. Put her hands up, surrendered her weapon, but wouldn't get into the back of my patrol unit for anything. Said I'd have to shoot her first. Then she gave me your name."

"Okay, we have some ruffled feathers here, but nobody got hurt. You want to see my identification, trooper, just so you can tell your boss you got a look?"

Rios smiled and shook his head. "You get transport from one of our aircraft, sir, I figure they checked you out plenty. You going to need a lift?"

"No, thanks, but I'd like Special Agent Olson's weapon back."

"Yes, sir."

Rios opened the patrol unit and handed the M-4 to John.

John made sure the state cop was well down the road before he returned the carbine to Maj.

She told John, "I've been out in the sun long enough. Let's go somewhere we can get a cool drink and talk."

He got on the back of the dirt bike.

It wasn't made for two riders. He had to scrunch up close. A hand on each of Maj's hips.

Law enforcement working in close cooperation.

Sitting in the back booth of a diner with gas pumps out front, Maj looked at John with a sneer and said, "Movie star? Hah! Big shot? Hah!"

John smiled and replied, "But you didn't mind bad-ass chick?"

Maj gave in and grinned. "It's not every female Ph.D. who can pull that off."

She still had her assault rifle with her, but it was tucked away as discreetly as possible.

A waitress brought Maj a milkshake and burger; John got by with a glass of lemonade.

When they were alone again, he asked, "Did you and Trooper Rios do anything but hiss, spit and threaten each other?"

"Sure, we discussed unwelcome trends in modern dance."

"Well, he certainly looked like a fan of the arts."

"He was a macho jerk, but once he heard you were flying to the rescue in a state helicopter, he grudgingly agreed to answer some questions."

"That was collegial of him. Would you care to tell me what you learned?"

"He told me he knew of no new rail track being laid into the nearby Mescalero Apache reservation."

"New rail?" John asked. That worked nicely with what he'd been thinking.

Always good to work with a compatible mind.

Maj finished a long slurp of her milkshake and smiled.

"How's that for an idea?" she said. "All along, I was thinking the Super Chief thieves were stuck on the existing rail system. Even using dark territory —" She stopped her narrative to explain the term to John. "Well, it seemed to me that *somebody* would have had to spot that train before too long. Once that happened, word would go up and down the system and we'd have heard about it."

"We haven't publicized the theft," John told her.

"Don't need to. If we were talking about some run-of-the-rails locomotive — old, grimy and undistinguished — nobody would give it a second glance. But a mint-condition Super Chief in full warpaint? That's worth talking about. Hell, somebody would've snapped a still photo or shot a video of it and put it up on social media."

John thought about that and nodded. "You're right. These days, anything worth noticing is worth sharing. I had a thought similar to your new rail idea."

He told her first about learning of Rick Engram, one of the Super Chief's crew, paying to get his assignment. "The FBI is now looking into whether he has any Native American connections, family or otherwise. My sense of things is he does. That fits in with the idea I had that somebody with structural engineering skills is working with the thieves, also likely someone with native blood."

Maj raised her glass to John. "Great minds think alike."

John sighed. "Hearing you talk about laying new rail, though, just made me wonder something. Besides having a structural engineer on hand, you'd also need at least semi-skilled labor, I'd think."

Maj bobbed her head. "You'd need Irishmen or their equivalent."

"Okay, I need some help with that one."

"Many, if not the majority, of laborers building the eastern two-thirds of the first transcontinental railway line were immigrant Irish, a lot of them right off the boat. I remembered that from my dissertation, but the importance of it didn't click until I thought of the idea of the thieves laying down their own rail."

"How much rail could they lay?" John asked.

Maj leaned forward, as if to share a secret. "During the building of the transcon, a hand-picked crew of eight Irishmen, with prep work done beforehand, laid ten miles of track in twelve hours. Driving spikes by hand."

"Damn," John said. "Makes me want to say people were tougher back then."

"They might have been, but who's to say a group of motivated Native Americans, doing the prep work ahead of time and learning to swing hammers accurately and with force, couldn't put down maybe six or seven miles of track?"

John thought about that. "Their work wouldn't appear on any existing maps."

"No, it wouldn't, and it might get trickier still."

"How's that?" John asked.

"Once I thought of the Irish, other tidbits of my doctoral research came back."

"Pertinent stuff, of course."

"Wouldn't bore you with it otherwise. Anyway, our Civil War was the world's first train war. The first time troops, weapons and munitions were moved by rail. Both sides quickly understood the importance of this, but the North had much more track, more experience organizing train schedules and more guys who, well, understood the whole concept of railroading. They were the tech geeks of their day."

"Getting to the relevant part," John said.

"Okay, so each side also understood the importance of sabotaging the other side's rail lines, right?"

"Makes sense," John said.

"What your guys couldn't destroy, though, they did their best to capture."

"Also logical."

"But the Union had this guy named Herman Haupt. He'd lay down track where he needed it and then *he'd* take it right back up before the rebels could destroy or capture it. That way he didn't have to wait for new rails or ties to arrive from the rear, and the Confederates weren't left with anything to capture and use for themselves."

"Huh," John said. "Wasn't all that work hard on the crews?"

"Not Haupt's concern. He probably told his workers they could get sent to the front, if they didn't like working for him, but I couldn't document that. Anyway, using largely *unskilled* labor, Haupt could lay down or take up a mile of track a day."

"A man ahead of his time," John said, and now he saw where Maj was going. "So you think it's possible the Super Chief thieves might have built their own tracks and taken them right back up?"

"That'd be a pretty good way to hide a train, don't you think?" Maj asked.

The waitress brought their check. John covered it and left a good tip.

"Maybe back in the nineteenth century," John said, answering the question.

"Meaning what?"

"Well, we have all sorts of spy satellites in orbit these days. The guys on the ground might think they've covered up their work well, but if the view from a hundred miles up looks like a railroad track had been impressed in the earth and then removed, I'd say we'd have a real clue, wouldn't you?"

Maj smiled. "That's good. Wish I'd thought of it."

"You did your part." John closed his eyes for just a moment. "You know where we have to ask the satellites to start looking, don't you?"

"Native American reservations, no question. I even wormed the fact out of Rios that the top people from the Mescalero reservation have jumped into their pickups and SUVs and are heading north."

"How'd you do that?"

"I told him that I know you, remember? And I might have mentioned the vice president."

John winced.

"What?" Maj asked. "I asked Rios if he knew of anything unusual going on at the reservation and he told me. After I dropped a name or two, that is. I figure if we do the same thing with cops in neighboring states, and if there's a big, pardon the word, powwow about to take place somewhere, maybe we can triangulate on it."

"You're right," John said. "Your idea's as viable as mine. One last question: How'd you recall all those details about train history?"

"Well, when Rios and I weren't sticking our tongues out at each other, I whipped out my phone and pulled up my dissertation online." Maj smiled. "I've never been more proud of my scholarship."

"With good reason," John agreed.

— CHAPTER 39 —

Ruidoso, New Mexico

John knew another way to find out if there was a clandestine gathering of Native American tribes — or at least tribal leaders — taking place anywhere in the country. Call Marlene Flower Moon. Hell, if something was going on in a place with modern amenities, Marlene probably had the presidential suite booked.

John made the call from the passenger coach of Maj's pursuit train. She'd let him have his privacy in case something above her pay grade was discussed. John thought he might get routed to Marlene's voice mail again but she answered.

"How much do you know, Tall Wolf?" she asked, not bothering with a hello.

"More about some things than you, less about others."

"And you called to share, no doubt."

"Don't I always?" He told her what he'd heard from Makilah Walsh and Maj Olson.

Marlene laughed. "Ever the ladies' man. How's your Mountie sergeant?"

She was referring to John's paramour, Rebecca Bramley.

"We're doing fine, thanks, and she's been promoted to lieutenant."

For just a second, John thought he heard a gnashing of teeth.

He asked, "Is Nelda going to apply for that museum job?"

"I told her she should, but she's waiting to see what happens with me first."

"I *will* push you for the cabinet post at Interior, Marlene," John said, "for whatever my humble recommendation is worth."

After a moment's pause, she asked, "So you've said, but *why* would you do that, Tall Wolf?"

"Because I know that kind of thing is important to you, and the two of us should always have a little daylight between us. Not be joined at the hip, organizationally, the way we are now."

"You still think I'm Coyote, though, don't you?"

"If not, only because you did Coyote in and picked his bones clean."

Marlene laughed. "That's the nicest compliment I've ever had — and that's what worries me about you. You're not only smart, you charm people effortlessly."

"Even you?"

"Even me, up to a point."

"Well, sure, you still want to have me for dinner someday."

There was no immediate verbal reply, but John could imagine Coyote nodding.

"I have some news for you, too, Tall Wolf, since you share so readily and have only my best interests at heart."

"You know where the chiefs are gathering," John said.

"I do."

"You're with them right now."

"I am."

"The train crewman, aside from the two in the hospitals, he's all right?"

"No harm done."

"And the inside man was Rick Engram."

"Very good," Marlene said.

John waited a moment to let her spring the big surprise, but Marlene was quiet.

"You're going to make me say it, aren't you?" he asked.

"You're doing so well all on your own, I can't resist."

John tried to throw her a curve. "Byron DeWitt said I could come work for him at the FBI. Prestige agency, probably a nice job title, more money, chance for advancement."

"None of which matters a damn to you," Marlene said.

"A man can change."

"If you'd told me you were emigrating to Canada to join your woman, I might have had a moment of doubt."

She was right, John thought. He should have used that as his feint.

He sighed. "All right, the chiefs are gathering on the reservation where I was born, right? And they have the Super Chief with them."

"Well, this reservation is a large place. I haven't actually seen the train."

"And that gives you deniability," John said. "But if you're on the rez with the Super Chief and don't call for help and —"

"The train will be returned, as good as new and maybe better."

That surprised John. "No ransom?"

"No conditions whatsoever."

No conditions from the tribes, John thought.

But what about from Coyote? The answer to that was obvious.

"You're going to deliver the ringleaders to the government," John said.

"Well, the main one anyway, and let's remember, in some small measure, I *am* the government."

"*L'état, c'est moi,*" John said, sure Marlene would be up to translating. "Far be it from me to argue that. Are you going to tell me the reason for stealing the train in the first place?"

"You should know that, too," Marlene said. "Oh, wait. I forgot you grew up white."

"White and brown," John reminded her. "So what I'll do, I'll ask Mom what she thinks is going on here."

John heard a low growl in his ear. Coyote was not amused.

Then she said, "But you'll still come, Tall Wolf. You won't be able to help yourself. This is one time you'll have to work a rez."

Try as he might, John couldn't find a way to deny that.

He didn't have to. Having gotten in the last word, Marlene had ended the call.

— CHAPTER 40 —

Sonoma County, California

Edward Danner found himself in a sweat, literally as well as figuratively. The usually temperate climate of the wine country north of San Francisco had turned hot and humid that summer. Warm and dry were his vintner's preferred growing conditions. The grapes harvested that year would be far from the best. Danner's future looked like it was turning to piss, too.

The last time he'd felt so personally aggrieved was when he'd found out how Brian Kirby had fucked him when they were kids, just as the two of them were supposed to go into business together. The only way Danner had gotten out of that was by doing something of which he'd never imagined himself capable. He'd professed that he'd gotten his science wrong. That deception had been rationalized by the fact that as soon as Brian had been disposed of, at the cost of every penny he had to his name, Danner had miraculously found the fix for his imaginary problem.

There was no doubt in Danner's mind that Brian knew all along he'd been screwed deliberately, and that awareness had made Danner's lie all the sweeter. He who laughs last and all that. Of course, they'd butted heads at every opportunity ever since, but they were well matched, each having his own strengths. All their battles had ended in draws.

Danner fully expected that should he be the first to die, Brian would try to shit on his grave.

A provision Danner had written into his will would counter that posthumous insult.

He was to be cremated. His ashes would be scattered from a plane flying high over the Pacific. If Brian wanted to pee in the ocean as a symbolic gesture, that would only show him how pathetic he was, how futile it was to try to best his one-time friend and long-time nemesis.

Now, though, thanks to that miserable cretin Merritt Kinney, Danner feared that Brian might be the one not only to have the last laugh but enjoy years of merriment at his expense as he rotted away in jail. There was no precedent in modern American history for a man with his money being convicted of a felony and actually forced to serve a lengthy sentence behind bars, but …

That would only make the opportunity to nail a multi-billion-aire for corrupting political officials all the more compelling for the Department of Justice. Any U.S. attorney in the country would beg for the opportunity to put Danner away. Hell, a *special* prosecutor might even be appointed.

With Patricia Darden Grant facing the prospect of impeachment by the House and facing trial in the Senate, dropping his ass in the fire would be just the thing for the president to do to distract the public from her own troubles. In her place, he'd do it in a heartbeat.

Danner looked at Chuck Elias, the CEO of the private investigations firm, SearchCo. Elias had been the young PI operating a one-man shop that Danner had hired on a whim to check into Brian Kirby's past. Sure, he and Brian had been pals at Stanford, but if you were going into business with someone, you'd better do your due diligence. Elias was the one who had discovered Brian's dirty little secret.

Changing the course of the lives of two of the most prominent men in American high tech.

Danner was so grateful to Elias he'd funded SearchCo and had Elias do background checks on everyone Positron did business with or hired. The investigations company worked for other firms, too, but Danner was the fountainhead of revenue and business contacts. Chuck Elias had no doubts who had made him very rich or where his final loyalty ultimately lay.

"You asked to see me," Danner said.

He couldn't thwart the flicker of hope he felt.

"Yes, sir. Possibly good news, possibly bad."

Danner hated equivocation, but held his temper.

"How's that?"

"One of my people in Louisiana called and told me the cops found a crewman from the stolen Super Chief, a man named Clarey. He was passed out in a bar in Baton Rouge. We did a quick look at Clarey's background. He's been employed by the railroad for twenty-two years, has had regular promotions and pay raises. He also has no criminal record whatsoever. So far, we've found no family or other connections in Louisiana."

"The man was drugged and left there, in that bar."

"Yes, sir. That's what I think."

"Possibly suggesting the thieves have taken the train they stole that far. Got rid of some baggage and moved on."

"That would be the possibly bad news, sir. The possibly good news, and I think it's more likely, is the bad guys are trying to pull a fake out. Forcing anyone searching for them to cast a far wider net and waste time, money and man-power."

"Why do you think deception is more likely?" Danner asked.

"Because the bar where Clarey was found is ten miles from the nearest rail line but only three miles from a general aviation airfield, a small place without even a control tower. A place it would be easy to get into and out of without anybody wearing a badge ever noticing."

Danner liked that. It was a hunch but it made sense.

"Assuming you're right, what conclusion do you draw?"

"The train and your property are somewhere nearer to California, say Arizona, New Mexico or maybe West Texas."

"That's still a lot of ground to cover," Danner said.

"It is, but if you think it's worth the chance, sir, I'll pull investigators in from all over the country to flood those states."

Danner nodded. "Do it."

"To confirm what you told me earlier, the homing chip in the item to be retrieved has a detection radius of fifty miles."

"That's right."

"I'll work that into the search parameters when I assign my people."

"Anything else?" Danner asked.

"Yes, two things. My agent in Louisiana said the bartender in the place where Clarey was left said he came in with two Indian-looking guys. Native Americans. The bartender thinks they're the ones who left him there. 'Indians' was the best description the bartender could offer."

"You think that could have something to do with the train being a Super Chief?"

"That's my only guess, sir. Well, that and the thought that maybe if the train is still in the Southwest, it could be on a reservation."

"Sovereign land," Danner said.

"Yes, sir, but if you want, I'll find the right people to go any-where."

"Yes, do that. What else?"

"I received a call from Sergeant Gallo of the SFPD. He asked me if there was any chance an explosive device was incorporated into the item we're to retrieve for you?"

Elias had maintained an impassive expression while asking his question.

Danner did his best to do the same. "Of course not."

The investigator accepted the response with a straight face.

"Yes, sir. Just what I told him. We won't worry about that then."

"Please don't, and when you find my property, package it for commercial express delivery."

Danner told Elias to send it to Brian Kirby's house, but he used Erika Bergdahl's address.

The private investigator recognized the discrepancy immediately, but neither commented nor objected. He also didn't ask if Edward Danner's return address should be used.

Danner knew that Erika, being the salt-of-the-earth rich type she was, would likely walk the package over to her neighbor's house. Brian, only too happy to cultivate Erika, would let her in and accept the package.

Then ... well, Danner would see who would shit on whose grave.

— CHAPTER 41 —

Ruidoso, New Mexico

John's backside throbbed. His arms and legs pulsed, too, but it was his rump that reported the most distress. After returning to Maj's train, she persuaded John it was time for him to log a little practice time on the dirt bike she'd secured for him.

"You really think that's necessary?" he asked.

"You tell me. I've never been on a Native American reservation."

"Neither have I, not since the first hours after my birth."

"Well, speculate for me then. You think reservations have terrific infrastructure? Miles and miles of well paved roads? Rest stops and fast-food joints. Or maybe the people there use off road vehicles, four-wheel drive and the like to get around rough terrain."

John had to concede her point.

"So," Maj asked, "what do we do if we need to catch up to bad guys who aren't considerate enough to stay on the blacktop?"

John agreed to go for a ride. His Yamaha YZ450F was red and white; Maj's was blue and white.

The seat height of his bike was just over thirty-eight inches; the handlebars were only slightly higher than that. The machine felt small, light and toylike to him. He'd had the same sensation riding close behind Maj on her bike, but, foolishly, had thought it would feel different if he ever had his hands on the controls.

Before he put on his helmet, having doffed his Ray-Bans, Maj could see the look of misgiving on his face.

"Don't have much experience here, huh?" she asked.

"Very little on a motorcycle, none at all on something like this. Where'd you learn?"

"My dad did some small-time motocross racing. He taught my brother and me. Mom stayed home because she couldn't bear to watch. We all came through it okay. My brother's a terrific rider; I'm not bad."

"Yeah, well," John said, "don't expect any Steve McQueen stunts out of me."

"You mean like in 'The Great Escape?' So you're *not* a movie star, huh?"

John shook his head.

"You ever ride horseback?"

"A lot more of that," he said. "My folks like organic rides whenever possible. That's what I learned."

"You ever ride a mount at a gallop?"

"Yes."

"Okay, so what you do is think of your bike as the quickest horse you've ever ridden. Able to both stop and turn on a dime. Capable of jumping like a horse, too, only higher and farther."

"You're saying this machine is powerful and highly responsive," John replied.

"Oh, yeah. So we'll take it easy until you get the feel of it. Just think you're on a horse, only it's got a lot more horsepower than you've ever experienced. And follow my lead."

That was exactly what John did. He trailed Maj, watching how she picked her way through the open grassland outside of Ruidoso. Before long, he started to get a bit more comfortable with the bike. It did help to think of the machine as a living thing, an extension of himself.

Cutting John a break, Maj led them back to the train on paved roads.

"Not bad," she said, "but we were riding on relatively level ground. When we get the opportunity, we'll try some hills and maybe even a mountain, so you can get a feel for climbs and descents."

"Can't wait," John told her, removing his helmet and putting his sunglasses back on.

"You say that, but I know you had at least a little fun."

John held a thumb and index finger an inch apart.

"Oh, well, if that's all," Maj told him, "we'll have to shoot your horse."

John shook his head. "Not yet. Maybe it's just a slowly maturing relationship."

He and Leo Taylor hauled the machines up to the back of the passenger car to store them.

With two men lifting each machine, they seemed lighter than ever.

Maj retired to her private compartment in the car, the one with the tiny shower stall. She said John would have to bend his knees to shampoo, but she was sure it would work for him. Give her thirty minutes, and she'd make way for him.

John said, "Sure. Thanks for the hospitality."

"Mi tren es su tren." My train is your train.

John closed himself in the car's other private compartment and called Byron DeWitt. He told DeWitt about the homing device in Edward Danner's missing journal

DeWitt laughed. "You know why the guy went analog, right? So his secrets couldn't be hacked by anybody. But he couldn't resist putting a high-tech touch in place."

John told him about his thought that Danner might have stuck some plastique in the binding.

"Why would he do that?" DeWitt asked, and immediately guessed the answer. "Oh, yeah, to keep from incriminating himself."

"Mmm-hmm," John agreed. "Even a small bang would work a lot better than a paper shredder."

"Maybe give him the pleasure of taking out the dirt-ball who stole his property, too," DeWitt said.

"So you like the idea?"

"I don't think we can ignore the possibility. You have any other news?"

"I know where the Super Chief is."

"You might have mentioned that first."

"I would have, but it's problematic."

John told DeWitt of his conversation with Marlene.

"So you're saying, what, Marlene has the whole thing wired, but she wants you on hand to bring the curtain down?" DeWitt asked. "Make the arrest?"

"I was hoping the Bureau might like to handle that, if not you personally."

DeWitt sighed. "Well, you know how that goes."

John did. The FBI had responsibility for major crimes committed on Indian reservations, but since a very unfortunate shootout in South Dakota back in 1975 that left two special agents dead, the Bureau had chosen to tread lightly, leaving the heavy lifting to the BIA whenever possible.

The BIA, after all, also had authorization to conduct concurrent investigations on reservation related crimes. On top of that, John at least *looked* the part of someone who could make a major bust on Indian land without cries of racism being raised. And with Vice President Morrissey so deeply involved in the case, appearances would matter.

"Had to give it a try," John said.

"Don't blame you, but I think you're the guy for this job. Hey, I do have some news for you, though. You were right about Brian Kirby. He *bribed* the judge of the model train contest. Otherwise Danner would've won."

John laughed without humor. "And years later Danner finds out just in time to screw Kirby out of a fortune and a feud is born. Talk about karma."

"Yeah, rich guys. What're you going to do with them?"

"Lock Danner up, I hope."

"That'd make for a nice change, wouldn't it?" DeWitt asked.

"Absolutely."

"You know how Danner's journal got filched, right?"

"Sure." John had been working on that all along. "Could've been only one way. He was too arrogant to think anyone would dare touch it. He left the damn thing out in the open somewhere instead of locking it up."

"And along comes Merritt Kinney, poor sap."

"I can empathize. I'm the chump being played here by Marlene. She's got some trick in mind for me."

"You want me to be the token FBI guy on hand?" DeWitt asked.

"I appreciate the offer, but you're right about paying attention to how things will look. Even so, how about you and some of your best people position yourselves nearby and ride to the rescue if I send up a flare?"

"Will do. You going to keep Maj Olson with you?"

"I'm sure she won't have it any other way."

Hearing himself say that, John felt an unexpected sense of comfort.

He ended the call with DeWitt and downloaded a copy of "Railroaded: The Biography of Theodore Judah" onto his Kindle. He wanted to see what the last thing Merritt Kinney had read might tell him about Edward Danner.

— CHAPTER 42 —

Northern New Mexico

Alan White River sat alone in the plush private train car attached to the Super Chief. None of the other chiefs ever wanted to enter it again. They knew what was coming and chose to stand well clear. The growing number of ordinary people arriving from tribes around the country — even Wampanoag, Oneida and Seminole people were flying in from the East Coast — would look on in amazement at the stolen locomotive and its passenger car but wouldn't linger in their vicinity.

Powerful forces were about to be summoned, and it paid to be careful.

White River, however, was past worrying about his fate in this world or the one to come. He wouldn't live long enough to care about what the white man's courts did with him, and he had faith that his fate as judged by his ancestors would be neither more nor less than he deserved. The only anxiety he felt was the growing certainty that he had led Bodaway in the wrong direction, started his great-grandson off on a path that would end in disaster.

If that turned out to be so, White River knew he would never find peace.

He sat and brooded in a leather chair meant for a rich white man. Its size was intended to project an aura of power. Its comfort, yielding yet supportive, was sensuous. Enough to bring back memories of his beloved, long-dead wife. That thought struck him immediately as being unworthy of such a fine woman.

Try as he might, though, the idea was not easily shaken. He could imagine entwining himself with Awinita on this very —

No, that was going too far. He pushed himself to his feet more spryly than he'd done in more years than he could remember. "Old fool," he muttered to himself in reproof.

Even in that moment of disapproval he couldn't keep a smile from forming on his seamed face. If his wife's spirit was one of those who would sit in ultimate judgment of him, and why wouldn't it be, his fate couldn't be too unkind. Maybe Awinita would even inspire him and work with him to find a way to save Bodaway.

What did the men who built the railroad use to save their spirits, he wondered. Anything at all? Or did they merely hope to indulge themselves so richly in the world of the flesh that any punishment that came afterward would be a small price to pay? White River had seen more of the white world than most of his people. He'd spoken at colleges around the country about the conditions in which so many of his people lived. He knew that there were great luxuries to be had in the larger country around him.

People from all over the world came to the United States, many willing to break immigration laws to do so, just so they might grasp a fragment of what had come to be called the American dream. Now there was an idea more seductive than any other: a country in which any man or woman might create their own idea of perfection.

He doubted even the spirit world offered such a compelling vision.

Then again, some dreams were just tissues of imagination.

As imperfect as they were fleeting.

Even the gleaming interior of a rich man's rail car could not keep dust away. White River dragged arthritic fingers through a thin patina of grime on a mahogany desk. He felt a small wedge of wood unexpectedly yield to the meager pressure of his hand and the door of a concealed compartment opened, surprising him. As if trying to avoid setting his foot in a snare, he tottered backward as quickly as he could manage.

A moment later, having suffered no adverse consequence, he bent forward and peered at the object in the unsuspected space. Reason told him a thing had to be valuable if it was hidden. He strained his eyes to see what it was, and it looked like a book of some sort.

A leather bound volume with gilt-edged pages. A handsome thing. White River felt himself drawn to it, but he held back. The book itself might be a trap, and it did seem to convey a sense of danger. After a moment, though, his anxiety made him laugh.

He'd conceived and helped to execute the plan to steal this train, and now he was going to be worried about a book?

"Old fool," he said to himself again.

He removed the book from its hiding place and closed the door. He found the spot in the dust his finger had touched and pressed it again. The door opened as before. Now *he* had a secret hiding place. He closed the door again and gently dusted the mahogany desk with his shirt sleeve to conceal the release point.

White River returned to the leather chair and opened the book's cover.

The first thing he saw was a warning: *Private Property. Read No Further. Violators Will Be Prosecuted. Edward Danner.*

The old chief chuckled to himself and turned the page.

— CHAPTER 43 —

Northern New Mexico

Arnoldo Black Knife quickly came to loathe the man who called himself Bodaway. The intruder had done in the blink of an eye what Arnoldo had been unable to do in a lifetime of trying. Warm the cold, dark stone that was his grandmother's heart. More than simply offering Bodaway a smile or two, she'd clasped his hands in hers and pressed them to her withered bosom.

Maria Black Knife had always played the harsh taskmistress with Arnoldo, drilling him on the endless obligations he must heed to maintain their family's position of tribal leadership. Warning him of rivals he must always guard against, especially John Tall Wolf. Every day since childhood, the old woman had forced him to observe a litany of behaviors that had all but strangled his soul.

He'd told himself that his self-sacrifice was worth it. The rez had always been dirt poor, but his family had done far better than most. If they ever lost their eminent standing, well, the alternative was unthinkable.

Perhaps more so now than ever when it seemed real wealth was within grasp.

In the old days, there had been no engine of prosperity. Now, in partnership with a national hotel chain, there was a casino. That had brought jobs and for the first time aspirations of a middle-class life for more than a few. Dwarfing that development was the news from the energy companies. The seismic tests had been done, the geological maps had been generated and the news was overwhelmingly positive. The reservation sat atop a vast supply of natural gas.

Revenues from its exploitation would be unlike anything the tribe had ever known — if the bidding process and the licensing agreement with the winning company were carefully drawn, monitored and enforced. Maria Black Knife felt she was just the woman for the job.

But she'd made plain to Arnoldo her doubts about his ability to maintain the family's preeminent position in the tribe. Their job was to make sure everyone else would feel lost without the Black Knife family to lead them.

"Who would feel helpless without you?" she'd asked Arnoldo.

He knew exactly what she meant. One time, just once when he was young, he had made the mistake of letting his grandmother see him cry. That night, she'd told him, "Your grandfather was strong and a great man. Your father was strong and he would have become great."

If he hadn't driven off a mountain road of substandard construction that crumbled under the wheels of his Jeep.

"You," Maria told him, "are strong only when I stand behind you, stiffening your spine and reminding you to hold your head high."

Erect posture was a cardinal virtue with Grandmother, as she insisted on looking down at the rest of the world. Arnoldo knew from that moment on that he would never truly lead the tribe as long as Maria Black Knife was alive. In all his life, Arnoldo had defied Maria in only one regard.

He would not allow her to choose a wife for him.

Her attempts at matchmaking had everything to do with building political alliances. Nothing to do with love or even the possibility of being able to converse comfortably with the woman in question. Not that grandmother had ever selected a woman for him. It was always young girls, only recently fertile, children who would be sure to cower before her.

Grandmother knew a mature bride might make an alliance with Arnoldo against her, and she would never stand for that.

Just as he wouldn't consent to marrying a child.

Leaving Arnoldo alone and childless.

"This stubbornness of yours is a threat to our family," Maria harped at him daily.

He'd once responded, "You can remarry after I die and give birth to a new chief."

Grandmother had taken advantage of the fact that he was seated at that moment and slapped his face. Arnoldo had welcomed it. His character may have been as insubstantial as the road that had failed his father, but his body was rock solid. The blow had hurt his grandmother's hand far more than it did him.

She never tried to hit him again. Her words were far better for leaving wounds.

None more so than when she told Bodaway, "You are the man I've been waiting for since my son Cesar died."

The two of them had been talking of ways to kill John Tall Wolf. Maria Black Knife had been delighted to hear that Bodaway had conceived the same idea entirely on his own. That was what had made her heart glow with affection for him. Here was someone as bloodthirsty in his ambitions as she was in hers.

Grandmother had always warned Arnoldo that his cousin, John Tall Wolf, was their greatest threat. Now, with great riches so close, he was more dangerous than ever.

For a very long time, Arnoldo had believed her and hated Tall Wolf, even though the two of them had never met. Tall Wolf was supposed to be a predator, but he'd never hunted them. Just the opposite, he seemed to have no interest in them at all. As time passed and no real evidence of Tall Wolf's menace ever revealed itself, Arnoldo's fear of his cousin left him and his hatred for him soon followed.

So why was Grandmother scheming with the intruder, Bodaway, to kill him?

Because in Tall Wolf's place *she* would have attacked?

Or was it simply a vile turn of mind to which she was addicted?

And why should it matter to Arnoldo that the old hag seemed to have found someone to supplant him? Riches would have only bound him further to a life he'd already come to hate. Living in Grandmother's suffocating shadow.

The idea of being dispossessed did sting, but only for a moment.

Then the fact that Bodaway had arrived from the outside world introduced a revolutionary thought to Arnoldo's mind. Maybe there was a place and a life for him somewhere *outside* the rez. Outside of New Mexico.

He was deeply ashamed that he'd never thought of that before now. The look of revelation must have shown on his face. Grandmother and Bodaway were staring at him.

"What?" he asked.

For the first time he could remember, Grandmother asked him, "Are you all right?"

"Yes."

"You have no problem with the idea of my killing your cousin?" Bodaway asked.

"Why should I? I don't know him."

The two of them nodded, satisfied. No reason they shouldn't be. Arnoldo had answered honestly. Only in the next breath, without saying a word, he changed his mind.

Tall Wolf had never done anything to hurt him.

Maybe Arnoldo should warn his cousin.

Let grandmother and the intruder see what happened to their plans then.

Then both Arnoldo and his grandmother were surprised to hear that Tall Wolf wasn't Bodaway's only target. He told Maria, "You know who represents the real danger to your family? Marlene Flower Moon."

Hearing that, Maria Black Knife shrank from Bodaway.

He laughed at her fear. "Yes, I know. She's supposed to be Coyote. But she's arrived just in time to seize control of my great-grandfather's plan. She'll steal all the glory for what he's done.

She'll also get credit from the white men for capturing Alan White River and landing him in their prison. So what's left for me to do but trick the Trickster? My bet is she'll die just like anyone else."

Grandmother began to tremble.

Then with just a few words Bodaway won her back. He said, "Whatever plans *you* might have, she'll steal those, too."

Maria Black Knife was thunderstruck. Bodaway had it exactly right. Marlene Flower Moon wouldn't let Maria keep the fortune that was about to land in her lap. Coyote would demand most if not all of it for herself.

That certainly was what Maria would have done, had she been Coyote.

It was hard for her to believe Bodaway might best Marlene Flower Moon, but where was the harm in letting him try? The only risk would be if Coyote found out she was involved. She turned to tell Arnoldo to remain silent about this plan. Never expecting any resistance from him.

Only he was already gone.

Having found even talk of such things to be more than he could bear.

That was how Maria saw things, and Bodaway thought little better of Arnoldo.

But Arnoldo had taken quite a different view of things.

He truly held no grievance against John Tall Wolf.

He was going to warn Tall Wolf of the threat Grandmother and Bodaway represented to him. Maybe he should even tell his cousin of Bodaway's mad idea to kill Marlene Flower Moon. But Arnoldo decided not to go that far.

It would be more interesting to see what kind of damage Coyote would inflict on Bodaway.

— CHAPTER 44 —

New Mexico, rolling north

John Tall Wolf lay on the tiny bunk in his train compartment, folded up not quite as completely as a closed accordion but nearly so. He ignored the physical discomfort to concentrate on recalling his recent conversation with his parents. His father had called and spoken only briefly with his son.

Haden Wolf had told John, "Your mother told me she'd talked to you recently. So I thought I'd put in my two cents. Just be yourself. There's very little your mother and I haven't prepared you for. Your law enforcement training and experience is likely to cover any small gaps we might have left."

Dad wasn't being boastful, simply confident in himself, his wife and his son.

Most times, John felt the same way. That night, however, a sense of misgiving had returned. He felt a small, deep chill in his craw that refused to be displaced. He didn't think the condition was physical or he would have told his father, a semi-retired physician.

He did tell his mother how he felt when she took her turn on the phone.

Speaking of John's trepidation, Serafina Wolf y Padilla told her son, "It's only natural. You very nearly died in your first few hours of life, after your birth mother banished you from her reservation. If you were able to return to that place without any concerns, then I would worry about you."

"So you think it's going to be smooth sailing?" John asked.

"I think you will navigate any storm to your own advantage."

"And Coyote?" John asked.

"You're the one who chose to work for the woman you believe to be Coyote. I've always thought that was one of the bravest things I've ever seen anyone do. And from what I know, you've always held your own with her."

"I only have to come out on the short end one time for everything to change," John said.

"Then don't let that happen. Are you feeling well?"

"Physically, yes. Emotionally, it's a challenge."

"Have you spoken to Rebecca about this?"

"No."

"Because?"

John laughed without humor. "It'd ruin my image."

His mother said with a sigh, "That or improve it. Is there anything in particular you'd like your father or me to do for you, John?"

"Just talking to you always helps. But Marlene said I would have known why the Super Chief was stolen if I hadn't been raised white. I told her I'd been raised white and brown."

"*Absolutamente.*"

"So can you tell me what I'm missing here, Mom?"

"Your new friend, this Maj —"

"It's not like that. We're colleagues. Purely professional."

"I was going to say," Serafina responded, "you pointed out to me that she told you of a large gathering of native peoples."

"Yes."

"And Marlene confirmed this, as well as saying the train would be released without ransom."

"Right again."

"Then if something is not going to be withheld, what might the purpose of all this be?"

It took John a moment before he said, "Something's going to be *added* to the Super Chief? What could that be?"

"You told me this train is being sent to a museum. What do such places trade in?"

"Knowledge. Conveyed by images and language."

Serafina said, "And, in this case, my guess is, songs. Perhaps even dreams."

John knew only too well the story of the nightmares Serafina was reputed to have sent to his birth mother, Bly Black Knife, after she sued to regain custody of John when he was six years old. The night terrors had persisted until Bly had dropped her suit. John's aversion to the rez was based not only on having been expelled from it in his earliest moments, but also the fear of being returned to it against his will as a young child.

"So you're saying, what, Mom? The Super Chief is going to be released, but the museum in Chicago is going to get a *haunted* train?"

Serafina told him, "I would say that anyone visiting these railroad cars will find it a saddening, perhaps even disturbing, experience. It will be filled with many distressing stories."

From the even tone of his mother's voice, she didn't seem to disapprove.

But then she had blood from the Tarahumara, a Native American tribe of northwestern Mexico. They'd once occupied much of the land that now comprised the Mexican state of Chihuahua. When the Spanish arrived in the 16th century, *los indios* fled to the mountains and canyons. John had no doubt his mother's native forebears would have their own tales of woe to tell, given the chance.

John said, "I suppose the museum's management, if they're smart, could prepare visitors for the emotional impact by providing graphic educational materials outlining the historical effects of the railroads on native peoples."

Exactly what Alan White River had asked for in the first place.

Serafina responded, "I'd like you to introduce me to whoever conceived this plan."

Said as if White River wouldn't be going straight to a lockup, John thought.

Then he had an idea. Maybe something other than a prison sentence could be worked out.

"I'll do what I can, Mom. Thanks for everything."

"Remember what your father told you, John. Be true to yourself."

That was the thought John held onto as he fell asleep

— CHAPTER 45 —

New Mexico, further north

More comfortable with her accommodations, Maj Olson lay asleep in her own compartment on the train as it moved northward through the New Mexico night. A phone call disturbed her rest. What the hell, she thought. Couldn't a doctor of philosophy get a little rest?

More often than not, the answer had been no. Starting out as a teaching assistant, moving up to a research assistant, finding a dissertation subject, writing the damn thing and then defending it against your superiors' attempts to pick it apart, she hadn't had much idle time. If you cleared all those hurdles, you were awarded your doctorate, the peak of academic achievement in these here United States and …

You got a job being a cop for Amtrak.

At least that was how things had worked out for her.

Sometimes Maj thought she should have become a professional dirt-track racer like her brother, Denny. Sure, that was dangerous and *dirty* work, but it was fun. The money could be significantly better than what your wet behind the ears college prof made, too. Maybe it wasn't too late to change careers. Denny would help her sharpen her racing skills.

A decent-looking woman could, pun intended, clean up in dirt track racing, if she posted a few wins.

Or Maj could write an insider's view of a true-crime story: the theft of the Super Chief.

Maybe become the author of a best-seller, if she played a big enough role in finding the train. Might even be a movie deal in the bargain. Hollywood liked a good train story every now and then. She could be the technical advisor. John Tall Wolf and that state cop, Rios, notwithstanding, she didn't see herself as a leading lady. Maybe a bit player, a walk-on, just as a hoot.

What she could see quite clearly, in her dream state, was becoming a celebrity scholar. A woman of both learning and action. Indiana Joanie, if you will. Someone all the best schools would want to add to their faculties. Then there would be the pile of guest lecturer money she could make and …

The damn phone, playing "Good Day Sunshine" had interrupted her fantasies.

She answered with a surly, "This better be good."

A woman's voice, unruffled by Maj's ill manners, told her, "If John should need you, you will be there for him."

"What? John who?"

"You will not let Coyote or anyone else harm him."

"A coyote? Are you nuts? We're on a train. Who is this?"

"You will be there for him."

You couldn't argue with loons. Every grad student learned that right off.

"Yeah, sure. Good night."

Maj clicked off. To her great relief, she picked up dreaming right where she left off.

With the decision that authorship and movies would be a better choice than dirt bike racing. And, who knew, maybe she did have unsuspected acting skills. Hours later she woke up, after getting another phone call.

Her ringtone played "The Anvil Chorus," the way it normally did.

A sound clip from a Verdi opera, not a Beatles ditty. Where the hell had "Good Day Sunshine," come from? Was that weird phone conversation she'd had last night a dream within a dream? Looking out the compartment's window, she saw her train was pulling into Albuquerque.

And FBI Deputy Director Byron DeWitt was talking to her.

"I'd appreciate it if you could do me a personal favor," he said. "Make sure your backup for Co-director Tall Wolf is spot on, okay? Working a rez is a tricky assignment for him."

DeWitt's request brought the weird dream back again. Maj wondered if she was *still* asleep.

But if the call was real and she had the chance to have DeWitt owe her one …

"Sure," she said. "Will do."

— CHAPTER 46 —

San Francisco

So you trust this Amtrak person?" Special Agent Abra Benjamin asked Byron DeWitt.

The two of them had just introduced themselves, including a display of federal badges, at the reception desk of SearchCo in San Francisco. Their arrival had been unexpected, and they had neither arrest nor search warrants, but they were greeted politely and assured that the CEO, Mr. Charles Elias, would be right out to see them.

The receptionist, a sturdy young man, went to attend to the task personally.

Before he left, though, DeWitt had said to him, "Please tell Mr. Elias that it would be a terrible idea to call Edward Danner. Doing that might open him up to a conspiracy charge."

Benjamin made no threat, but she was timing how long it took Elias to appear.

"From what I've learned of Ms. Olson," DeWitt told Benjamin, "she's both capable and trustworthy."

Benjamin said, "Something's got to be wrong with her, an Ivy League Ph.D. doing gumshoe work for Amtrak."

"Nothing's been documented in the matter, but I was told in confidence that a moment of indiscretion might have caused her academic career to … go awry."

Benjamin grinned. "You were going to say 'get derailed,'

weren't you?"

"I'll never tell," DeWitt replied.

"So what was her indiscretion? She slept with the wrong guy, someone who couldn't get her a good job?"

Benjamin had made sure DeWitt would be able to help her before sleeping with him, but they'd also had real feelings for each other. They'd had a kid, too, but Benjamin had put him up for adoption. Despite that, and maybe because he didn't want to face a lawsuit, DeWitt hadn't done anything to hurt Benjamin's career. On the contrary, he'd helped it.

But he'd never slept with her again. A fact that Benjamin had come to regret.

"No, that wasn't it," DeWitt said. "The word I got was she took exception at the end of a job interview when the head of the department, as he ushered her out the door, decided to test the muscle tone of young Dr. Olson's heinie."

Benjamin's eyes widened. "Grabbed her ass?"

"Hard enough to leave a bruise is the story."

"And?"

"Olson responded with an elbow to the schnozz. Fractured cartilage and a gusher of blood resulted."

Benjamin laughed. "I love it. I want to meet her."

Before that possibility might be discussed, Chuck Elias arrived.

Under two minutes, Benjamin saw. Still, she asked, "You call your lawyer, Mr. Elias?"

He said, "My secretary has him on hold."

"A reasonable precaution," DeWitt allowed.

Within moments the three of them were in Elias's office, and DeWitt said, "We have reason to believe Edward Danner has corrupted several state officials in furtherance of his plan to build a high-speed rail link between San Francisco and Los Angeles. We're here to give you the chance to come down on the right side of the tracks."

Benjamin kept a straight face, but she knew DeWitt had just told her she'd been right.

He had been about to say derailed.

Chuck Elias wasn't concerned with the inside jokes of two former lovers.

He had his own misgivings about Danner and told the two feds everything they wanted to know. He reasoned that just because someone made you rich that didn't give him the right to bring you down and get you locked up for the rest of your life.

Elias even volunteered the use of his people to help the feds find Danner's journal.

— CHAPTER 47 —

Albuquerque, New Mexico

The Amtrak rail line stopped well short of the Apache reservation northwest of Taos. John wanted to secure the use of a government four wheel drive SUV to continue their journey, but Maj raised an objection. "Where are we going to put our dirt bikes? Even if you don't want yours, I want mine."

John took her point of view into consideration.

Not waiting for him to come to a disagreeable conclusion, she added, "If you don't bring your bike, of course, and there's a chase across badlands, you'll be leaving me all the credit for bagging the bad guys."

Maj didn't know John as well as Marlene did. He genuinely preferred to deflect praise, divert credit to others and go about his work quietly. What did matter to him was making sure anyone who helped him got to go home in one piece at the end of an investigation.

He'd never consider letting Maj face danger alone.

That was part of being true to himself, as Mom and Dad had advised.

So John called Washington, asked for and got a Ford SVT Raptor, a huge pick-up truck reputed to be able to climb and descend steep, rocky inclines like a mountain goat, though without the same mileage. He made sure the optional 36-gallon fuel tank was topped off. The dirt bikes were fastened to the bed of the truck.

John drove. For the first couple of hours, at least, the roads were well paved. Not even a pothole.

Maj had been impressed by how quickly a local Ford dealer had delivered the truck. It showed her the vice president's muscle continued to support the investigation. Or maybe how much pull John Tall Wolf had in Washington. For an employee of the always cash-strapped Amtrak, either possibility was impressive.

Having endured a long, if not uncompanionable, silence by then, she asked John, "You mind if I put on some music? Looks like this thing has satellite radio."

"I'd prefer a little more quiet," he said. "I have to sort out a few things."

"Okay … Listen, don't take this as a slight, but is something scaring you?"

John gave Maj a glance. "Yeah. I've always thought that if I ever set foot on this particular rez something awful would happen."

Maj gave it a beat. Something like that, an unspecified fear, deserved a measure of privacy. Then again, possibly going into a dangerous situation here, she felt she really should know of any limitations the big guy sitting next to her might have. If she were to count on him in a tight spot and —"

John preempted her next question. "What I'm afraid of is being vengeful, especially against the people who turned me out, my biological family. I might do something unfortunate."

"Uh-huh. I think you've left a few dots unconnected there. But I won't pry."

She didn't have to; John told her his story. Including the fact that his maternal grandmother perceived him as a threat to her power. According to Marlene Flower Moon, anyway.

"And you also think your former boss, now your co-director, is a supernatural entity known as Coyote?"

John nodded. "Could well be. If you think that's nuts, that I'm off my rocker, I can pull over and let you ride your bike back down the road."

They were climbing through the foothills now, fir trees growing thick along the roadsides. The truck was pointed toward the town of Agua Pura, the population center of the rez. Beyond that, near the state line with Colorado were mountains, an offshoot of the Sangre de Cristo range.

Maj said, "Thanks for the offer, but I'm a stick-to-it kind of woman. You can't grind your way through a doctoral program without being persistent."

John nodded to a sign alongside the road. *Native American sovereign territory. Travel permit required for non-tribal persons.*

There was no border crossing station. No armed customs officials. No barrier to be raised for automotive traffic. John kept driving, entering a rez for the first time since infancy.

"I guess entry works on the honor system," Maj said. "But with your BIA status, I assume you're okay. You'll vouch for me, right?"

John smiled at her. "I'm guessing you have as much Native American blood as I do Viking blood, right?"

"Maybe I have just a bit more," Maj said. "I'm one sixty-fourth Pequot. That's a Connecticut tribe. I think all the members now work for insurance companies and stock brokerages."

John laughed. "You're making that up. You're not blonde, but you do have blue eyes, and you're one of the fairest-skinned people I've ever met."

"I'm also a historian, so I looked into my family history. Well, the Mormons did it for me. Online. Still, there's a Pequot on my mom's side, way back when."

John stuck out his right hand and Maj gave it a fist bump. Solidarity.

"I suppose your sixty-three sixty-fourths Caucasian blood accounts for your looks," he said. "But you're Indian enough to qualify for membership in some tribes. Maybe even a leadership position."

"Never liked politics. I'm just a scholar who has police training and likes to ride dirt bikes."

"Always good to be well rounded. So help me out here a bit

from your scholarly side."

"Sure," Maj said, "what do you need?"

"Well, I have it on the very best authority that the Super Chief is nearby."

"You heard that from Coyote?"

"I did. But we've come a fair piece from the Amtrak station. I don't think a whole Irish village could have quickly laid and taken up enough track to bridge the gap."

Maj smiled. "Heck that one's easy. Wait a second and I'll get you the exact numbers." She took out her phone and fiddled with it. "Here we go. Quoting from my research: In 1916, when the U.S. rail system was at its most extensive, there were 254,037 miles of track in the country. In 2010, when I successfully defended my dissertation, there were 94,200 miles. Officially."

John knew a cue when he heard one. "And unofficially how many miles are there?"

"Nobody knows. A lot of old rails were taken up and sold for scrap, but not all of them were. Some were simply abandoned, left untouched even by scavengers." Maj paused to smile and lift her rump to reach a back pocket of her jeans. "And who knows how many miles of track were repurposed and are still in use today?"

She waved a four-color brochure. John took a glimpse, thought he saw a picture of an old train, before putting his eyes back on the road. "What's that?" he asked."

"Could be, probably is, a clue."

"Found where?"

"A rack of tourist attraction pamphlets back at the Amtrak station. I spotted it while you were arranging this cowboy limo for us."

"And the punchline is?" John asked.

"Guess which Native American reservation already has its own little steam-powered choo-choo, cow-catcher, railroad tracks and all, to take the tourists to see all its pretty places?"

"Sonofabitch," John said.

"At the very least. My guess is the thieves on this rez didn't have to lay too much new track, after all. Just enough to suit their needs."

John was about to ask when Maj had intended to share this gem of serendipity with him as he rounded a bend in the road and had to slam on the brakes. Two Indians stood in the middle of the blacktop. The bumper of the truck came to a halt within spitting distance of them but neither one flinched.

Both of them were tall. One was old, the other middle-aged. John put the gear shifter into park, and he and Maj got out of the truck.

"You Tall Wolf?" the middle-aged guy asked.

Maj thought she saw something of a resemblance between the man and John.

"I am."

"My name is Arnoldo Black Knife. You know who I am?"

John had never seen the man before but had no trouble recalling the name. Marlene had told him this was his rival for power within the tribe. "My cousin."

"Right. You and me, we need to talk."

"Okay." John turned to the old man. "Are you Alan White River?"

Maj thought the old man bore an even stronger resemblance to John.

Jeez, she hoped all Native Americans weren't starting to look alike to her.

"I am. I stole the train you seek."

All by himself, John was sure the old man would claim.

Unless Cousin Arnoldo cared to share the blame.

"Before you place me under arrest, I have something to give you," White River said. He put a hand under his denim jacket, and Maj, quick as a cat, had her semi-auto pointed at him.

John forestalled any untimely gunfire with an upraised hand.

White River didn't move, until he smiled at Maj.

"My wife would have liked you," he said. "May I?"

"Go ahead, but take it slow," John told him.

The old man brought out a leather-bound book. He extended it to John.

"Edward Danner's journal?" John asked.

White River nodded.

"Did you read it?" John asked.

"Every word. Mr. Danner is a bigger crook than I am."

John took the journal, tried to judge the heft of it in his hand.

Was it heavy enough to hold a bomb? Had he come this far only to get blown to pieces?

While still pondering that thought, Arnoldo told him, "We better get you, the lady with the gun and your truck out of the middle of the road. Might cause an accident."

SUPER CHIEF

— CHAPTER 48 —

Northern New Mexico

Maria Black Knife handed Bodaway an antique revolver. She'd just taken it from the bottom of a trunk in her bedroom. Accepting the gun, Bodaway felt the weight of it, marveled at the length of it. Damn thing was near an artillery piece.

"This belonged to my husband Cesar's great grandfather. He took it from a blue devil horse warrior he killed."

"U.S. Cavalry?" Bodaway asked.

"Yes, one of their chiefs not just a brave."

"How did he kill the man?"

"Dug a hole on a path the blue devils used, filled it with soft mud, covered the mud with grasses and leaves."

"He made the man's horse stumble," Bodaway.

"The animal broke its leg and the blue devil fell to the ground. Mangas crushed his skull with a war club. Took his weapons."

She showed him a cavalry sword, too.

Bodaway turned his attention back to the gun and looked at the rounds in the chambers.

"This ammunition, it's not from the nineteenth century."

Maria shook her head. "My late husband Cesar bought it."

It still looked plenty old to Bodaway. Might have been in the weapon fifty years or more.

Maria had told Bodaway that her husband had died of natural causes but the younger Cesar, her son, had lost his life in a car accident. The mountain road beneath his vehicle had washed away in a rain storm. She'd pointed out the mountain on which her son had died. Said the road had never been repaired. Her tone had implied she'd seen to that.

Maria's intention was the whole mountain would remain a memorial to her child.

Bodaway found the old woman's ruthlessness and egotism amusing.

"Did Mangas ever use this gun to kill a man?" he asked.

Maria shook her head. "Only the horse that broke its leg. He apologized to its spirit, butchered the animal and brought as much meat as he could carry back to the village to eat."

Practical, Bodaway thought. Mangas probably preferred to use his hands to kill his enemies. The gun was more of a totem than anything else.

"Do you know if this gun shoots straight?" Bodaway asked.

"Why would it not?" Maria asked.

Lack of maintenance, Bodaway thought. Decay of the ammunition in it. Manufacturing defects that would make it unsuitable for anything except showing mercy to a crippled horse.

Bodaway decided not to give a lecture.

Humoring Maria, he said, "It probably does."

Still, he asked, "Do you have a kit to clean this weapon?"

Maria shook her head.

"Did your son buy any more ammunition for the weapon so I can test fire it?"

"No, just those. Is that not enough to kill John Tall Wolf?"

The rounds were .44 caliber. "Sure. One shot in the right place would do it."

"Then shoot straight," Maria said in a voice of command.

"Uh-huh," Bodaway replied.

He wondered if he should take just one test shot at her.

But she was too close to miss, and he didn't want to gun her down in her own home.

"One other thing," Bodaway said, "I don't think we should

leave Arnoldo behind to talk. He knows what we're planning. If he ever were to find himself in trouble, he could say to the police, 'Hey, let me tell you what Grandma and this Bodaway guy did.' There's no statute of limitations on murder, and killing a BIA agent will put federal pressure on the whole rez."

"I will take care of Arnoldo," Maria said. "He has always been a disappointment."

No great loss, Bodaway interpreted.

He might have to watch out for the old witch himself, once he got the job done for her.

So he started to make plans. For his getaway.

— CHAPTER 49 —

San Francisco

W e're leaving a loose end here, Abra," Byron DeWitt said. The executive jet detailed to him, a Gulfstream G550, had just rolled up to the gate in the general aviation terminal of San Francisco International Airport.

Special Agent Abra Benjamin looked at her boss and former lover. "What kind of loose end?"

"Well, back when Edward Danner and Brian Kirby were kids they competed in a model train competition, right?"

"That's what I confirmed for you, Mr. Deputy Director," Benjamin said, not wanting him to forget where credit was due.

"And you also found out Kirby bribed the contest's judge to give him an undeserved win," DeWitt said, acknowledging Benjamin's good work.

"Only because John Tall Wolf has a better mind for spotting sneaks than either of us."

Much as she hated to give credit to others, Benjamin had found a measure of honesty actually worked to her benefit. Made her seem less ruthlessly ambitious. She longed, though, for the day when such artifice was no longer required.

"That was a heckuva call on his part," DeWitt agreed.

He liked Tall Wolf. Would have hired him in a minute. Groomed him to take over his slot. Doing that would put Abra's nose severely out of joint, but tough noogies. DeWitt had found, much to his surprise, that he'd enjoyed dancing with Jean Morrissey — and it didn't take a genius to see that the vice president was going to need a husband before she ran for the presidency.

DeWitt flattered himself that he was going to be her choice. The VP had had a good time, too, dancing with him.

They'd have to see how compatible they were in other planes of interpersonal relationship, of course. But his guess was that would work out just fine as well. The only problem was he'd about had it with federal law enforcement. He wanted to go back to California full time. Teach at UCSB, if the school would have him.

Would the future Madam President be willing to have a commuter marriage? Might she even prefer one? And how would the political optics of that situation work out?

So he might either follow in Jim McGill's footsteps or leave government involvement behind entirely. Meaning he wouldn't have to worry about Abra Benjamin's ire whatever he did.

"In fact," DeWitt said, "Tall Wolf inspired me to take a look a Brian Kirby."

"What do you mean?" Benjamin asked.

"Well, think about it. Kirby's been mighty cagey so far. Refusing to take possession of Danner's stolen journal. Advising Merritt Kinney to do 'the right thing.' But Kirby and Danner are playing trains again, this time on a multi-billion dollar scale. For all we know, being cheated out of first place in the model train contest is what inspired Danner to take criminal actions this time."

"He might say as much in his journal," Benjamin said.

"Right. So what kind of schnooks would we have to be to think Kirby, with all that money on the line, isn't cheating again?"

"He is cheating, he *has* to be." Benjamin kicked herself for not thinking of that first.

"You know what the best way for Kirby to cheat Danner again would be, don't you?"

There were times when Benjamin knew she was a half-step behind DeWitt, but she was good at playing catch up. She smiled at DeWitt and nodded. "Yes, I do."

"And the answer is?" DeWitt asked.

"Kirby would need to find out, using his own private investigators, who Danner had bribed and then corrupt those people's superiors with even bigger bribes. So even if Danner's stooges tried to steer things his way, Kirby's better placed crooks could overrule them."

"Yeah, that's the way I see it," DeWitt said. "Kirby's corruption of public officials is the loose end. It also explains why he could so easily turn down reading Danner's journal. He'd already found out what he needed to know by other means. So why don't you tidy things up, Abra? Find out who Kirby bribed."

"You're leaving that to me?" Implicitly asking if she could claim credit for bagging a billionaire.

"Sure."

"What are you going to do?"

DeWitt said, "Make a quick trip to Washington. Brief the vice president on where things stand. Turn around and jet back to New Mexico. Be ready if John Tall Wolf needs some help."

— CHAPTER 50 —

Northern New Mexico

Our grandmother is gonna try and kill you," Arnoldo Black Knife told John.

John and Maj had pulled off the road into a clearing in the forest; Alan White River and Arnoldo had followed. The four of them clustered around the huge Ford pickup. Maj's dirt bike had been off-loaded, but John's remained in the truck.

"For failing to acknowledge our relationship?" John asked.

"For being a threat to her. There's big money coming and she's sure you're gonna make a try for it. She's been scared of you ever since she wasn't able to rope you back onto the rez where she could have put her thumb on you when you were a kid."

Arnoldo's summation sounded like one born of experience to John.

But he raised a point John wanted to have answered.

"I always thought my biological mother wanted me back."

"She did, but the old lady planted that seed. She told me so. She used Bly, your mom, to carry her water, you know. That way, if things went wrong, and they did, Bly'd get the blame not her. Grandma didn't want Grandpa to get on her for creating another mess."

"The first mess being me," John said.

"Yeah, you being born and not getting eaten by Coyote."

So his family on the rez knew about that, too. John could only shake his head.

He said, "I take it our grandmother isn't the kind to do her own dirty work."

Arnoldo shook his head. He looked at White River.

"Sorry to tell you," he said to the old man, "that young guy, the one you came here with, he had it in mind himself to kill my cousin."

"Bodaway?" White River asked.

"Yeah, that's him."

"What grudge does he have against me?" John asked.

"He thinks you're gonna mess up this guy's plans." Arnoldo hooked a thumb at White River.

Maj had been content to observe and listen, but now she asked, "Did he say how he planned to kill a federal officer?"

Arnoldo shook his head. "Didn't hear that."

White River asked Arnoldo, "Why aren't you part of their plan?"

Arnoldo shook his head and laughed without humor.

"Grandma would never trust me with something like that. And I thought my cousin here, he never did anything to hurt me. Why should I want to see him die?"

None of the three who heard Arnoldo's words doubted his sincerity.

His truthfulness was only buttressed when he added to John, "Besides that, I wanted to ask, you think you might help me find a job off the rez? I think when you got away young, you were the lucky one."

After being spared from Coyote, yeah, John thought.

"I'll see what I can do," he said.

Maj told John, "What we'd better do is call in the FBI. If there's an active plan to assassinate you, we can't take any chances."

Arnoldo shook his head. "That's not gonna happen. Any tourist on the rez is gonna get sent home real soon. Guys with rifles'll be posted on all the roads. No outsiders let in. Only people who look like us get in."

With a wave of his hand, Arnoldo indicated himself, John and White River.

"You're gonna have to leave, lady."

Maj gave him a look, went to the truck and took out her M-4.

She looked at Arnoldo and asked, "Wanna bet?"

John told his cousin, "She has native blood."

Arnoldo looked at Maj and said, "Her?"

"Pequot," John said.

Arnoldo returned a blank look.

White River was the one to tell him, "An eastern tribe."

"Really? Never heard of them. But so what? What d'you have, lady? One ounce native blood?"

"She has enough for me to vouch for her," White River said.

That made Arnoldo think twice. He knew White River had masterminded the train theft. The old man was the reason native people from all over the country were pouring into the rez. Arnoldo shrugged.

"Okay. Have it your way."

His implication was clear: Don't blame him if things went wrong.

"Is there room on your machine for two?" White River asked Maj.

The old man was nearly as tall as John, but he had to be fifty pounds lighter.

"Not really," Maj said, "but that hasn't stopped me. You think you can hold on tight?"

He nodded. Maj slung her M-4 over her back, donned her helmet and the two of them mounted Maj's dirt bike.

"Care to tell me where you're going?" John asked Maj.

"To find this Bodaway guy. Have a long talk with him."

White River nodded. He had exactly the same idea.

John looked at the old man, trying to decide if he could be trusted.

"Anything bad happens to my Pequot friend, I'll do more than talk," John said.

The old man nodded. Maj gave John a wink. Then they took off.

"You want to go meet Grandma?" Arnoldo asked John.

"Later. First I want to see Marlene Flower Moon. Do you know where she is?"

Arnoldo nodded. "Best suite in our new casino's hotel."

— CHAPTER 51 —

Northern New Mexico

The accommodations weren't called the presidential suite. That would have been too culturally dissonant. Marlene was ensconced in The Sky Lodge. Same idea: a penthouse with all the creature comforts anyone who wasn't an emperor could want.

John looked around when Marlene let him in and asked her, "You putting the tab for this place on your expense account?"

She closed the door, strolled past John and brought him a bottle of Arrowhead sparkling water from a nearby bar. One hundred percent spring water, the label said. John saw the seal on the cap was intact, and trickster though Coyote was, he doubted Marlene had her own bottling plant.

They sat next to each other in a pair of arm chairs with a view of mountains in the distance and a gleaming lake below.

"I spent some time in the movie business, as you know," Marlene told John. "I made a bit of money and I can afford to indulge myself now and then, if I choose."

"You made a *lot* of money is my bet, and you're still going to expense this place."

Marlene smiled at John, showed him her long, pointed incisors and shook her head.

"I don't have to do that. My suite is being comped."

"Of course. I should have known."

"So is this rez, the place you tried so hard to avoid, what you thought it would be?" Marlene asked.

"The scenery is terrific. The view from up here is great. What I'd like to know, though, is how the schools are. What's the unemployment rate? How many people have substance abuse issues? Gambling problems?"

Marlene asked, "Are you an anthropologist like your mother or just a part-time social worker?"

John cracked the top on his bottle of water, paying close attention to the amount of force required and the sound of separation. Both elements seemed legit. He took a sip, ready to spit it out if need be, but all he tasted was clean water.

"What I am is an investigator," he said, "and I've already learned my grandmother means to kill me."

Marlene looked surprised, but understanding came quickly.

"Arnoldo told you, betrayed the woman who raised him."

"Not with any great warmth or affection apparently. He'd like me to help him find a job off the rez, away from Grandma. Maybe she has a contract out on him, too."

Marlene laughed. "If not now, as soon as she learns of his treachery."

John took another look around the suite. "How big a share of this place does Maria Black Knife control?"

"The tribe has a two-thirds ownership position; the hotel chain that built it has the rest."

"Impressive. A two to one stake for the locals over the city slickers. Granny must be a tough old bird. Smart, too. She saw an advantage in having the gathering of native people from around the country for the Super Chief haunting here as well. What's she got in mind? Giving Vegas a run for its money as a convention destination? Ski resorts are next?"

Marlene gave John a brief round of applause.

"You figured out what will happen with the train. Or did Mommy tell you?"

"She did, and I find no shame in that. You'd do well not to underestimate her. You more than anyone, really. Coyote."

Marlene sank her hands into the arms of the chair in which she sat, splitting the fabric.

For a moment, John thought she might spring at him, changing shape in midair.

He didn't flinch. He was a very big man in the prime of life. Ready for the fight.

If the rez was where he was meant to have his final battle with Coyote, so be it.

Then the moment passed, put off to another day. Marlene slumped back in her chair.

John picked up the thread of the conversation. "Are gambling and tourism the extent of Maria's ambitions or is there something else?"

Marlene stood up, got a bottle of water for herself. Used it to clear her throat. As if she might have growled at John otherwise. Retaking her seat, she said, "A new opportunity presented itself recently. Natural gas. Huge amounts of it."

John looked out at the natural beauty of their surroundings, took a hit of water and asked, "Fracking? Here?"

His preconception of the reservation had featured neither a casino nor natural resources. Now, it seemed the place had both. Big money and huge money. And who was in the best position to control everything? His grandmother, the woman who wanted him dead.

According to Arnoldo, she feared he'd screw up her plans. Make a grab for her power. She'd been unable to seize him as a child just as Coyote had failed to do. Not to eat but to mold into her own creature. So he'd become a threat and had to die.

John put aside worries of despoiling nature for the moment.

"What do you know about this man called Bodaway?" he asked Marlene. "He's supposed to be the one to do Grandma's dirty work."

"He's Alan White River's great-grandson. Another Native American raised white. Studied engineering in Georgia. He helped get the train here, but thinks giving it back is a mistake."

"He doesn't believe in the haunting?"

"No. Two ideas captured his imagination: stealing the train and besting you. He thinks that would give him real status."

"Besting as in killing," John said.

"Yes."

John asked, "And how would you feel if he did that, taking your prize from you once more?"

Marlene shook her head. "I won't let him do that."

"No? What if he should target you, too?"

The very idea shocked Marlene. *Me?*

"Why not? How many engineers have any fear of the supernatural? If they can't reduce the world to mathematical equations, it doesn't compute for them. And remember, Marlene Flower Moon is something of a Washington big shot. Someone whose murder would certainly bring notoriety, if not fame."

John could see Marlene parsing his logic, and she found no fault with it.

Except one. She couldn't believe Bodaway could pull off killing her. Ego.

"Let him try," she said. "It will be the hardest lesson he'll ever learn."

"What's his English name?" John asked.

"Thomas Bilbray."

"And when does the haunting of the train begin?"

"Tonight at the zenith of the moon."

John took another drink of water, set the bottle on an end table and stood.

"Thanks for the hospitality."

"Don't you want to know where the train is?"

"I'll just follow the crowd tonight," John said.

— CHAPTER 52 —

Northern New Mexico

Maria Black Knife had people all over the rez watching for John Tall Wolf's arrival. She'd flattered herself that if he was half the man he was reputed to be he'd come for her first thing. Had he done so, he would have found a dozen armed men waiting for him, including Bodaway. A violent argument would have followed — instigated by Maria if necessary — about just who represented the law on the reservation, and the outcome would be fatal for the representative of the federal government.

But Tall Wolf didn't pay Maria the compliment she felt was her due.

Instead, Maria learned, he'd spoken with Arnoldo and Alan White River. Maria was perversely pleased her grandson had found the courage to defy her. She'd been trying all his life to provoke some semblance of manhood in him. Aside from refusing to let her choose a bride for him, that had never happened. Now, at least he'd have a brief moment of thinking he was his own man before …

Well, he was no longer needed even as a figurehead.

The deal she'd struck with Bodaway had been agreeable to both of them in terms of how the money would be shared and their roles in managing the affairs of the tribe. Bodaway would ultimately try to displace her, she knew, and if he succeeded she'd die a happy woman, knowing she'd finally found an heir as ruthless as herself.

The only problem with Bodaway was he still loved his great-grandfather. Well, she had plans for Alan White River, too. If Bodaway was sentimental enough to try to save White River's life, then Bodaway would be yet another disappointment. She'd have to start searching for a truly villainous protégé once again.

Such thoughts made her long for her late husband, Cesar.

There was a man who did whatever was needed to get whatever he wanted.

Of course, after being the *de facto* leader of her tribe all these years, she'd probably plot against Cesar, too, if he was ever made flesh and blood again.

Bodaway watched the old woman daydreaming. She'd been angered that Tall Wolf hadn't made a suicidal charge at her. Then she'd started to … daydream was the only way Bodaway could think of it. The lines on her face softened as her mood mellowed.

The transformation reminded him of his great-grandfather. That a man of White River's age could conceive of the theft of a train iconic to the white man had thrilled Bodaway. That he wanted to return it covered with nothing more than a wash of superstitious moanings had disappointed Bodaway grievously.

Maybe becoming soft in old age was inevitable, he thought. Muscles withered, bones became brittle and thoughts of mercy dimmed the fires of righteous vengeance. If Bodaway ever saw those signs of decline in himself, he would end his days by his own hand. With an inward smile, he added an image of his leaving the world in such a spectacular explosion that all who saw it — the ones who lived — would always remember his passing.

He stood and told Maria, "It's time for me to go. I have preparations to make."

He had to leave the rez to get what he needed.

He wasn't going to rely on an antique weapon.

He set his mind to approaching the task of ending John Tall Wolf's life with the mathematical precision he'd learned in engineering school. Although he'd been warned not to do so, he added Marlene Flower Moon's name to his hit list. Coyote, my ass, he thought with a laugh.

Well before he left the rez, he tossed the old Colt handgun out the window of his truck and into a stand of trees. Five rounds of dubious ammunition. He might as well throw the gun at Tall Wolf as try to shoot him with it.

— CHAPTER 53 —

Northern New Mexico

After John left Marlene, he went down to the hotel's reception desk and told the clerk, a pretty young Native American woman, "I'd like a room, please."

She looked at him, tried to sort out his standing in the hierarchy of the new arrivals. Liked his imposing height, the way his polo shirt stretched tight across his chest and shoulders and most of all the way he wore his Ray-Ban sunglasses. She said, "You're in luck. We've got one room left."

"That's all I need."

A look of mischief entered the young woman's eyes.

"What would you have said if I'd told you there weren't any rooms left?"

"I'd have said Marlene Flower Moon sent me."

The clerk immediately looked chastened. "I … I'm sorry, sir. I shouldn't have said that."

"That's okay. I got the idea you were going to offer to put me up at your place."

Now, the young woman blushed deeply.

Good circulation, John thought.

He said, "Unless I'm just trying to flatter myself."

She shook her head, not daring to verbalize things further.

"I'm a bit old for you, and I'm spoken for. By a Canadian Mountie."

The young woman's jaw dropped.

"A female Mountie," John clarified.

He supposed there were gay Mounties; maybe even gay BIA men.

Nothing wrong with that. Equal opportunity was a public virtue.

The reception clerk told him, "I could move you to a suite, sir. Put someone else in that room."

John shook his head. "The room is fine, but I have something I'd like you to put in the hotel safe." He handed her Edward Danner's journal.

She put it in an envelope bearing the hotel's logo, and gave John a receipt.

"If you could tuck that item in a corner away from other people's things, I'd appreciate it."

He didn't know if a bomb planted in the journal could be remotely detonated inside a safe, but why damage other people's valuables if it could be avoided?

"Yes, sir, I'll see to it."

John thanked her, went to his room and called Byron DeWitt.

"I don't think a radio signal can penetrate thick steel," DeWitt told John. "But I can't say for sure, so I'll check it out."

John had just told the FBI deputy director where he could find Edward Danner's journal, if something unfortunate happened to him.

"What kind of misfortune are you anticipating?" DeWitt asked.

"My cousin tells me my grandmother plans to kill me."

"She couldn't just write you out of her will?"

"Seems she's more aggrieved than that."

"Because?"

"She's the queen bee of the rez, and Marlene tells me the land here is chock full of natural gas. Worth a lot of money to the tribe."

"And?"

"And I might be a bastard child, but Granny thinks I might still be able to make a claim to the throne."

DeWitt's tone changed. "So this is a *real* threat?"

"I'm taking it as such. I've got a name I'd like you to check: Thomas Bilbray. He might be on that list of FAFSA applicants I asked you about. You did compile the list, right?"

"I had it done, yeah, but I haven't scanned it yet. Let me bring it up on my computer."

DeWitt was silent for a moment before telling John, "Yeah, here he is. Thomas Bodaway Bilbray. Georgia Tech. Bachelor of Science in structural engineering. Dean's list. Magna cum Laude graduate. Hmm. Switched from a Pell Grant to full ride courtesy of the ROTC."

John said, "The guy's had military training?"

"Hold on, I'll see what I can access from the DOD."

"You can do that?"

"Just between you and me, the VP has clearance from the president to get us whatever information we need."

John whistled, truly impressed.

DeWitt said, "Yeah, that's called giving your preferred candidate for the Oval Office a running start. Okay, here's Bilbray's file and … there's nothing top secret in it. He served in the army. Supervised construction projects, left the service honorably with the rank of captain. Ribbons for overseas service and … damn."

"What?" John asked.

"Our boy Bilbray — the engineer — earned himself an army marksmanship qualification badge: sharpshooter."

"With a rifle?" John asked.

"Yeah. Could be worse. The guy could've shot *expert.* But you'd better be careful."

"Might not be possible. Maj Olson is out looking for him right now, and she's packing an M-4."

"Well, hell," DeWitt said. "Hold on. Let me dip into Amtrak's files." That didn't take long. "Well, I'll be damned. Our Columbia Ph.D., she's the one who shot *expert.* Both rifle and pistol. Maybe I'll recruit her."

"In the meantime," John said.

"Right. I'm in the air, on my way to D.C., but I'll turn the plane around and be in Albuquerque in under two hours. I'll have a team waiting for me and we'll blast on up to the rez to backstop you."

John remembered Arnoldo's warning of braves with rifles guarding the rez roads.

"Let me see how much it means for me to be a co-director. If I can manage it, I'll have a BIA team at the airport, too. We'll put a native face on the joint effort."

DeWitt said, "Good thinking. Sorry to hear your grandma's gunning for you."

"It's always some damn thing," John replied.

— CHAPTER 54 —

Santa Fe, New Mexico

The default mask for modern anarchists, both the street thugs and the digital provocateurs, was Guy Fawkes. Bodaway felt, however, that visage had become a cliché. Besides that, it was definitely paleface. He was far more taken by something he saw in a Santa Fe store window.

He was unsure of the word to use. His Native American vocabulary still needed work. Headdress, he'd guess. Someone had caught and skinned an animal, preserving and spreading out the beast's face, upper jaw, teeth and body. The beast was a coyote.

The face of the mannequin on which the coyote was draped had its face painted white with parallel vertical black lines running along its lower jaw from ear to ear. A sign said it was a replica of what a Cheyenne warrior had worn into battle.

As far as Bodaway knew, his bloodlines were Apache and maybe Navajo. But the Cheyenne persona beat Guy Fawkes all to hell in his eyes. He went into the store and paid seven hundred dollars cash for the animal skin and the face paint.

The store had security cameras but Bodaway wore sunglasses and an Arizona Diamondbacks cap. He also kept his gaze down so the cameras wouldn't catch much beyond the bill of his hat. Nobody would be able to identify him from his visit.

His other three stops in town were a firearms store, a motorcycle dealer and a place called The Big First Step. From the arms dealer, he bought a Bravo Company BC-M4, a semi-auto carbine similar to the one he'd shot in the army, and a weapon not dissimilar to the one Maj Olson carried. From the cycle shop, he purchased a high-powered dirt bike. The Big First Step catered to the needs of BASE jumpers.

Bodaway took the calculated risk of paying for his assault rifle, dirt bike and jumping equipment with credit cards he'd stolen from the crew of the Super Chief. When each sale went through without a hitch, he felt a warm glow. If he'd been the least bit gullible — superstitious — he'd have thought a higher power had approved of his mission. As it was, he knew he was simply playing the odds correctly.

The numbers were in his favor, nothing more.

That was the way he'd gamed his whole plan. He'd made calculated choices and would position himself to take advantage of them. The primary decisions were based on the assumption that both John Tall Wolf and Marlene Flower Moon would show up at the ceremony to haunt the Super Chief, and before they made any law enforcement moves they'd both wait until all the people who wanted to curse and wail at an inanimate object had disburdened themselves of their emotions.

To try to preempt the haunting would cause an uproar and resistance. The much easier choice, the smart move, would be to let the frenzy turn into exhaustion. Then take action. Bodaway felt sure Tall Wolf would be present throughout the moaning and weeping and Flower Moon would turn up near the end so she could claim credit for the train's return.

Once Bodaway's pick-up truck was loaded with all his purchases, he made a call to Maria Black Knife before heading back to the rez.

"You know where he is?" he asked without identifying himself.

He referred to Tall Wolf. The old lady still opposed Flower Moon's death .

"Yes, but there is a woman with him."

Flower Moon? No, she was supposed to be Tall Wolf's nemesis. So …

Had an unknown variable been introduced?

Something like that could screw up all his plans.

"What woman?"

"She claims to be Pequot, but she's white."

So *not* Coyote. That was good.

"Why is she important?"

"She carries a weapon, a rifle. She rides a motorcycle."

That was serious. "A federal agent?"

"She works for Amtrak."

Great punchline, Bodaway thought. He almost laughed.

"We won't worry about her then. She might be returning lost luggage."

Maria didn't comment on that. She told Bodaway where Tall Wolf and the woman were.

At the casino's hotel.

"I'll be back soon," he said.

— CHAPTER 55 —

Northern New Mexico

Delshay Crow Wing was twelve years old. He was smart in both a book sense and in observing the ways power flowed from one person to the next. Physical strength, he'd learned, was the foundation of much power. To make himself strong he ran miles every day and climbed rock faces until his arms and legs ached. But standing in the tribe, he also understood, depended even more on intelligence. That and making people like or fear you, as called for by the moment.

He studied Maria Black Knife. She was an *old* woman. But everyone knew she was the most powerful person in the tribe. The one who made the decisions that affected all their lives every day. Her grandson Arnoldo was simply the man through whom Maria spoke.

It was easier for both her and the tribe to have everyone think they were following a big man rather than a small woman. Delshay had come to understand that strategy only last year. At first, he was outraged by the pretense, but then he realized it was a useful thing. Not everything had to be as it first appeared.

Some things worked better when people agreed to pretend a lie was the truth.

The boy, soon to be a young man in his mind, was trying to find such a strategy that might work for him. He hadn't reached the point of thinking he might lead the tribe — yet — but he knew he would have special standing among his people. Wouldn't just scratch out a living by the strength of his back. Or by dealing cards at the casino.

Nor would he be content using only his mind.

Being strong in every sense was his plan.

He'd come to see it was to his advantage to help those who could help him.

That day, running his miles across the rez, he came upon an opportunity to do just that.

He found a large pistol in the trees, just off a road. He couldn't imagine how it got there. People on the rez valued their firearms. Took good care of them. He picked the pistol up and saw initials had been etched into both of the grips: BK. Black Knife.

Delshay smiled. Here was an opportunity to gain favor.

There was only one Black Knife family on the rez.

He would return the gun to Maria Black Knife.

That was bound to earn him some sort of reward.

— CHAPTER 56 —

Northern New Mexico

Maj Olson was a sight. The thing about riding a dirt bike was you got dirty. Her hair was matted from sweating under her helmet. Her body odor wouldn't remind anyone of springtime in Paris. And her every muscle fiber throbbed from carting Alan White River around for hours on a machine meant for one rider. That and having the weight of her M-4 slung across her torso.

She'd seen the Super Chief, had witnessed it move as it left its hiding place under the cover of a stand of trees and rolled out into an open glade at the foot of a fairly big mountain. On newly laid track. Seeing that was really something. Validation and a thrill wrapped into one.

But she hadn't been able to find Bodaway — or get anyone else to admit they even knew of him. One sixty-fourth Pequot didn't cut much ice with this crowd. She was tolerated only because she was accompanied by White River.

Maj had called John after White River promised her the Super Chief wouldn't be moved again for the next twenty-four hours. John told her where he was. She said she'd top off her gas tank and see him soon. The reception clerk on duty at the front desk took one look at Maj and had no trouble telling her there wasn't a vacant room in the building.

Maj was only reluctantly informed that, yes, John Tall Wolf was a guest.

She was put through to his room and explained her problem.

John thought of suggesting that Maj use Marlene's name to secure lodgings, but he said, "My room has two beds and you can shower as long as you like without interruption."

"On my way up," she said.

She entered his room looking like an extra from "Mad Max," but cleaned up nicely, emerging from the bathroom in an old Amtrak T-shirt — *America is getting into training* — and a pair of gym shorts from Columbia's track team.

John asked, "What was your event?"

"Ran the 400-meter hurdles as an undergrad. Wasn't too shabby either, for the Ivy League. Probably what put me over the top with the admissions office."

"A scholar and an athlete," John replied.

"And a gun-toting federal officer. Don't forget that."

"Impossible to do."

"You mind if I ask you a favor?" Maj asked.

"Asking is free."

"Would you take off your sunglasses just for a minute?"

John's Ray-Bans had polarizing lenses. He left them on indoors as often as not. Even bright electric light could cause his eyes discomfort. But he obliged Maj.

She studied his face for a moment and nodded to herself.

"Okay, that's good."

John put his glasses back on. "You going to tell me what that was all about?"

"Just checking my powers of perception. I saw a family resemblance between you and your cousin Arnoldo, but I also thought I saw a likeness between you and Alan White River. Then I thought I must be imagining things."

"And were you?"

Maj shook her head. "Unh-uh. White River has a million lines on his face and you have only a few, but it's there. The two of you have similar faces. Could be a coincidence or …" She shrugged her shoulders.

She had John thinking. He never had found out much about his biological father or his family. Only knew that the guy had worked for a rodeo and was probably Navajo. Any resemblance between him and Alan White River *had* to be happenstance.

Didn't it? He moved on to another topic.

"You decided not to arrest Alan White River," John said.

"What, before he gets to do his thing with the train? No way."

"He told you his plans?"

"Right away. Said he was to blame for the whole thing and as soon as he got done with the Super Chief, he would turn himself in. Told me you and I could take the credit for his arrest."

"You found that a compelling idea?"

"I found it inevitable. If we tried to grab White River before he gets to do his thing, we'd make General George Armstrong Custer look like a military genius. We'd also get *planted* on this rez. Besides, my one-sixty-fourth Pequot thinks what he's doing is cool."

"And by working with White River …"

"We're cool, too, with the rez cops and pretty much everyone but Bodaway."

"And my grandmother," John said.

"Yeah. White River's going to talk with her."

John grunted. White River, he was sure, would continue to look for Bodaway first. Then, if he found the time and if the past was any guide, he'd find Maria Black Knife to be completely obstinate.

Maj reclined on the spare bed and closed her eyes.

"I've got to take a cat nap. You'll wake me when it's time to go to the ceremony? That and make our plans, whatever they might be."

"Sure," John said.

She closed her eyes and said, "You know what the name Bodaway means?"

"Yeah. It's Apache for firemaker."

Maj cracked an eye and looked at him.

"It's one of those names you hear occasionally," John said, "if you're Native American and grow up in Santa Fe."

She closed her eye and said, "Okay. White River told me the meaning. In this case, though, it might as well mean arsonist. Seems like there's always a troublemaker in every family. The old man's worried about his great-grandson."

"Any concern about a certain rising star in the BIA?"

Maj laughed, but kept her eyes closed. Yawned wide and long.

"He is, in fact. He noticed the resemblance between the two of you, too. Made him curious."

"Did White River say if he thought he could make Bodaway see reason?"

John didn't get an answer. Maj had fallen asleep.

— CHAPTER 57 —

Northern New Mexico

The casino's hotel proved more hospitable when Deputy Director DeWitt arrived. The manager, William Sharp Eye, not only found a room for him, he also made a conference room available to the twenty-four federal agents — half FBI, half BIA — DeWitt had brought along with him.

DeWitt had a brief personal chat with the first two Apache riflemen who were stationed on the main road into the rez to keep outsiders away. In a soft voice he'd told them nobody would interfere with what Alan White River had planned for that night. But if he and his people were not admitted without delay the next callers would be far more numerous and less likely to be as culturally sensitive.

The BIA contingent had added that a death threat had been made against one of their top officials, and they were going to come in *right now,* so the two guys with their rifles might as well let the FBI in, too. They did just that.

John made one fruitless attempt to rouse Maj and then joined his federal colleagues in the hotel conference room. Both he and DeWitt had a word with the hotel manager.

John told the man, "What's happening here is bigger than a family quarrel or rez politics. You need to understand where your best interests truly lie. Don't tell anyone anything about this group meeting here tonight."

DeWitt added, "Few things in life are worth having federal law enforcement take a serious interest in you. Do you understand?"

Despite John's advice and DeWitt's implicit warning, Sharp Eye found the candor to tell John, "She's really afraid of you, you know."

Neither John nor DeWitt had to ask whom he meant.

John said, "My grandmother has no reason to fear me. Once we have the train, after the ceremony, I'll be gone, and if it's up to me, I won't be back. You can tell her that at the appropriate time."

"You're really not going to spoil White River's plans?" Sharp Eye asked.

"No," John said. "We're not."

"Not at all," the deputy director said.

"Okay," Sharp Eye said, "I don't talk. My people don't talk."

"Be sure you keep your word, William."

That warning came from Marlene Flower Moon. A moment earlier she wasn't present, and then she was. The two agents on the door looked at each other with the same expression.

How the hell did she get in here?

Their reaction was secondary to Sharp Eye's response: fear. Marlene intimidated him far more than DeWitt had. More than even Maria Black Knife had.

The FBI guys, with the exception of DeWitt, were puzzled.

The BIA agents felt Marlene's power, too, and they were on edge.

John broke the tension by saying, "Co-director Flower Moon has always taken a special interest in me. Me and my welfare."

DeWitt smiled at the joke. So did the BIA men, after Marlene put a hand on John's shoulder and said, "Anyone who threatens John Tall Wolf threatens my interests."

She smiled at the others, but the look she directed at Sharp Eye, flashing her razor-sharp incisors his way, chilled his soul. He gave a quick nod of both understanding and submission. Nobody on the hotel payroll would be talking to anyone.

Everyone would be warned of the risk of incurring Coyote's

wrath.

Just as the hotel manager turned to leave, the door to the room opened. Maj Olson was there. With her were Alan White River and Arnoldo Black Knife.

They made way for the departing William Sharp Eye.

"So what'd we miss?" Maj asked.

— CHAPTER 58 —

Northern New Mexico

Arnoldo Black Knife put on a pair of Ray-Ban aviator-style sunglasses, the same type John wore.

Maj said, "The casino gift shop sells them. So what do you think?"

She'd asked the question of John in particular and the conference room group in general.

"Passable resemblance," John said. "A haircut would make it more so."

Arnoldo wore his hair shoulder length.

"I've got an appointment with a stylist here for a cut in thirty minutes," Arnoldo said.

"So do I," added White River. "I'm getting a dye job and a facial, too."

Merriment danced in Maj's eyes, but John asked, "Why?"

Maj rolled her eyes, but DeWitt answered, "I think the older gentleman wants in on the act."

White River nodded. He also put on a pair of matching sunglasses.

John said, "The two of you plan to act as decoys for me?"

He ignored the point that White River did bear a striking likeness to him.

He continued with what he felt was the more crucial point. "Bodaway might gun either of you down as easily as me. I'm sure you know that. But maybe what you didn't think of is he might get *all* of us. He's supposed to be quite a marksman."

"So am I," Maj said. "I bet a lot of the other guys in this room are, too. Unless the three of you are standing in a clump, and we know you're all too smart for that, Bodaway won't know for sure who to shoot. Assuming he'll try a long-distance shot. Maybe he'll even see that we're on to him and take a pass on shooting anyone."

Marlene admired the wiliness of the idea. "I like it."

John gave her a sidelong look.

"It does have merit, along with an element of risk, I'll admit," DeWitt added.

John shook his head. He didn't like the plan at all.

He turned to Arnoldo and White River. "Why would either of you risk your life for me?"

Arnoldo said, "I asked you for a favor; I'll do you a favor. Besides, it'll show our grandmother what I'm made of. If I spoil her plans, too, I'll get a good laugh out of it."

There was nothing funny about White River's answer. "I've led my great-grandson down the wrong path. I'd never have stolen that train if I'd known this would be the price I'd have to pay. I can't find him now, can't talk sense to him. If he were to kill me instead of you, that'd be just what I deserve."

The old man still wore the Ray-Ban sunglasses, and John felt certain they shared a bloodline.

"What if I don't want either of you to die?"

Arnoldo said, "I've stopped letting anyone else make decisions for me."

"I have no choice," White River told John. "I must accept the consequences of my actions."

John looked at DeWitt. The deputy director said, "Family can be a pain, mess things up, but it also has its advantages."

Marlene said nothing aloud, but her expression told him, "Don't be a fool. Think of yourself."

As for Maj, well, the plan was her idea.

White River told John, "Who can say? Maybe the real reason I stole the train was so I could meet you. Let's hope we all live a little longer. I'd like to talk with you."

"Me, too," Arnoldo said.

"Damn," said John.

Even so, he nodded. He'd go along with the idea.

— CHAPTER 59 —

Northern New Mexico

Delshay Crow Wing stood before Maria Black Knife's door and hesitated. He'd raised his hand to knock, but stopped short. He looked around for a doorbell. That'd be a more polite way to announce his presence. Only he didn't see one. Hell, he didn't know anybody who *had* one.

He also didn't know anyone who had a house as fancy as the Black Knife place. It was done in log cabin fashion. Not the old-fashioned kind. The exterior of this house gleamed. There were no gaps in the walls or cracks in the windows. It looked to Delshay like it might stand for a thousand years and look every bit as good as it did right now.

The place was big, too. By far the biggest home he'd ever seen.

He and his entire family could live in a small corner of it and still have twice the room they did now. He'd bet they wouldn't have to worry about a leaky roof either. No problems with being cold in the winter or hot in the —

Delshay heard a buzzing sound. Not the kind that came from bees. No, sir, it was air conditioning. In all his young life, he'd never encountered that amenity in a private home, only in government or commercial buildings.

The idea that a person's house could be comfortable year 'round impressed him more than anything else. It spoke of true wealth and power. He decided then and there he had overstepped himself. It would be better for him just to leave the revolver on the doorstep.

Forget about currying favor and —

The door opened just as he lowered his hand.

Maria Black Knife stood in front of him wearing a scowl.

"Who are you, boy? What do you want?" Then she saw the gun in his hand and took an involuntary step backward, frightened. Delshay made sure to offer it to her butt first, and she soon recovered her haughtiness. She took it from him and asked, "Where did you get this?"

Delshay gave her his name and said, "I found it."

He readied himself to run, if she pointed the weapon at him.

"Where?"

"In the woods." He described the location.

"How did you know to bring it here?"

He inclined his head toward the gun. "Your initials. They're right there."

Maria looked at the BKs etched on the grips.

"Did you fire this gun, even once?"

Delshay shook his head.

"Are you expecting a reward?"

He shook his head again and started to edge away.

"Stop."

The boy stopped, but remained ready to run.

Maria said, "You expected something from me. Don't lie. What do you want?"

Delshay answered honestly. "I don't know. I just thought … it would be a good idea."

Maria Black Knife's crooked smile didn't reassure Delshay at all.

She told him, "What you had was half an idea. Now, you've learned a lesson. Know what you want before the chance comes to ask for it. That knowledge in itself is a gift."

The old woman was right. If he'd wanted money or only a pair of new shoes, he should have been ready to ask for it. He been a fool.

Then, looking at the gun dangling at Maria's side, Delshay knew exactly what he wanted.

To get far away from the old woman. He turned and ran.

Hearing her call out to him, "I'll keep my eye on you now, young Crow Wing."

— CHAPTER 60 —

Northern New Mexico

There were Indians everywhere. In front of, in back of and on both sides of the Super Chief and its passenger car. The glade was filled with people old and young. The faces of Pre-Columbian North America had gathered to tell and hear their stories.

The train had no choice but to sit and listen.

Absorb recitations of pain, rage and sorrow.

Several Native Americans wore tribal garb and paint. Giving the impression that the past was reaching out to seize the present. Shake the twenty-first century until it acknowledged the sins of the past.

John Tall Wolf stood on a small knoll on the fringe of the glade and took it all in. He recalled Maj Olson's comment about the fool-hardiness of trying to arrest Alan White River and seize the train before the night's purging of tortured souls took place. She'd said it would make Custer look smart. The analogy was more apt than John had first realized. A premature move by law enforcement would indeed have resulted in a massacre: theirs.

Maj had positioned herself at John's side and said in a quiet voice, "Looks like I'm the only paleface here, huh?"

The FBI contingent, with help from the state police, was watching all the roads out of the rez. DeWitt had summoned up a helicopter and a marksman to take to the air in the event Bodaway tried both an assassination attempt and an off-road escape. DeWitt had told John and Maj, "Try not to get killed. I think both of you show promise."

John had laughed. After DeWitt had left, though, Maj had asked, "Was that just a bit of pep talk or do I have a law enforcement future beyond Amtrak?"

"Let's see how things go, before we do any career planning," John had said.

Now, he asked Maj, "You really weren't kidding about your Pequot heritage, were you?"

"Unh-uh. If the Mormons were straight with me, and that's their reputation, then it's real."

"That's the case, don't worry about your skin color. This is a solemn occasion, but it's not a religious ceremony that has to be kept secret."

John looked for the BIA agents who had spread out through the crowd. The problem with that was, he'd met them only that day, their faces weren't familiar and they were dressed like all the people who'd worn contemporary clothing: flannel shirts, jeans and boots. They were armed, of course, but it was likely most of the adult men — and plenty of the women — were, too.

Nobody had a peep to offer about seeing the M-4 Maj had slung over her shoulder.

Neither that nor her fair skin.

A few of the younger men and women who passed by did cast admiring glances at the Yamaha YZ450Fs dirt bikes resting behind John and Maj on their aluminum kickstands. Maj took a watch out of a pocket and glanced at it.

John said, "That looks like a timepiece a conductor would use not a cop."

Maj smiled. "My father gave it to me as a joke when I got my Amtrak job. But it keeps perfect time. And it always reminds me of how my dad makes time for me anytime I need it. If White River's on schedule, we should be seeing him right about … now."

The old train thief appeared on the near side of the locomotive. The sun had just dipped behind the nearby mountain and torches, both flaming and electric, were lit against the growing darkness. Alan White River didn't look anything like John now, not in terms of the way he was dressed. He wore a beaded leather war shirt and buckskin pants and moccasins. His recently cut and dyed hair was covered by an eagle feather headdress.

White River mounted a wooden platform that had been placed opposite the point where a train crew would enter the locomotive's cab. He waited for the people on the other side of the train to join the crowd in front of him. Everyone made accommodations, seemingly with the ease of tributaries joining a main water course. No shoving or jostling was evident, only a fluid rearrangement that provided the best sight lines for all concerned.

Maj was impressed. She looked at John and said, "These people are working together here."

"United," John said.

Dropping her voice, Maj added, "I'd always wondered if that sort of headdress White River is wearing is authentic."

John nodded in affirmation. "It's more often associated with Great Plains tribes like the Sioux and the Kiowa, but there was a cultural drift that extended westward, too."

Maj was about to ask another question when she noticed John tense.

"What's wrong?" she asked.

Looking around, straining to see against the deepening night, John said, "Maybe a couple things. Occupying the high ground is usually a good thing, but not when it makes you a target."

Maj understood. "You're thinking Bodaway has a rifle?"

"A rifle and a night scope. Maybe he can see us and we can't see him."

"Damn, I should've thought of that. Let's —"

John placed a hand lightly on her arm. "We'll move in just a minute."

"Why wait?"

"Because if White River and Arnoldo played us all for suckers and intend to turn all those loyal followers down there against us, we'll hear of it any moment now."

The old chief in native clothing began to speak, but neither John nor Maj understood a single word of what he said. They didn't speak Apache. For that matter, neither did most of the crowd. After a moment, White River switched to English, the *lingua franca* of Native North Americans in the twenty-first century.

White River said, "We are here to remind the world, or at least those who will visit the museum where this train will reside, that the progress the railroads brought to the white society was purchased by lies, theft and murder."

Many heads in the crowd bobbed in agreement, but otherwise the gathering was silent, intent on hearing White River's every word. Even the wind had died, letting the old chief's words carry to the far reaches of the crowd. That was good for communication, but it brought the same disturbing thought to both John and Maj.

Calm air made accurate shooting much easier for a sniper.

The dancing and weaving torchlight complicated things.

But the bright, steady light of a full moon would be available soon.

More than enough illumination for a marksman using a night scope.

White River continued, "Before we are finished here, you will hear stories of broken treaties, stolen hunting grounds and outright mass murder. More important, this train will hear them, too. The sorrows of our people will become as much a part of it as its steel. Anyone who comes to look upon this train will feel our heartbreak, know of the crimes committed against us. They will never be able to forget a part of their history they have never learned or have chosen to ignore or forget. What we do here tonight will force all those who look upon this train to open their eyes to our history, too."

Another old man in buckskin climbed onto the platform next to White River.

He introduced himself as Daniel Four Bears of the Cheyenne and began to speak of the Sand Creek Massacre in Colorado in 1864. More than a hundred members of his tribe, mostly women and children, were slaughtered — and this was perfectly in keeping with the policy of the territorial governor, John Evans, that policy being the genocide of the native people.

"The military and the railroad men put it more bluntly," Four Bears said.

"They called it disposing of the Indian menace."

Maj felt her jaw tighten in outrage, and then John tapped her shoulder.

She looked and saw him lift his eyes. The moon was rising.

It was time for them to find Bodaway, before he found them.

Bodaway nestled among a cluster of bushes on a mountain foothill perpendicular to the speaker's platform outside the Super Chief. From his position he could put a round into the right ear of whoever was talking up there. Comfortable in a kneeling position, his head rose no higher than the tallest shrub. He was all but invisible.

Even if a high-def camera found him, though, all it would see was an individual wearing the face paint and the headdress he'd bought in Santa Fe. If he had to run, he'd be able to rise to his feet quickly. Not that he intended to escape on foot. His dirt bike lay on its side five feet behind him. He'd disappear in a heartbeat.

If things really went to hell, his ultimate means of escape was strapped to his back.

The Leupold scope on his weapon diminished any reflections off its lens, kept the image quality sharp and increased the amount of available light that reached his eye. Bodaway smiled when he saw his great-grandfather step onto the platform to address the crowd. The guy was as old as the hills, but he still looked every inch a man who was meant to lead others into battle.

Not just symbolic fights. Not mystical conflicts. Not rhetorical debates.

Bodaway couldn't hear the old man's words, but he'd read his speech.

The audience seemed to be buying into it. If hundreds of people had started to jeer and boo, he would have heard that. Nobody objected vocally. Not that he could tell.

That was enough to make him sigh.

When would the country's first people pick up arms?

Only when they were about to vanish from the earth?

By then it would be too late.

In Bodaway's earlier incarnation, as Thomas Bilbray honors graduate in engineering, he had thought to request an assignment to the infantry. Only he happened to run into a down on his luck Vietnam Vet, a fellow Native American, one night shortly before reporting for duty. The guy had been wearing an old-fashioned army utility jacket and holding up a sign: *Will work cheep.* It was the misspelled word that most touched Bilbray. He gave the man fifty dollars and told him it would be his honor to buy him dinner.

They ate in a chain steak house, sat in an out of the way booth. The vet needed a bath among other things. He wouldn't have been allowed in on his own. But Bilbray's appearance was not just immaculate, it was starched. He also slipped the hostess a twenty and whispered to her that the old guy was his uncle and had been wounded in service to his country.

That last bit turned out to be true. The vet said he'd been an 11-Bravo, an infantryman. He'd been in-country three months when he got shot in the leg. The enemy round took out the bottom half of his right calf and he hadn't been able to walk right since. Made it damn hard for him to hold down any kind of a job, what with just a sixth grade education.

"Damn thing was, *I* never got to shoot anybody over there," the vet said.

"Why not? Just the way it went?"

"For one thing, those little bastards were sneaky as hell. You're out humpin' the boonies, you never see 'em. You're walkin' through a ville, hey, they're all just rice farmers out walkin' their water buffalo. It was up to me, I'd've dinged 'em all. Only they had these damn things called rules of engagement. Don't shoot the papa-san unless he's handin' you a live grenade. Shit. We never had a chance over there."

When Bilbray told the vet he'd be reporting for active duty soon, he got a piece of advice for his generosity. "Stay the fuck out of the infantry, whatever you do."

With those words fresh in mind, Bilbray took the engineering job the army gave him, thinking he could always ask for a transfer after he got the lay of the land. But he never did. The brass put endless limits on its front line soldiers. Rules of engagement still applied.

The old vet had it right. You got into a fight, the only rule should be ding 'em all.

That being far from the case, Bilbray served out his four year ROTC commitment and was discharged. Along the way, though, he picked up every military skill he could, marksmanship being prominent among them. Others included demolition and jumping out of airplanes. The brass humored him that way because he was good at his job and hinted he might want to go infantry when he re-upped.

Only he didn't reenlist. The people he'd deceived weren't amused, but there was nothing they could do. He'd fulfilled his obligation and done it at a superior level.

During his time in service, as he matured intellectually and emotionally, Bilbray came to ask himself for which causes would he actually be willing to ding people. Being as egocentric as anyone else, he decided he would be willing to kill and, if he couldn't avoid it, die for his own people. Native Americans.

It wasn't six months after his discharge that his great-grand-father came to him with this insanely great idea: steal a train that symbolized the white man's conquest of the red man. By that time, he thought of himself by his true name, Bodaway, and he jumped at the chance to play a part. Only to be bitterly disappointed in the end.

Great Grandpa intended to *give* the damn train back.

After just singing and shouting at it.

Hell, one go at the train with a power washer, it'd be good as new.

But then he'd learned about two people, John Tall Wolf and Marlene Flower Moon, who'd do their best to foil what little symbolism his great-grandfather hoped to achieve. Two Native Americans working against their own kind. He knew better than to think there was any short term way to displace white domination in the U.S., but now he had it in mind that it would be cool to twist the power structure's damn noses every so often.

Steal a Super Chief and fill it not with the grievances of his people but with their shit.

Then give it back.

Come up with other ideas like that. Have fun pulling them off.

If creeps like Tall Wolf and Flower Moon were obstacles … well, then they had to go.

And there was no time like the present to start getting rid of them.

The moon was rising and Bodaway started to search the crowd through his scope.

John and Maj slipped through the crowd surrounding the Super Chief. People let them pass without comment, as accommodating as ever. Most listened intently to the speakers on the platform, often with tears in their eyes or with expressions of barely repressed rage on their faces. But mothers and fathers also took care of their little ones, letting them sleep in their arms or carving out small patches of grass for them. Husbands and wives placed supportive arms around each other. Older couples held hands.

Everyone present felt waves of emotion sweep over them. So much tragedy. So much sorrow. But there were moments of triumph, too. Battles won even as the war was being lost. All this went into the train. Bodaway had it exactly backward. Excrement could be washed away; the stain of their agonies would be indelible, a part of the Super Chief until it was melted down for scrap. By that time, everyone who had seen it would have learned their stories.

John and Maj, though intent on finding Bodaway and staying alive, couldn't help but be affected. Even so, they kept moving, looking for the man who would turn an occasion of healing into yet another episode of innocent blood being shed. As the moon rose, set and yielded to the sun of a new day, John and Maj kept moving and searching. Several times, they spotted both Arnoldo and White River also passing through the throng. The other two men created credible replicas of John, all the more so at the kind of distance from which a sniper might work.

The only giveaway John noticed was the pace at which White River moved. At his age, he walked with a far more measured step. Some of that, though, could be ascribed to the limitations of threading his way through a crowd. At least that was how it might look through a telescopic sight. Or so John hoped.

Arnoldo, on the other hand, was closer to John in both age and movement. The similarity struck John deeply. He'd never had a sibling, hadn't expected to feel a sense of family with his cousin, but there was one. It was unexpectedly real and welcome.

Still, White River was the one who aroused a deeper curiosity. Was he family, too? Through John's biological father? John would never think of anyone but Haden Wolf and Serafina Wolf y Padilla as his real parents. It would be very interesting to think he had, what, a grandfather, he might come to know?

The last thing he'd ever expected to find on the rez was family he'd welcome.

After all, his maternal grandmother was the one who wanted to put him in the ground.

Maj tapped John on the shoulder. Gave him a nod of her head. The two of them took shelter behind a ponderosa pine.

She said to John, "Either this Bodaway guy is one patient SOB, he can't sort out who's who or he's decided not to pull his trigger."

"I haven't seen White River for a while. Maybe he found Bodaway. Talked him out of becoming a killer."

Bodaway was tired but determined. He'd now assumed a sitting position, his legs crossed in almost a tailor fashion. He had to concentrate to keep his heavy head from drooping. He thought he'd seen Tall Wolf several times last night. He'd almost taken the shot on the first sighting, but then passing behind his target he thought he'd seen another man who resembled Tall Wolf.

He'd quickly acquired the second target and, yes, this man looked like Tall Wolf, too.

He tried to go back to the first target to compare the two, but that man had lost himself in the crowd. When he tried to go back to the second man— a decoy or the real Tall Wolf? — he, too, was gone.

Over the course of the night, Bodaway had found there were at least three men who looked like Tall Wolf moving through the throng, as far as he could tell through his scope. There may even have been others he had missed spotting. Shooting the genuine target would have established a reputation for Bodaway as someone willing to kill for his people. Taking out the wrong man, an innocent person, would make him look like a fool to everyone.

A bloodthirsty madman who deserved nothing more than to be hunted down.

The rising sun made closer examination of his target possible, but Bodaway had never seen Tall Wolf in person, only in the photographs Maria Black Knife had clipped and shown him. The real BIA man might have left by now, gone to make arrangements to take possession of the newly haunted Super Chief. Shooting an impostor who lingered below would give him some satisfaction, but knowingly doing that would make him look worse than a fool. He would be revealed as a spiteful loser. The kind of man no one would ever follow.

Then, again, maybe he was never meant to lead.

Bitter now and more tired than ever, Bodaway took one last sweep of the setting below him. He didn't see either the real Tall Wolf or any decoys. What he did see was his great-grandfather wearing his headdress and once again standing on the platform next to the Super Chief. With him was a woman he'd also never met in real life, but whose pictures he'd also studied: Marlene Flower Moon.

Unless there were decoys of her on hand, too. For that single moment, Bodaway gave up on the idea of shooting anyone. Maybe he'd just build highway bridges the rest of his life.

The damn country certainly had plenty of civil engineering work to be done.

Then, after a photographer snapped some pictures of great-grandfather with the woman who might be Marlene Flower Moon, Alan White River removed his headdress and Bodaway's life changed forever. Great-grandfather who'd had long white hair for as long as Bodaway had known him now had short black hair. Styled just the way John Tall Wolf wore his. Cut like it belonged on a white cop not a Native American chief.

The realization that the most revered member of his own family had helped to thwart his plan enraged and energized Bodaway. He centered great-grandfather in his crosshairs and squeezed the trigger. Doing so just a split second too late.

As if she'd known what was coming, Marlene Flower Moon shoved the old man off the platform and stepped dead center into Bodaway's sight picture. Her eyes burned with fury. Her mouth pulled back and her teeth flashed white and sharp. In that quick-silver moment, Bodaway believed for the first time this woman might really be Coyote.

Then his round hit her and she went down.

— CHAPTER 61 —

Northern New Mexico Mountain

John and Maj had been on their way to the platform when the crack of the shot jolted what had been a peaceful setting. They both saw White River shoved into space before the bullet struck Marlene and slammed her off the platform, too. Their training and the possibility of further rounds being fired compelled them to ignore the initial victim and look for the shooter.

John knew there was no chance a handgun could match the effective range of a rifle — Bodaway's assumed weapon of choice — but if he could spot the assassin he could still harass and distract him with his shots. There was no telling when dumb luck might be more lethally accurate than skill. Even if fate didn't lend a hand, taking fire that was nearby would degrade the shooting accuracy of anyone but the most hardened combat marksman.

"There he is," John said, pointing to a figure who'd just jumped up from a clump of bushes on a foothill maybe five hundred feet distant. Gimme range for a rifle with a scope.

"See him," Maj said, and that was when John realized she still carried her M-4.

She shouldered it, the weapon looking completely familiar and comfortable in her hands.

Maj took the shot and the small figure in the distance went down.

John remembered DeWitt telling him that Maj had shot expert

with a rifle.

"You got him," John said.

Maj shook her head. "No, I didn't. The sonofabitch fell just as I took my shot. He went down *before* he could be hit."

Sometimes dumb luck worked against you, John thought.

Then they heard a proof of life: the buzz of a high-performance engine roaring to life.

"That bastard has his own bike up there," Maj said, "probably one like ours."

The two of them raced to get back to their Yamahas.

John yelled, "No way the shooter will come down this way. Not after you shot at him."

"He'll go up the mountain, look for another way down," Maj shouted back.

She flashed a good deal of her old college track form, but John ate up considerably more ground with each stride. They ran side by side as people who had been sleeping on the ground or sitting in small circles of conversation scattered in random directions, many of them screaming, all of them fearing there might be more shooting than the two rounds that had already been fired.

Just short of reaching their bikes, a knot of four people saw John streaking toward them. His size and speed dictated that they clear a path. Doing so, they stepped directly in front of Maj. For a heartbeat, she considered trying to leap over them, but the hurdles she used to jump were never *that* high. She slowed and saw a small gap between the two women at the center of the group and aimed for that opening. She stopped striding and skidded past them on the dew-wet grass like she had ice skates on.

With running room ahead of her now, Maj put on the jets, as if in a final burst for the finishing line. A small part of her mind told her she'd never run faster, not even in her salad days. But by now John was already on his bike and taking off to pursue the shooter.

Then, as if someone were running at her shoulder, Maj heard a woman's voice in her ear.

"Catch him. Don't let him come to harm."

Not worrying about whether she might be hallucinating from fatigue or going a bit nuts from the adrenaline overload, Maj took the woman's words to heart. Any SOB who wanted to kill John Tall Wolf would have to go through her first. And that wouldn't be easy.

Maj jumped on her bike and took off after John.

She was maybe five to ten seconds behind him, but she was a better rider.

She could make up the difference.

The woman's voice in her ear urged her to do just that.

Bodaway knew he was lucky to be alive. Maybe luck was all that mattered. But he never counted on that. Calculation was more to his liking, and in picking his shooting site he'd taken into account the chance that he might draw pursuit. Aided by Maria Black Knife's story of how her son, Cesar, had died, he'd also planned his getaway in a fashion no one could match.

Not unless the SOB had one-in-a-million foresight.

If that was the case, his luck would have turned a hundred and eighty degrees.

He might as well not have tripped and been hit by that first shot.

No, he decided, the odds that he'd both been lucky enough not to be dead already and that any pursuer might have prepared for what he had in mind were beyond reason.

Feeling reassured by logic, he wondered what the chances were that John Tall Wolf might come after him. The odds of that seemed far more probable. If Tall Wolf deserved his reputation as a BIA hotshot, he might even lead any pack trailing him.

Bodaway didn't see any reason not to play things that way.

What the hell? He'd already gotten Marlene Flower Moon, if only inadvertently.

Maybe he could goad Tall Wolf into making a fatal mistake and get him, too.

***

John found that the road up the mountain was a thrill ride designed by nature, moderated by man, but amplified by years of neglect. The two narrow lanes — one up, one down — were paved in asphalt. No doubt this was a great improvement over the dirt track that had preceded it. But potholes of varying sizes and depths afflicted the pavement like a bad rash.

John hit one as he started his climb and the jolt nearly unseated him. Not a happy prospect as he got a close-up view of a drop-off that was already more than fifty feet. Guard rails were not an amenity the rez's road builders had included in their plans. He regained his place on the Yamaha and brought the bike back under control, knowing that going over the edge as he ascended the mountain would be a fatal event.

He might have made allowances for the driving conditions and slowed down.

Instead, he chose to go as fast as he could while swerving around the holes and staying on a relatively smooth surface. This obligated him to make full use of both lanes, from the precipice on his right to the bruising rock face on his left. One small mistake on either extremity and he was done.

A part of his mind warned him that he was behaving irrationally.

He should slow the hell down.

After all, Bodaway, or just maybe somebody else, had shot Marlene Flower Moon.

His nemesis. Coyote. The beast who had almost devoured him as an infant. The shape-shifter he'd felt compelled to go to work for as a man so he could keep track of her while she, no doubt, watched his every move.

Perverse though the thought was, he felt possessive about Marlene/Coyote. Conniving woman or creature of legend, she was *his* antagonist. If anyone was going to best her, it would be him. An outsider who interfered in their competition would answer to him.

For a fleeting moment, John wondered if it was even possible to kill Coyote.

With a bullet anyway.

He pushed his dirt bike even harder, and that was when he first heard the engine note of Maj's bike. She had to be right behind him. He heard her shout. The sound and tone of her voice were clear, but he couldn't make out her words. He could guess what she wanted, though. To take the lead.

There was no way John could look back. Taking his eyes off the cratered road for even a moment would likely mean disaster. Even lifting a hand from the handlebars to wave her back would be risky. He had to content himself to give a measured shake of his head.

Maj didn't back off, not at first anyway. John could feel her riding his bike's rear end. That made things even more tense. Most times, he didn't care who got the credit for solving a case or making an arrest. This time, he did. It was as personal as if his mom or dad had been the victim.

In that very moment, as they approached a sharp turn to the right, Maj eased off, giving John some space. He thought somehow she'd come to understand the importance of what he was doing. He couldn't have been more wrong.

No sooner had the gap between them increased and John had slowed to take the turn than he heard Maj's bike roar as she opened her throttle wide. She didn't try to take the curve in the road at top speed. She jumped her bike over the interval, shooting over a drop of thousands of feet, landing on the far side of the road, just ahead of John now, before gravity could swat her out of the sky.

John was stunned by the suicidal recklessness of the maneuver. But he had no way to voice his disapproval except to follow Maj around the next sharp turn in the road, this one breaking to the left, and let her know when they finally stopped how mindless she'd been.

Making the turn, John was the one who had to dial it back, easing off the gas and slowing abruptly. Maj had all but stopped just ahead of him. They were two-thirds of the way to the crest of the mountain now. She held up a hand and stopped.

John might have tried to race past her and take the lead again.

But this time the cautionary voice in his head held sway. He stopped.

Maj turned her head and he saw her mime a word. *Listen.*

John did just that. Over the soft buzz of their idling motors he could hear the engine note of another bike just up ahead, around the next bend. Someone — Bodaway — waiting to ambush them?

Bodaway heard their bikes, too. He'd timed things perfectly. Allowed his pursuers to get close to him just before he'd spring his trap. He savored the moment for a heartbeat and then revved his engine to the redline. Whoever was behind him would have to think he was making one final, desperate effort to get away. Any lawman worthy of the name would feel compelled to give chase.

Maj was sure John was about to do just that. She shared the impulse to race forward, too. But the woman's voice in her ear said, "Not now." She spurted ahead, but stopped her bike before the blind curve and turned it sideways on the road.

If he'd dared to do it, John could have skirted her barricade, but he'd have been on the thin, crumbling edge of the pavement. Blacktop that looked like it would dissolve if given a dirty look. John chose not to risk it. He stopped his bike and dismounted. Crept forward to where Maj was about to peek around the curve.

Heard her say, "Jesus Christ!"

John looked over her shoulder and felt his heart rise into his throat.

The road ahead had fallen away for a stretch of at least fifty feet. A jump of that distance on a dirt bike likely would have been impossible coming down a straightaway at top speed. Taking a sharp turn at reduced speed and finding it right in front of you would have meant certain death.

Unless you were wearing a parachute. Like the guy who'd tried to sucker them into following him. He had a ram-air elliptical rig. The high maneuverable design was used by sport chutists. The would-be killer was riding the currents, making his escape toward the forest below.

If he hit a tree, he'd be in trouble.

If he was any good, though, and that looked to be the case, he'd find an open patch of ground, land safely and be on his merry way. John and Maj couldn't follow, and once he was under the cover of the forest they wouldn't be able to see which way he'd fled.

Maj had saved their lives but —

She said to John, "Give me a little room."

He took a step back, asking, "What are —"

Maj yelled, "Stop, federal officers!"

The chutist was unable to effect a mid-air arrest of motion.

Maj raised her M-4 and fired two rounds before John could say a word.

She hit the parachute, tearing and partially collapsing its canopy. The fabric drooped on one side and gaped on the other. The man beneath the chute accelerated toward the earth at a far greater speed, with a seeming lack of directional control.

In a matter of moments, the chutist disappeared beneath the leaf cover of the forest.

John wondered if Maj was really that cold-blooded or if she'd momentarily lost her mind.

She responded to the unasked question by saying, "A little voice in my head told me to do that.

Now, John felt sure he understood. Maj had fallen under the spell of a *bruja*. A witch. He knew who had influenced Maj's over-the-top behavior and why. His mother had been responsible, and there was no question how ruthless Mom was.

"We'd better get going," John said. "Get a search started."

"Sure. But we'll take it easy getting back. Even going downhill, this road won't be a picnic."

— CHAPTER 62 —

Northern New Mexico Forest

The first tree branch that hit Bodaway made him think he'd broken his back. Things only got worse from there. He kept getting slammed. His arms, his legs and the back of his head all took blows. His headdress got ripped off by a branch. Somehow, he managed to think of pulling the three-ring release system on each of the risers of his chute harness. The last thing he wanted to do was to have his rig get snagged on a branch and leave him hanging to die of exposure, thirst or getting picked apart by crows while he was still alive.

Better to take a big fall and embrace oblivion in a single burst of agony.

The release rings worked just as they had been designed to do. Gravity yanked him free of the harness just as the chute did catch on a branch. He fell faster now. But not nearly as far as he thought he would.

And then he hit the ground feet first.

Bodaway felt bones and tendons in his ankles, knees and back give way as he slammed into the earth. Despite all that, he still remained self-aware. He couldn't even manage to close his eyelids. He also was unable to keep from hearing something ferocious approach him.

With all the pain occupying his mind, he still felt his bladder let go.

A sense of shame joined his suffering, but not for long.

Soon terror left room for nothing else.

The face of the largest coyote he'd ever seen looked down at him.

It's eyes were red and its fangs dripped blood. Worse, it seemed to bear him a personal enmity. The animal took his throat in its mouth and growled. Bodaway felt death was more certain now than when he was falling out of the sky. He was also sure the agony he was about to endure would be worse than anything he'd suffered already.

His hair stood on end as he recognized that within the vibrato of the creature's growl he could recognize words. The animal was *talking* to him. Logic told him this was the product of a traumatic brain injury. His heart told him he was trying to deny reality.

The coyote said to him, "You shot me, you vile speck of mouse shit. I should disembowel you. Let you watch as vultures feed on your entrails."

Bodaway began to twitch in terror.

The involuntary movements only deepened the beast's hold on his throat.

"You tried to kill White River, a man so much better than you that —"

The animal pissed on him. Its stream scalded him, added to his own stink. He wanted to scream but couldn't produce the slightest sound. Fear and a vise of lacerating teeth prevented it.

"Worst of all, you tried to kill Tall Wolf — and his fate belongs to me."

That was when Bodaway knew: *Coyote was real.*

And had saved the worst news for last.

"You will live, Bodaway … and now I own you."

He pleaded for mercy and tried to curry favor.

Told Coyote of Maria Black Knife's part in the plan to kill Tall Wolf.

And her intention to kill her grandson, Arnoldo, too.

Coyote released his throat. It proved no balm for his suffering.

Especially when the creature told him, "I know all that."

— CHAPTER 63 —

Maria Black Knife's House

Arnoldo decided to pay his grandmother one final visit. For the first time in his life he didn't knock before entering. He shoved the door open hard enough to make it slam against the wall. It bounced back at him and he kicked it out of his way. The imprint of his boot left a mark of his contempt.

Under normal circumstances, some menial would be called on to remove the stain. Maintaining appearances was one of the pillars of holding on to power. You let the way people viewed you slip, your days of domination were over.

Arnoldo waited for Grandmother to appear. He hoped she would try to berate him. Scold him. Diminish him. He would throw her every word back in her face. Or maybe he'd throw her through a window. When she didn't appear, he felt disappointed. But only for a minute.

He improved his mood by breaking things, starting with an oil portrait of his grandfather, Cesar Black Knife. A truly vicious bastard, as Arnoldo remembered him. Arnoldo put a fist right through the canvas. "How you like that, old man?" he asked. The he tore the frame apart and scattered the pieces throughout the living room.

Still no Grandmother.

He continued his rampage, smashing a Tiffany lamp, its leaded glass shade commissioned specifically for the Black Knife family, showing the occasion of Grandmother and Grandfather's wedding against the background of a mountain landscape. Arnoldo thought it had never looked better than when he smashed it into a thousand pieces.

That felt so good he destroyed everything that came to hand.

Arnoldo was about to take an heirloom tomahawk — sharpened stone head, wooden handle, rawhide bindings — off a wall and start in on the furniture when Maria Black Knife finally appeared. Arnoldo looked at her and smiled.

"How do you like what I've done with the room, Grandmother?"

By way of an answer, Maria withdrew from a deep pocket in her skirt the revolver that Delshay Crow Wing had returned to her.

Arnoldo seemed not to notice or think it was important, if he did.

"Did I tell you I met my cousin, John Tall Wolf?" he asked. "Great guy. Said he'd help me find a job, if I decide to leave the rez."

Maria raised the gun and pointed it at her grandson.

He made no move to run. Showed no sign of fear.

"I know you've lost faith in me," Arnoldo said, "but I wouldn't count on that Bodaway guy too much. You know how dumb he is? You want me to tell you who he shot just now?"

The old lady was intent on the task at hand, but that last question ruined her focus.

"Who?" she asked.

"Marlene Flower Moon."

That drew a response. Maria looked suddenly stricken.

Arnoldo nodded. "Yeah. How stupid can you get? We all know the stories about her, right? Guess Bodaway is learning the error of his ways about now, huh?"

The gun in Maria's hands started to move in a downward arc.

"Of course, you were in on the plan with him, weren't you?" Arnoldo asked.

"No!" Maria yelled. "I told him to stay away from her. He was only to kill Tall Wolf."

"So you were in on a plan to commit murder. Something you

never needed to do. John told me he has no interest in ever returning to the rez."

"He said he would never come here at all," Maria said, "but he did come. He doesn't control his fate; it controls him. He will be back and the time will come when —"

"He'll seize power from the Black Knife family? That's why he has to die?"

"Yes."

"And it's my fate never to lead the family and run the rez? Get all the power and most of the money that will come from our natural gas reserves?"

"Yes." She raised the gun again, held it in front of her eyes. Pointed it at Arnoldo's chest.

"So I have to go, too. Just like John. Neither of us can be allowed to make a claim that might spoil your plans. But with Bodaway gone, who will your successor be?"

Maria's face became a stone mask. "I'll find someone."

"If Coyote lets you," Arnoldo said.

Maria pulled the trigger of a gun that hadn't been fired in more than a century — hadn't been cleaned or oiled in who knew how long — and it blew up in her face.

Several pieces of sharp, flying metal barely missed Arnoldo.

Far more struck Maria Black Knife. Two pierced her eyes. One went through her windpipe and into her spine. Another severed her external carotid artery. She seemed to Arnoldo to compress as if an invisible handle was pushing her into the floor.

"All that planning, and what good did it do you, Grandmother?" Arnoldo asked.

He supposed he should have been frightened when she tried to kill him, but he'd felt all along how things would work out: with his survival and his grandmother's death.

He'd thought the ghost of a long-dead cavalry officer might make things right.

But he'd felt far more certain Coyote would have her revenge.

Whatever the case, he was the true head of the Black Knife

family now.

Wasn't sure he wanted the title though. However much power might come with it.

Look where it had gotten the rest of the family.

Except for John Tall Wolf. He'd gotten out and … Okay, he seemed to have Coyote as a full-time problem. So maybe he wasn't a good example.

But if he, Arnoldo, didn't get out he might become as power hungry as all his relatives.

He called the tribal police to come to the scene and take care of the immediate mess.

He'd sleep on what to do next.

— CHAPTER 64 —

Albuquerque, New Mexico

The doctors tell me you're not going to die," John told Marlene in her hospital room.

Byron DeWitt's waiting helicopter had medevacked Marlene to Albuquerque.

"Of course not," she replied.

"The surgeons who worked on you were amazed by the narrowness of your wound path."

"Were they?"

"Yes, the round that hit you didn't tumble on impact, as expected. Just went straight through."

"Lucky me," Marlene said.

Her complexion was pallid. The outline of some sort of bandage was visible under her hospital gown in the area just above her right breast. But a monitor showed her heartbeat was within normal range and steady. Her hair looked like she'd just had a stylist come in and fix it.

Taking his cue from that last point, John asked, "You going to have someone do your makeup before the TV people get here?"

Marlene's eyes flashed, telling him he'd nailed it.

John nodded. "You're right. It might help you get a leg up for that cabinet post."

She smiled, showing appreciation for John's mind rather than affection for him.

"I'd have missed you, if Bodaway had killed you," she told him.

"The search party hasn't found him yet. You'd think someone who fell out of the sky would be dead, and the cadaver dogs wouldn't have any trouble locating the body. Unless, of course, someone else got to him first. Say a few locals who'd be only too happy to do your bidding … and only because Bodaway is still alive."

"I don't know what you're talking about."

"Of course not. But just in case you're keeping a little secret, think about this. I'm all but certain there's a family connection between Alan White River and me. That would mean Bodaway is my kin, too. You really want to have two of us to deal with?"

Marlene smiled again. "There's no one like you, Tall Wolf."

Though he knew better, he couldn't stop the compliment from pleasing him.

Even so, he said, "I shouldn't tell you this, but assuming you really are Coyote, you're immortal. And I'm not. I will die someday, and it is possible you might eat my remains."

"But?" Marlene asked.

"You might not like the way I taste."

Marlene frowned. That was clearly a thought she'd never considered.

With a scowl she told John, "Go take care of White River. Get him as little prison time as you can."

John nodded and left.

With John lightly grasping his left arm, Alan White River surrendered to FBI Deputy Director Byron DeWitt, saying, "I'm the man who stole the Super Chief."

"All by yourself," DeWitt added.

"Of course not."

"And your accomplices are?"

"I'm old. My memory's not so good."

"Well, I believe half of that. What's that in your hand?"

"Something I found on the train. I thought you should have it."

White River handed Edward Danner's journal to DeWitt. "You've read it?"

"I don't recall, but my feeling is it should come to the law's attention."

"Nicely worded," DeWitt said.

He looked at John to see how much he might have coached White River.

John kept a straight face, as did White River. Two wooden Indians.

"You're cooperation will be noted," DeWitt told the old man. "It might be considered a mitigating factor when you come to trial."

John said, "One billionaire and maybe two for —"

DeWitt's phone interrupted with the tone of an incoming text.

"Excuse me for just a moment," he said. He stepped away to read the text. What he saw made him chuckle. He returned to John and White River. "Two billionaires. Special Agent Benjamin has just taken sworn testimony from corrupt state and county officials in California that Brian Kirby bribed them to overrule the officials Edward Danner had bribed."

John nodded. "So with that testimony and Danner's journal, you do have two crooked billionaires in the bag — with the help of one little old man who has a failing memory but a strong sense of doing what's right."

DeWitt grinned. "Little? He's almost as tall as you are. If his memory improves to the point where he can remember what he read in the journal and testify in court that he chose to preserve this journal to deliver to the FBI in the interest of justice, that might go a long way toward shortening his sentence."

White River shared a few words with John, whispering into his ear.

"It's possible," John said, "his memory might improve selectively."

"Whatever is the best he can do, provided he gets the judge to buy his story."

White River nodded. He could work with that.

But DeWitt wasn't done laying things out.

"Given there's no tangible harm done to the train, there shouldn't be any major concern there, but when the train was taken, the crew was kidnapped. That is serious."

"They all survived," John pointed out.

"Just barely in two cases. Otherwise, it'd be capital murder and there'd be no wriggle room."

"How much is there now?" John asked. "Keeping in mind that at Mr. White River's age any prison term is likely to be a life sentence."

DeWitt sighed. "He's going to do some time. That can't be helped."

White River nodded in acceptance.

"It might even look like there'd be no way he could outlive the sentence."

"Might?" John asked.

"Someone in the federal government, say a senior law enforcement official, not me, might petition President Grant for clemency for Mr. White River in the waning days of her second term, less than two years from now."

John nodded. "I can do that."

DeWitt continued, "If for some reason President Grant can't find her way clear to do that, and her vice president should succeed her in the Oval Office, a senior government official in law enforcement might petition the new president for clemency — and that would be me."

John said, "Thank you. There's something else you might do in any case."

"What's that?" DeWitt asked.

"After Danner and Kirby are convicted?"

"Yeah?"

"See if you can get the powers that be to put them in the same cell."

DeWitt loved the idea. Even White River smiled.

As a courtesy to John, DeWitt let him have a few minutes alone with White River.

"Don't know if you've thought about it," John said, "but your plan for sending the Super Chief on to the museum in Chicago has a flaw in it."

Suspicion entered the old man's eyes, and he asked, "What's that?"

John replied with a question of his own. "Who's going to want to drive a haunted train? Not the crew that had the job in the first place. They probably don't ever want to see the thing again. You have someone else in mind?"

From the look of consternation that crossed his face, White River didn't.

"It's always some damn thing," John said in sympathy. "I won't ask you to implicate your inside man on the original crew by having him do the job, but you should ask Marlene if she knows two or three Native Americans who can do the skilled work."

White River bobbed his head. "I'll do that."

"I know some people who can provide security, make sure nothing unexpected happens to the train again," John said.

"Who's that?"

"Me, my parents, a Canadian Mountie I know and the Amtrak cop you met who's one sixty-fourth Pequot and loves a good train story."

White River's eyes moistened. "You warm my heart, but I have to warn you: The spirits on that train are real and their sorrow is enduring."

John told him, "I know. I hope I'll come to understand them better than I do now."

The old man reflected on what he'd done. "Do you think *anyone* will come to visit the train? Will it be too frightening? Too sad?"

John shook his head. "I think if the stories are explained well, the aura will make it all the more compelling. People will flock to it and will see the country's history in a whole new way."

John didn't say so, but he thought Disney would kill for an exhibit with even a whiff of the truly supernatural. Something that made people weep and rage and defied rational explanation.

Well written and illustrated supporting exhibits could give a factual underpinning for the strong feelings the train would arouse.

John added, "I think the Chicago museum could sponsor guest tours, too. The Super Chief should ride the rails again on a regular basis, visit cities across this country and in Canada and Mexico, too. Spread the stories that train can tell far and wide."

Now, Alan White River's eyes overflowed. He took John's hands in his.

"You are a very interesting young man. I hope I'll have the time to get to know you better. Will you come visit me in prison?"

"I will," John said.

Before heading east, John made a phone call to L. A., talking to Ellen Feazell, the reporter who'd put him on to Danner and Kirby. He told her to pack her bag for San Francisco. Two Bay Area billionaires were about to be arrested by the FBI. She could get the jump on what was bound to be a horde of newsies.

Ms. Feazell thanked John.

Agreed to refer to him as an anonymous source.

— CHAPTER 65 —

Washington, D.C.

John arrived at his new office after riding the Super Chief to Chicago with all of the people he'd mentioned to Alan White River: Haden Wolf, Serafina Wolf y Padilla, Rebecca Bramley and Maj Olson. Everyone got along famously.

They coexisted comfortably with the spirits aboard, too. Listened to their stories and songs. Understood every word, no matter the language that was spoken. Offered their respect and condolences.

A picture postcard from the rez in northern New Mexico lay on the unstaffed secretary's desk outside John's new BIA digs. The photo looked a whole lot like the mountain on which Maj Olson had kept him from dying. He turned it over and read a note from his cousin Arnoldo.

Thought you should know. I got a promotion, too. Elected chief of tribal council. Let's send each other cards from time to time. Show each other we care — from a distance.

John smiled. He could live with those boundaries.

There was a knock at the door to the outer office and a handsome young woman entered.

She was Native American in appearance, except for her eyes.

"I'm your new secretary, Johona Green Eyes. Just a temp until you decide whether you want to keep me on or bring in someone else."

She didn't seem bothered by the idea that John might replace her.

"Are you one sixty-fourth Irish?" he asked.

"One eighth Scot."

He had one other question for her.

"Did Marlene send you?"

"Marlene who?"

Perfect answer — for someone who was either innocent or well coached.

No matter, he'd find out soon enough.

"Never mind. Tell me what skills you have."

The list was lengthy. She could keep his professional life well organized.

"Where would you like me to start?" she asked.

"We'll get a jump on my Christmas card list," John said. "Begin with Arnoldo Black Knife."

ABOUT THE AUTHOR

Joseph Flynn has been published both traditionally — Signet Books, Bantam Books and Variance Publishing — and through his own imprint, Stray Dog Press, Inc. Both major media reviews and reader reviews have praised his work. Booklist said, "Flynn is an excellent storyteller." The Chicago Tribune said, "Flynn [is] a master of high-octane plotting." The most repeated reader comment is: Write faster, we want more.

Contact Joe at Hey Joe on his website: *www.josephflynn.com.* You can also read excerpts of all of Joe's books on his website. All of Joseph Flynn's novels may be purchased online.

The Jim McGill Series
The President's Henchman, A Jim McGill Novel [#1]
The Hangman's Companion, A JimMcGill Novel [#2]
The K Street Killer, A JimMcGill Novel [#3]
The Last Ballot Cast: Part 1, A JimMcGill Novel [#4]
The Last Ballot Cast: Part 2, A JimMcGill Novel [#5]
The Devil on the Doorstep, A Jim McGill Novel [#6]
The Good Guy with a Gun, A Jim McGill Novel [#7]
The Echo of the Whip, A Jim McGill Novel [#8]
The Daddy's Girl Decoy, A Jim McGill Novel [#9]
The Last Chopper Out, A Jim McGill Novel [#10]

The King of Mirth, A Jim McGill Novel [#11]
McGill's Short Cases 1-3

The Ron Ketchum Mystery Series
Nailed, A Ron Ketchum Mystery [#1]
Defiled, A Ron Ketchum Mystery [#2]
Impaled, A Ron Ketchum Mystery [#3]

The John Tall Wolf Series
Tall Man in Ray-Bans, A John Tall Wolf Novel [#1]
War Party, A John Tall Wolf Novel [#2]
Super Chief, A John Tall Wolf Novel [#3]
Smoke Signals, A John Tall Wolf Novel [#4]
Big Medicine, A John Tall Wolf Novel [#5]
Powwow in Paris, A John Tall Wolf Novel [#6]

The Zeke Edison Series
Kill Me Twice, A Zeke Edison Novel [#1]

Stand Alone Novels
The Concrete Inquisition
Digger
The Next President
Hot Type
Farewell Performance
Gasoline, Texas
Round Robin, A Love Story of Epic Proportions
One False Step
Blood Street Punx
Still Coming
Still Coming Expanded Edition
Hangman — A Western Novella
Pointy Teeth, Twelve Bite-Size Stories